Final Jeopardy

A Jake Sledge mystery

B.D. Lawrence

J.V.R. Publishing, LLC

Book Cover by Gary Val T.

First edition 2026.

Also by B.D. Lawrence

Chilled to the Bone: A Jake Sledge Mystery

The Marble Hill Crime Blotter

Killer Redemption

The One-Armed Detective series

The Coyote and a One-Armed Man

An Angel and a One-Armed Man

A Vigilante and a Two-Armed Man: The Lefty Bruder Origin Story

(a novella), including the short story *The Finger Snatcher and a One-Armed Man: Lefty Bruder's First Private Detective case*

And visit B.D. Lawrence's website at https://www.bdlawrence.com to download and read many more short stories.

Contents

One

Before we could prove his innocence, we needed to find Barker Dupree. His sister, Jeopardy, hired us yesterday to prove that Barker did not kill Sandy Akins, a nurse's aide at the River Bluffs Residential Treatment Center. Barker walked away from River Bluffs eight days ago. Someone murdered Sandy Akins the day after. According to Jeopardy, Barker called her that same day and said the police might come looking for him and he had to disappear. And disappear, he had.

Bobo Johnson, my partner at the Sledge Hammer Detective Agency, sat in one of the worn vinyl armchairs in front of the desk. He hunched over his laptop, compiling background research on River Bluffs Residential Treatment Center. The top of his massive, shaved head glistened with sweat, as it always did, especially in August in River City. Yeah, that's right, we live in River City. And there's always trouble in River City.

Outside temperatures had climbed into the nineties with matching humidity. Our air conditioner limped along, keeping the office a balmy eighty degrees. The ceiling fan whumped and circulated the warm air. The office smelled musty. Maybe it was time to get an air freshener.

I stood, slipped off my green windowpane sports coat, and hung it on the coat rack next to the light green fedora. Yes, I wear a fedora. It's a necessary accessory for a private eye. Then I took off the shoulder holster holding my Beretta .45, one of two Berettas of that caliber I owned. River City PD held the other one as evidence, along with its cousin, my Colt 1911. They'd assured me they'd return them soon. However, soon to the River City PD meant within the next century.

My undershirt clung to my torso, and sweat stains spread from my armpits. "Dude, why don't we go somewhere that has better air-conditioning? Someone should really talk to the landlord and get the air conditioners replaced."

Bobo didn't bother to reply that I am the landlord. I guess he'd heard me use that line too many times.

"Okay by me," Bobo said. "How about The Bean Shop? We can walk."

Walk? In ninety-plus temperatures? Whatever.

Bobo packed his laptop into a backpack and slung it over his shoulder. He wore his usual jeans and a dark T-shirt. How anyone could wear jeans during a Missouri summer baffled me. I wore light tan chinos. Leaving the sports coat and shoulder holster, I donned my fedora and grabbed my laptop. Because of our recent case where we'd battled skinheads, I was wary of leaving the .45 behind, though I still had a .40 Smith & Wesson Bodyguard strapped to my ankle. I followed Bobo out of the office.

We waded through the late morning humidity. Not another soul out walking. Obviously, everyone else had more sense than we did. About halfway there, my cell phone belted out Santana's "She's Not There."

"Who's that?" Bobo asked.

"Our client." I pulled my cell phone out of my pants pocket. "Ms. Jeopardy Dupree." I punched the answer icon, then put it on speaker. "Ms. Dupree. How are you today?"

"Did you find Barker, yet?" Not as much Southern twang as usual.

"We just started looking for him."

"Any leads? Where are you? And where are you looking?"

Bobo raised his eyebrows. He'd not met Ms. Dupree yet. In that, he was fortunate.

"Right now, we're heading to the coffee shop. Care to join us?"

"Coffee break, already? You should be looking for Barker. That's what I'm paying you for, Mr. Sledge. What coffee shop are you at?"

I told her where we were going. "Why don't you join us?"

"Busy right now, Mr. Sledge." She hung up.

"Not in a very good mood today, is she?" Bobo asked.

"You noticed. Odd, though. She's usually ... how can I describe it?" We stopped outside a glass door where letters spelling "The Bean Shop" encircled a giant coffee bean. "Let's just say, Ms. Dupree has a thing for me. She's usually trying to come on to me."

Bobo shook his head. "Jake, according to you, that describes every woman in River City, doesn't it?"

I shrugged. What could I say?

We entered the coffee shop. Small joint. Six round tables in all. Five construction-type men occupied two of the tables. Bobo sat at one of the vacant ones, and I went to order our usual from the child working behind the counter. I still hadn't worked up the courage to ask her how old she was. She looked twelve. I ordered my mocha and Bobo's chai tea, then returned to the table. The young girl said she'd bring them to us when ready.

By habit, I sat facing the door. "We need to visit River City PD and see if they'll tell us anything about the murder of Sandy Akins. Then let's visit River Bluffs and see what they'll tell us about Barker."

Bobo nodded. "Unusual name he has."

"You have no idea. His full name is Barker Robert Dupree."

Bobo's forehead creased. "As in Bob Barker?"

"You got it, big guy. Papa Dupree's favorite game show host."

"And Jeopardy?"

"Another favorite game show. And get this, Jeopardy's alter ego, the one that tried to kill me, named herself Concentration."

"Wow."

And that's all one could say about the Dupree family.

"I remember that case." Bobo rubbed one giant paw across his head. "It's when I was traveling to a Hall of Fame get together. Wasn't Mr. Dupree murdered?"

"He was. By Connie. That's the name Concentration Dupree went by."

"You're saying our client murdered her own father?"

The young barista placed our drinks on the table. She gave Bobo a huge smile. Did I mention, everyone smiles at Bobo?

"Physically, yes, Jeopardy murdered her father." I took a sip of the coffee, then wondered why I'd ordered something hot. "But supposedly, she had dissociative disorder, so it was Connie that really killed him."

"That's a big word for you."

"True that. Jeopardy explained it to me yesterday."

Bobo chuckled. "Do you think her brother killed that nurse's aide?"

"No idea. He has schizophrenia, so Jeopardy says."

"Wow, two big words in the same day."

I shook my head. "Look, smart guy, what do you want to contribute to this case?"

We went back and forth for forty minutes, ingesting our caffeine, looking things up online, and discussing who we could talk to about finding Barker Dupree. It came down to the same conclusion we started with. Visits to River City PD and River Bluffs Residential Treatment Center.

We left the comfort of cool dry air and ran smack into a wall of wet, hot weather. Some idiot agreed to walk to the coffee shop, and now we had to walk back to my building's parking lot to get the rental car I was still driving. Riley Perkins of CS Auto had told me two or three more days before he'd finish pounding out all the bullet holes. He was also waiting for the back-ordered plastic rear window for my classic 1975 convertible Delta 88. My poor baby had been through a lot the last month. And so had I.

We swam through the humidity to the corner of River Road and Willson Drive. I was scrolling on my phone, looking for the River City PD number that bypassed the switchboard. I stepped onto Willson Drive. Tires screeched. An engine roared. I looked up. A dark SUV headed right at me. Fast. Bobo grabbed my collar, pulled me off my feet, and threw me a couple yards onto the sidewalk. The SUV swerved at us. It ricocheted off the curb. Because of the tinted windows, I couldn't make out the driver. The SUV turned into our office parking lot, its tires screeching as it made a U-turn and drove out. It beelined toward us. Bobo dragged me back close to the coffee shop. The SUV jumped the curb but stopped before hitting the street sign. Bobo ran toward it. With more screeching, the SUV backed onto the street, turned sharp right, and accelerated west on River Road.

I sat on the pavement. My body shook uncontrollably. I felt cold in the ninety-plus heat and humidity. My teeth chattered. Muscles in my back and shoulders seized. I couldn't move.

Bobo knelt beside me. "Jake, you okay?"

I couldn't speak. I could barely shake my head. A gray veil spread over my eyes. Bobo wrapped his arms around me and pulled me up. He steadied me as we walked. By the time we reached the building, the shaking had stopped. My vision had cleared, but a blanket of fear enveloped me. Nothing I'd ever felt before. Bobo helped me into the building, up the stairs, and to the office, where he sat me in my executive chair behind the desk. He towered over me, watching me.

I could finally speak. "I'm fine. Not sure what came over me, but I'm fine."

Bobo narrowed his eyes. "You need to see someone."

"I see you."

"I mean, you need to go to a counselor."

"Why?" I pushed the chair back and stood. Dizziness swam through my brain, but I steadied myself. "I said I'm fine. Let's go. River City PD."

I brushed past Bobo. He sighed hard but followed.

Two

Bobo drove.

I assumed he was leery of my shaking fit. Frankly, so was I. Where in the world had that come from? I've been in many dangerous situations before. Just last month, I was nearly killed three times, and I never had that type of reaction.

"Did you get a look at the driver of that SUV? And better yet, did you get the plates?"

Bobo eased to a stop at Westline Road. "Whoever it was wore a baseball cap. No insignia I could see. White person." Bobo pressed the accelerator. "Couldn't tell gender, but I didn't see any hair hanging down. Could have been tall, as their head nearly reached the headliner. Didn't look heavy. Sorry, no plate. There wasn't a front one and I was busy with you when it drove away."

"Their head reached the *what*?"

"The headliner. That's what the inside top of the car is called."

"Huh." I learned something new. "The person wasn't a skin-head?"

"Wearing a hat. Couldn't tell."

I had hoped our war with the neo-Nazis had ended. And it wasn't Edwin T. Masewich, resident killer, as that wasn't his style. He'd shoot me in the back. Who else in River City wanted me dead? Or were they going for Bobo? Unlikely. Everyone likes Bobo. Even the bad guys.

We arrived downtown at the fourth precinct of the River City Police. Sergeant Willow stood at his post behind the desk.

"Bobo, my man. Sledge. Good to see you guys."

Bobo and Willow slapped skin. I shook his hand.

"What brings you here? And be warned, Kazminsky is in his office and not in a good mood."

"Is he ever?" I asked.

"Not usually."

I leaned on the desk, trying to case some of the pain throughout my torso. Recovery from the two gunshots — one in the chest and one on the shoulder — was taking time. The vest had kept me alive, but it still felt like someone had hit me with a hammer. Not to mention my ribs, stomach, face, and other body parts that had been punched and kicked. I had started healing, when two skinheads drove their white van into my car. That last case took a toll on my body and my baby, the Delta 88.

"Who's the detective assigned to the Sandy Akins murder?" I asked.

"Why?" Willow asked.

Bobo answered, "Between you and us, Barker Dupree's sister hired us to find him."

"Ah. The prime suspect, so I hear."

"Any warrant out on him?" I asked.

"Not yet. And the lead detective is Phil Morris."

Didn't know him. Name wasn't familiar. When I left the force, I didn't know a lot of the patrol officers.

"Do you think he'll talk to us?" I asked.

Two uniformed officers walked in, dragging a disheveled and belligerent white dude with long hair sticking out in all directions.

"Snatched a purse from a lady on the street," one officer said. "Right in front of Duffy, here."

"Take him to booking," Willow said. "I'm a little busy right now."

They dragged the guy down the hall.

"What was your question, Sledge?"

"Do you think Morris will talk to us?"

Willow shrugged. "I don't know him that well. Here." Willow pulled out two guest badges on lanyards and handed them to us. "Go talk to him. I think he's in the bullpen. Hasn't checked out that I know of." He placed a clipboard with a sign-in sheet on the desk.

We added our signatures and headed down the hall to the detective's bullpen. Unfortunately, we had to walk past Lieutenant Kazminsky's desk before getting to the detectives. And that was as far as we got.

"Sledge!" Kazminsky came out of his office and intercepted us. "Mr. Johnson, how are you?"

Bobo and the lieut shook hands.

"Doing well, Lieutenant. And you?"

"Still cleaning up that mess you guys made."

"Mess?" I asked, probably a little too curtly.

"That's what I said. What are you doing here?"

"Coming to talk to Phil Morris."

Kazminsky jammed his fists on his hips. The unbuttoned top button, the loose tie, and the missing suit jacket confirmed the bad day the lieut was having.

"About what?" he asked.

"The Sandy Akins murder."

"You got a badge?" Kazminsky pointed at me.

"No."

"Then Detective Morris isn't talking to you. What's your interest in the case?"

"We have a client who has an interest," Bobo said.

"Who's that?" Kazminsky asked.

"Client confidentiality." I peered into the bullpen. Three detectives at their desks. The oldest of the bunch, Arnie Hassenberger, and I went way back. Decent detective. Two blond guys. Detective Schumann I knew and wondered why he was still employed. We had suspected he was feeding information to the ringleader during our previous case. Using my well-honed detective skills, I surmised the third guy had to be Morris. Short blond hair. Sharp facial features. Early thirties. I started toward the bullpen.

"Where do you think you're going, Sledge?"

I waved and kept walking. Hassenberger shouted a greeting.

"Hey, Arnie." When I reached Morris, he looked up from his computer screen.

"Can I help you, sir?" Morris said.

"Sir? Ouch. Not necessary, Detective Morris."

I felt someone come beside me. Lieutenant Kazminsky stood shoulder to shoulder with me but said nothing.

"You know me, but I'm afraid I don't know you."

Bobo joined the party.

"You probably don't want to know him," Kazminsky said.

"Sir?" Morris stood.

"Nothing but trouble."

That was my opening. "There's always trouble in River City."

Kazminsky shook his head. Morris frowned, puzzled.

Bobo stuck his hand out. "Bobo Johnson. Nice to meet you."

"*The* Bobo Johnson? Cincinnati Bengals?"

Bobo grinned and nodded. Always a sap for fans.

"Wow. Pleasure to meet you." Morris then eyed me. "And you're Jake the Hammer Sledge?"

"That I am. Or was." I shook his hand. "Now, I'm a partner in the Sledge Hammer Detective Agency, and I have some questions about the Sandy Akins murder."

Arnie Hassenberger joined the party. Detective Schumann walked out of the bullpen. Party pooper.

Hassenberger asked, "You working for the prosecuting attorney's office again, Sledge? What's their interest in this murder?"

"Sorry, Arnie. No badge this time. Private client."

Kazminsky said, "No badge, no information. It's an active investigation, Sledge. You know the rules."

Morris shrugged. "Sorry, Mr. Sledge, like the lieutenant said. It's an active investigation."

"Can I get a copy of the police report?" I knew that was a long shot.

Kazminsky asked, "Did you recently get your law degree?"

I flashed my best sarcastic look at the lieutenant.

"Then no copy of the report."

I sighed. "Fine. Let's go, Bobo. No help here."

We turned to leave.

Kazminsky said, "And don't bother going to records. McMurtry isn't there. He's out on medical leave."

Dang it. That was my next stop. McMurtry was a former partner of mine, one for whom I served a two-week desk suspension to keep him out of Internal Affairs' crosshairs, though he deserved to be fired.

"What's wrong with old Joey?" I asked.

"Had a heart attack two days ago. He'll be out for several weeks." Kazminsky's smug expression showed his delight with the roadblock to me getting case files. "And besides, the case is still open, so the file isn't down there yet."

True, but McMurtry could have made a copy for me. And Kazminsky knew that.

"Pleasure meeting you, Detective Morris," Bobo said.

"Likewise."

We headed out but stopped again at Willow's post.

"One more question, Sarge," I said. "Who did the scene for the Akins murder?"

"Geoffrey."

Nice. Geoffrey Poindexter. Probably better at crime scene analysis than anyone even in Kansas City. Lived with his eighty-year-old mother, otherwise, he could have easily run the crime lab in KC.

"Thanks, Sarge." I started toward the elevator to go to the third-floor crime lab but stopped. Kazminsky stood in the hall glaring at me. I decided to try Mr. Poindexter later, when Kazminsky wasn't around, so as not to get my favorite crime lab person in trouble. I turned around and headed to the outside door.

We left the precinct building. Next stop: River Bluffs Residential Treatment Facility. Time to visit the funny farm and see what we could find out about Barker Robert Dupree.

Three

Bobo and I had an incredible lunch at Sweetie Pies on the east side of downtown. Sweet potato pie and collard greens for the big guy. The same for me, but I added a half rack of barbecued ribs. During lunch, I continually steered the conversation away from my weird episode on the street corner. Bobo was persistent, and I knew he would bring it up again.

After lunch, we headed to River Bluffs Residential Treatment Facility. As I drove the rental Mazda CX-90 through River City to the far east side, my phone belted out, "She's Not There". Bobo chuckled and shook his head. He still had not met our bedazzling, baffling, and completely batty client.

"Ms. Dupree," I answered. "What can we do for you?"

"Hello, Mr. Sledge. I hope you're having a great day." Her full Southern accent had returned. "I was calling to check on the search for my poor brother."

"Not much more progress than when you called us a half hour ago."

Silence.

"Yes, well, I also wanted to apologize as I may have been a bit abrupt and rude when I called earlier."

"Apology accepted. But unfortunately, there's no new progress. We're on our way to River Bluffs."

"Oh? I hope they are forthright with you, considering all the money we've paid them."

"I'll let you know."

"Thank you, Mr. Sledge. It's always a pleasure to talk with you." She disconnected.

Bobo and I glanced at each other. Our brows raised, and we both shook our heads.

"You really need to meet her."

"Not sure I want to," Bobo said.

I turned left onto Marian Road and drove toward the river. The road ended, and I turned right onto a long driveway that wound through a manicured lawn. The building ahead of us had a stone front, a green roof, and dark brown stained 4x4s set in stone columns supporting a porte cochere. Yes, I know what a porte cochere is. Okay, I had to look it up. Anyway, I drove through the porte cochere and to the parking lot beyond. The first five parking spots were two handicapped and three visitor spaces. The way my body felt, I considered a handicapped space, but I knew Bobo would object. I parked in the first open visitor space. We walked into the building.

Behind a dark stained desk sat a thirty-ish woman with short black hair and bangs that extended to just above her stenciled black eyebrows.

She smiled at us. "How may I help you?"

I gave her my best smile. "We'd like to speak to the person in charge of this facility."

"That would be our director of operations, Dr. Lila Charnow. Do you have an appointment?"

We shook our heads.

"That's no problem. Let me see if she's available." The receptionist picked up a desk phone and punched a number.

Beyond the desk, three off-white vinyl sofas formed a U in an open area. In the middle of the sofas sat a large coffee table holding books, magazines, and a stack of coasters. Three men sat on the sofas, one on each, engaged in conversation. All casually dressed in jeans, khakis, one with a collared short-sleeved shirt, the other two in T-shirts. I wasn't sure if they were patients or staff.

"She'll be right up," the receptionist said, pointing at two cushioned chairs behind us. "Please have a seat."

We sat and waited. The man in the open area with the collared shirt walked to the back of the building and turned, I assumed, down a hallway. The other two continued their conversation. One of them, a twenty-something-year-old with dark, curly hair, glanced at us repeatedly.

After a few minutes, a tall blonde wearing a beige pants suit and white dress shirt strode toward us. Her tight ponytail streaked with gray emphasized her sharp facial features. I guessed her to be in her mid-forties.

I stood. Bobo slouches when he sits, so when he unfolds in front of someone, the reactions can be comical. Dr. Charnow's eyes widened as she watched Bobo extend to his full height. Then she smiled and put out her hand.

"You're Bobo Johnson, aren't you?"

Bobo grinned. He grasped her hand.

"I'm so pleased to meet you. I'm Dr. Lila Charnow, but you can call me Lila. When you played, I became a Bengals fan. Normally a Chiefs fan, but I loved watching you play defense."

Another woman in River City infatuated with Bobo. His grin widened, showing all his pearly whites. I cleared my throat. Dr. Charnow studied me a bit.

"And I'll bet you're Jake the Hammer Sledge. The hit you put on that receiver in your fourth game. Wow. I jumped out of my chair."

This woman was alright in my book.

"Yes, ma'am, I am Jake Sledge. We're partners in the Sledge Hammer Detective Agency."

"Clever." She shook my hand as well. Strong grip, constant eye contact. "And what can I do for you? Is one of you in need of our services?"

"He is." Bobo pointed at me.

"No, I'm not."

"Trust me," Bobo said, "he needs some help. Maybe not today, but we'll be back."

I glared at Bobo who gave me an impassive look. To Dr. Charnow, I said, "We've been hired to help Barker DuPree. I believe he was a patient here."

Dr. Charnow's smile faded, and a cloud fell over her countenance. "I am familiar with Mr. DuPree. And when you say help him, what exactly do you mean?"

"I'm sorry, that's client confidential. All I can tell you right now is we're trying to find him." Dr. Charnow said nothing, so I continued. "We understand he escaped from this facility on July 28. Any idea where he might have gone?"

"First, Mr. Sledge, no one escapes from River Bluffs. All clients are here by choice. They are free to leave anytime."

"Okay, he left then. Any idea where he went?"

"Unfortunately, I can't even officially tell you he was or is a client here. Due to HIPAA regulations, we can't tell you anything without his written permission."

"What does a hippo have to do with regulations?"

Bobo chuckled. Dr. Charnow grinned. I raised my hands. "What?"

"It's HIPAA, Jake. H-I-P-A-A."

"Oh. And what does that stand for?"

Dr. Charnow said, "Health Insurance Portability and Accountability Act. It's a law that protects a person's health information."

"Oh, that's what all those forms were that I signed at the hospital."

Dr. Charnow raised her brows, but I didn't elaborate. "Okay, we won't ask you about his treatment here. But what we need to know right now is if you know where he might have gone?"

The curly-haired guy, now alone in the open area, watched us.

"Again, I can't acknowledge he was here. I can't tell you any address. And we can't tell you about anything he may have revealed to us if he was, indeed, in therapy here."

Wow. I considered some hypotheticals, but decided she'd not budge. I sighed.

Bobo asked, "When he signed his forms, did he mention anyone else that could have the information, like maybe his sister?"

Dr. Charnow's frown deepened. "He wrote her name as someone definitely not to release information to."

Nice job, Bobo. "He was here, then," I said. "If he signed forms, that is. And besides, we know he was here. His sister told us."

Dr. Charnow's shoulders slumped. "Fine, you got me there. He did sign some forms."

"And he named Jeopardy Dupree as someone not to release information to?" I asked.

"It's the only sister he has."

"Well, sort of." I explained about Concentration Dupree.

"Ah, yes. I'm familiar with Ms. Dupree's dissociative disorder. Is she who hired you?"

"Sorry, can't tell you that. No fancy acronym to back it up, but still client confidentiality."

"I understand."

"Thank you, Dr. Charnow. When we find him, we'll get him to sign something so you can talk to us."

She nodded. "Anything else I can help you with?"

"Do you do outpatient therapy?" Bobo asked.

"We do. What did you have in mind?"

"Not for me, Dr. Charnow. For him." Again, Bobo pointed at me.

I glared at Bobo, shook Dr. Charnow's hand, and left the facility. After about thirty seconds, Bobo caught up to me. I could only imagine what he told Dr. Charnow. As we approached the car, Bobo was mumbling to himself.

I asked him, "Where do we go next?"

"To where I always go when I'm stuck. To God." He continued praying quietly until we reached the car.

I threw my sports coat in the back seat. We both got in the car.

"Seriously, big guy, now what?"

"I *was* being serious, Jake. God will provide a path. Have some faith."

Someone pounded on the driver's side window. I jumped and turned. A man with a bald head stared at me. The guy held a long pipe. Adrenaline coursed through my body. I gripped my .45.

Bobo grabbed my arm. "Jake, what are you doing?"

I looked at Bobo. "Don't you see that guy?"

"Yeah, it's a dude from the facility. The guy who was watching us from the lobby."

I turned back. Not a skinhead. No pipe in his hand. The guy from the lobby. I started the car and opened the window.

"Sorry, man, that I startled you."

"Sure. What do you want?"

"Um, well, I couldn't help overhear you back there." He pointed his thumb over his shoulder. "Are you looking for Barker?"

Couldn't help overhearing? Yeah, right. "Do you know Barker?"

He nodded. "He's a friend of mine. We met here about a year ago."

"You've been here a year?"

"Yessir. I'm making good progress. Barker was here even longer."

"Glad to hear. What about Barker?"

"Well, he had another friend in here, a guy named Benny Frazer."

"Frazer? Where have I heard that name before?"

Bobo said, "We busted him maybe ten times. Meth-head and dealer."

I nodded, remembering good old Benny. He used to deal out of a ramshackle two-story just north of downtown.

The guy from the facility leaned on the door. Good thing it was a rental. No one leans on my baby.

"Yeah, that's him. Came here to supposedly kick his meth habit."

"Why do you say supposedly?" I asked.

"I think he came here to get more clients."

"Sounds like Frazer," Bobo muttered.

"Where's good ole Benny hanging out these days?"

"Far as I know, his house is around North 12th Avenue."

Same place where we'd busted him many times. "Thanks. We'll check it out. Anything else you can tell us about Barker?"

"Yeah, he didn't kill Ms. Akins. He loved her. Worshipped her."

Someone shouted from the facility entrance. "Mr. Connors, what are you doing?"

Connors pushed back from our car. "Sorry, gotta go. Come back and I'll tell you more." He jogged back toward the facility.

I backed out of the parking space. "Let's go pay Benny Frazer a visit."

Four

Five years ago, the last time I busted Benny Frazer, the house had been falling apart. Shutters hung askew. A first-floor window was boarded up. A yard of weeds and dirt. In five years, things had further decayed. Now, two first-floor windows were boarded up. Paint peeled off the graying boards of the porch. Along with the weeds, a tricycle, a large, dented play firetruck, and other assorted children's toys decorated the dirt lawn.

Bobo and I cautiously walked up the stairs. Wood creaked but held. I debated yanking the screen door off its lone hinge, but there was no need since the top of the frame was missing its glass. I banged on the interior door.

Inside, a woman yelled, and a child screeched. I pounded again.

"Coming!" a man shouted.

We waited. Squealing from a child. Rapid footsteps from someone upstairs. Finally, the door opened. Benny Frazer stuck his bearded face out, hiding the rest of himself behind the aluminum door.

"What do you want? You cops?"

I ripped the screen door off and shoved the interior door open. Benny staggered back, tripped on a toy car, and landed on his rear.

"What the heck, dude. Who do you think you are?"

I entered. Bobo came in behind me.

"You don't remember us, Benny?"

This house sat smack in the middle of Bobo's old beat. I had busted Benny once on suspected murder and again on assault, but Bobo had arrested him half a dozen times on drug charges.

Benny's eyes widened. "Officer Johnson. I ... I haven't seen you in some time." Benny stood. "What brings you here?"

"He's not Officer Johnson anymore. We're private. Not cops. Where's Barker DuPree?"

Benny looked over his right shoulder toward the back of the house.

"Good enough." I shoved Benny down again and walked toward the back room.

"Hey," Benny yelled.

Bobo stayed by him, so the drug dealer remained sitting on the floor.

Footsteps pounded down the stairs behind me. A moment later, a small child scooted by me. A disheveled woman wearing holey jeans and a stained T-shirt brushed past me in pursuit of the boy.

"Come back here, Simon."

A bumping noise came from a room down the hall to my left, followed by a loud screech, like nails scratching on a blackboard. I ran to the door. Locked. I kicked it in. A scrawny man dressed in jean shorts and a black T-shirt turned from the window and stared at me. The window was about half open. Not quite enough for anyone to squeeze through. The man had a mop of dirty blond hair, three days of stubble, and the same facial bone structure as Jeopardy DuPree.

"Barker DuPree?"

He looked both ways, then tensed his body.

"Don't bother. You won't get past me. And I'm not here to hurt you."

"Are you a cop?"

"Private eye. Hired by your sister to help you out."

"Jeopardy? You know her?"

I nodded.

He relaxed, then leaned against the windowsill. "How are you going to help me?"

"First, let's get you out of this meth-head's house."

"Benny's okay. He's making a real effort to quit the junk. Hasn't had anything since I've been here."

"Yeah, he's a real upstanding citizen. It's chaotic here. Let's go to my office where we can talk in peace and figure out how to help you."

His eyes became vacant, staring clean through me. He shook his head several times. "No. He won't do that."

"What are you talking about?"

No response. More head shaking. Then a nod and his eyes refocused on me. "Okay, I'll go with you."

"Anything you need to get before we leave?"

He walked to the side of the twin bed, leaned over, and when he straightened up, he clutched a travel bag. "This is it."

Barker DuPree followed me out of the room toward the front of the house. Benny still sat on the ground, Bobo hovering over him.

"Barker DuPree, this is my partner, Bobo Johnson."

Bobo stuck out his hand. Barker grasped it. They shook.

"Nice to meet you, Mr. DuPree. By God's grace, we'll be able to help you."

Barker released Bobo's hand. "Uh huh. I hope so."

With Barker in the back seat, I put the Mazda into gear and accelerated. I glanced in my rearview mirror. Half a block behind us, a cop car eased away from the curb and followed us. I drove north on W. 7th Street about five miles. The cop stayed behind us. No flashing lights and no closer than three car lengths. We stopped at a red light at the corner of 7th and River Road. I studied the driver through my rearview mirror. No one I recognized. Young guy. The light turned green, and I turned left toward my office. The cop did the same. For another three miles, he stayed behind us. But when I turned into the parking lot for my office, he kept going.

I parked and led the way to the office. Barker followed, then Bobo. At the entrance, I held the door open for them, then scanned the parking lot and road. No cop. We walked the stairs to the second floor of my three-story office building.

"*Sledge Hammer Detective Agency*," Barker read. "Kind of ominous. Do you pound out cases?"

Clever dude. "Close. Our motto is 'Got a problem? Let *Sledge Hammer Detective Agency* pound it out.'"

Barker rolled his eyes.

"Sit." I pointed to one of the vinyl chairs fronting the desk.

Barker sat.

Bobo asked, "You all want something to eat?"

I shrugged. Barker nodded.

"What do you like, Mr. DuPree?"

"Please, call me Barker. Burgers?"

"That works," Bobo said. "I'll go to Bob's Drive-in. I assume you want the usual, Jake?"

I nodded. The usual was two double burgers, large fries, and a large chocolate shake. Bobo's usual was two grilled chicken sandwiches and a diet soda. He'd have some of my fries.

Bobo left. I took off my sports coat and hung it on the coat rack. Barker's gaze tracked my .45. His hands did acrobatics in his lap.

"Don't worry, I won't shoot you."

A wan smile was Barker's response.

"At least as long as you behave yourself." Wrong thing to say.

He got up and walked to the door, muttering to himself.

"Halt!"

He did but didn't turn around and continued muttering.

"I'm kidding. Your sister hired us to help you. Please come sit down."

He rotated and inched his way back to the chair. His head hung and the muttering continued. I couldn't make out anything intelligible. He sat, went silent, and looked up at me.

"Tell me about Sandy Akins."

His eyes glistened. He wiped the back of his hand across them. "I loved her. She was the reason I left. We ... we were going to start a new life together."

"You didn't kill her?"

He leaped out of the chair, baring his teeth, eyes popping out. "Of course not! I just told you I loved her."

I backed up and held out my hands. "Calm down. Just covering the bases."

He returned to the chair.

"Any chance you flipped out or entered some type of psychotic state?"

"What? No. I was on my meds and doing well."

"Was?"

"Yeah, was. I ran out four days ago."

That explained the muttering and the weirdness at Benny's house. I started to ask another question, when a shadow crossed my frosted glass door. It wasn't tall enough to be Bobo. I waited to see if someone would knock.

The shadow grew and shrank and then grew again until widthwise it covered the glass. There was whispering and some shushing. Someone slowly turned the doorknob. I rested my right hand on the grip of my .45.

The door flew open. I started to extract my gun. My vision grew fuzzy and the people at the door faded in and out. Young men. Shaved heads. Black T-shirts and jeans. I eased the Beretta about halfway out, but hesitated. I shook my head. So much noise. Shouting. I couldn't make out the words. The men advanced. One had a gun pointed at me. Finally, something registered.

"Hands up! Now! Get your hands up."

My vision cleared. Three uniformed officers stood in my office. One had Barker up against the wall. I released my gun and put my hands up. All three officers were ten to fifteen years younger than me. None of them could have been out of the academy more than a couple years.

The closest officer was in a shooting stance; gun pointed at me. Another one, not engaged with Barker, stepped toward me. He pulled my gun from my holster.

"Turn around. Keep your hands up."

I complied. The officer slapped cuffs on my right arm and pulled it down behind my back. He pulled down my left hand next and cuffed me. I shook my head to clear the fuzziness.

"Do you know who I am?" I asked.

"I assume Sledge based on the sign on the door."

"Yes. Jake Sledge. Former detective first-class for River City PD. What are you taking me in for?"

"Harboring a fugitive." The officer turned me around and read me my rights.

The other officer, not holding Barker, told my client he was under arrest for the murder of Sandy Akins. The officer read him his rights. The three of them escorted us out of my building. Fortunately, none of my tenants were in the hallways. One officer shoved me into one car. Another one shoved Barker into the back of another car, and they took us to the jail downtown. None of the drive registered as I dwelt on what had happened to me, realizing I'd come inches from shooting a cop and being gunned down.

Five

My stomach rumbled.

I'd been arrested too late for lunch, and dinner hadn't come yet.

I wondered if Bobo had eaten my two double burgers, Barker's burger, and his chicken sandwiches from Bob's Drive-in.

A county deputy opened the holding cell door.

"Sledge, you're free to go."

I followed the officer out.

"Second time in a month, isn't it, Sledge?" Officer Crouch asked.

"But this time I didn't do anything."

"Not what I heard. The uniforms that brought you in said you almost pulled your gun on them."

"Didn't know who they were at first."

"Mm-hmm."

We climbed the stairs to the first floor. Bobo and Lieutenant Kazminsky waited for me in the lobby, both with stupid grins on their faces. I retrieved my personal items from the county deputy. Kazminsky chuckled as I approached them.

"What are you laughing at?"

Kazminsky shook his head. "Sledge, you're a lucky man. You could be dead if those officers had been more experienced." He shoved a large, heavy envelope into my chest.

"Or not arrested at all. Who were those yahoos?" I looked inside the envelope. My guns. The .45 I had supposedly almost pulled on the cops and my .40 I was wearing on my ankle.

"Newer guys." He laughed some more. "I dressed down their sergeant. No way they should have entered the way they did."

"What was that all about, anyway?"

Bobo answered, "They issued a warrant on Barker."

"How did they know where he was?"

Kazminsky grinned. "I asked patrol to have someone follow you guys."

"Seriously? That's got to be a violation of our rights. Why didn't anyone call to tell us about the warrant?"

"You don't work here anymore, Sledge. We went over that."

"Where's Barker?" I hadn't seen him in the two other holding cells I passed.

"In another cell in the other hall. Where he'll stay until his bail hearing Monday."

"Monday? What about tomorrow?"

"The judge is on vacation, and no one stepped in to take over. His bail hearing is Monday."

I shook my head, turned, and walked out of the building. Bobo followed.

"Whose car did you bring?"

"Mine," Bobo replied.

"I assume the rental is still at the office?"

"It is. Want to stop there?"

I nodded and climbed in Bobo's Range Rover.

"Where are my burgers, fries, and shake?"

Bobo pulled onto 2nd Avenue and headed east. "Burgers are in the fridge in the break room. We don't have a freezer, so I drank the shake. I left you my diet soda, though."

"Gee, thanks. And the fries?"

"What fries?"

"Funny guy. You ate them, didn't you?"

He just grinned. He had paid for them, so I couldn't be too mad. "Did you eat Barker's food?"

"Nope. It's in the fridge with yours."

Good. I'd get three burgers and a regular soda.

We rode in silence for about five minutes. Bobo turned north on Willson Drive toward the office.

"What happened with the officers?" Bobo asked.

"What do you mean? They arrested Barker and me."

"You know what I mean. They told me you nearly pulled your gun. What were you thinking?"

I didn't say anything for a moment. But Bobo and I had been friends forever, and this wasn't the time to hold back.

"It was freaky. They weren't cops when they entered."

"Let me guess. You thought they were skinheads."

"Yeah. And things got fuzzy. The shouting all blurred together. I froze."

Bobo stopped at the light on Riverside Avenue.

"You need help, Jake. Let me set something up for you."

"Why do I need help?"

"I think you're suffering from PTSD." The light turned green. Bobo accelerated.

"I don't have PTSD. Why would I have that?"

Bobo sighed. "Well, let's see. In the last month you were beaten up, rammed by a van, had two people assassinated right next to you, shot and killed four people, and shot three others."

"All in a day's work for a private eye, dude."

"Really? How many times did you shoot your gun on the job?"

He referred to my cop days, of course.

"I don't know. Three or four."

"And how many people did you kill as a cop?"

"None."

"Last week you killed four people."

"Those weren't people. They were animals that kidnapped my niece."

"They were still human beings. Killing another person takes something out of you. There's no shame in seeking help."

"Whatever. And I suppose you know someone who could help me?"

"I know a couple Christian counselors. I'll find out if any of them treat PTSD."

"Fine."

Bobo pulled into our parking lot.

"What time is it?" I asked. My smart watch and phone were still in the envelope from the county jail.

"Just about seven."

I swore.

Bobo punched me in the shoulder. It would leave a bruise. "Language, man."

"Sorry. I was supposed to meet Allie for dinner at six." I ripped open the envelope and extracted my cell phone.

"Put it on speaker."

"You nosy or what?"

"Just curious. And besides, I can vouch for you."

Bobo had a point. I dialed Allison Rogers, an amazing woman I'd met a few weeks back. We'd been on one whole date. Though I did spend the night at her house a week or so ago. In the guest room. Alone.

"Hello, Jake. I hope you have a good excuse for standing me up."

Even upset, her voice was pleasant.

"That woman is way too nice for you."

"Is that you, Bobo?" Allison asked.

"Yes, ma'am. How are you?"

"That depends on Jake's excuse."

Bobo chuckled.

"I was in jail."

"Oh my gosh. What did you do?"

I decided the dramatic approach would work best. "I almost shot and killed three police officers."

Bobo shook his head.

"Why would you do that?"

I told her about the cops breaking into my office, about mistaking their identity for the bad guys we'd dealt with a few days ago and then being taken to jail.

"They thought I was harboring a fugitive. River City PD issued a warrant for our client, but no one bothered to tell us."

"And before you ask," Bobo said, "I can vouch for everything he said. Except he didn't almost shoot the cops. He didn't even draw his gun."

She chuckled. "That's good. They might have shot you."

Obviously, she didn't know me that well yet. No way three rookies would have gotten the drop on me. A person drawing on a stationary target is almost always faster than the one already pointing the gun. Television gets that wrong most of the time.

"Can I make it up to you? Tomorrow evening? Same time? Same place?"

A pause. Some tapping noises. "Just checking my calendar." Another pause. "Sure, that would be great. Same place works. I didn't eat there. Came home and warmed up leftovers."

"Cool. See you there. And again, sorry about not letting you know earlier. Just got out of the slammer."

Bobo shook his head again. But at least he didn't say anything.

"Do you have your car back yet? If you do, you can pick me up."

"Not yet. Won't be until Monday. Glad to pick you up anyway."

"That's okay. We can meet there. See ya. Glad you're okay."

"Bye."

We disconnected.

Bobo stared at me.

"What?"

"I'm calling those two counselors tomorrow."

"Fine." I got out of the Range Rover. "See you tomorrow. Let's meet here about nine then go visit our client. You'll have the pleasure of meeting Ms. Jeopardy DuPree. Twice the woman most women are."

Bobo laughed. I got in my rental Mazda and drove home, thinking what else could possibly go wrong with this case. As it turned out, plenty.

Six

We arrived at the DuPree mansion. Even for River City, which had several neighborhoods with executives from Kansas City, the DuPree house was large. A Southern colonial, three stories, with four thick white columns on the portico.

"You ready for this?" I asked Bobo.

He shrugged.

I rang the bell. The tune to "Carolina in My Mind" played faintly inside. Cute. One side of the massive double door opened, and there she was. Ms. Jeopardy DuPree. I'd called her earlier and told her we were on our way, as we had news about her brother.

Jeopardy wore a beige pleated dress that fell to her calves. Her blond hair was back in a ponytail. An off-white scarf with brown ponies held the ponytail in place. To top it off, she wore three-inch spiked heels that matched her dress color.

I gave a wan smile. "Ms. DuPree, may I present to you Bobo Johnson. Bobo, may I present to you the two-of-a-kind woman, Jeopardy DuPree. And sometimes Concentration DuPree."

She fired a brief glare at me, then offered her hand to Bobo, who engulfed it with his.

"It's such a pleasure to meet you, Mr. Johnson." She turned to me, dipped her head a bit, and looked at me as if she were looking over a pair of glasses. But she didn't wear glasses. "And I've told you, Mr. Sledge, Connie is gone forever."

Despite the gone-forever Connie having nearly killed me, Jeopardy's southern accent pleasantly reverberated through my body. Possibly, probably a lunatic, but a gorgeous and charming one.

Bobo said, "It's very nice to meet you, too, Ms. DuPree. And you look beautiful."

Jeopardy blushed. She made a motion with her right hand. If she'd been holding a fan, she'd have fanned herself. Such the Southern belle.

"Thank you so much, Mr. Johnson." She batted her enormous eyelashes at Bobo. "And you, Mr. Sledge, you look dashing as always."

I tipped my light brown fedora to her and left it off as we walked into the house. For the occasion, I wore my purple windowpane sports jacket, light tan collarless short-sleeved shirt, and light tan linen pants. Of course, I had a .45 under my jacket in a shoulder holster and my .40 on my ankle. One cannot be too careful around nutcases.

We followed Jeopardy through the massive entryway. A crystal chandelier hung on what had to be a fifteen-foot chain from the top of the three-story house. A spiral staircase wound up to the second and third floors. I'd traveled that staircase once to the master bedroom, where Concentration DuPree nearly impaled me with a butcher knife. Plantation paintings still decorated the wall along the staircase. I hoped Bobo wouldn't notice them.

We entered a sitting room.

"Please." She gestured toward the chairs. "May I get you some lemonade?"

"No. Sit." I wasn't letting her out of my sight.

Bobo glared at me.

I flashed a huge smile. "Please. We won't be here long."

Jeopardy smiled and demurely perched on the edge of a brushed suede sofa. Bobo sat on a large easy chair, but like Jeopardy, he didn't relax back. I remained standing.

"You said you have news about Barker?"

"Yup. Good news and bad news."

She said nothing, just stared at me with her sparkling blue eyes and fluttering lashes.

"The good news is we found Barker."

She brought both hands up to her chin in prayer-like fashion. "That's wonderful. How is he?"

"That's the bad news. He's in jail. His arraignment is Monday. He's being charged with the murder of Sandy Akins."

Her eyes widened, and her hands dropped to her lap. "Oh, my. I just know he didn't kill that poor girl."

"And how do you know?" I sat on a straight-backed carved wood chair with a cushioned seat.

"That's just not his nature. He's always been such a sweet person. Even when he had his episodes, he was never violent."

Bobo asked, "Does he hear voices, ma'am?"

"He does. But as far as we know, he's never had voices tell him to do something violent, or even illegal."

"We?" I asked.

"Daddy DuPree and I, of course. When he was alive." She looked at her hands. "What can I do to help? How do we get Barker out?"

"At the arraignment, he'll have bail set. Maybe. The prosecuting attorney may ask for no bail, calling him a flight risk. Do you have a family lawyer?"

"We do." She stood and went to a small antique table. Upon it sat an old-fashioned phone with a dial. On close examination, I noticed it wasn't usable. No cord was plugged into anything. She opened the one drawer, rummaged through it, then pulled out a card. She brought it to me.

"Well, what do you know?"

Bobo asked, "What?"

"The Duprees have the same lawyer as our resident gangster friend."

Bobo's eyebrows shot up. "Really?"

"Yeah. And that's a good thing. He should be willing to work with us, since we snatched his client from the jaws of death."

"Oh, please do tell." Jeopardy sat on the edge of the sofa and leaned toward me.

"Sorry, client confidentiality." The client we'd rescued was Ricardo Patricci, who'd been kidnapped by the same animals that had taken my niece. Theodore Jorgenson, Patricci's lawyer, had hired us to find him. And we did. Unharmed. "We'll visit Mr. Jorgenson today. I suggest when we leave you call him, Ms. DuPree, and tell him Barker is in jail. Also, please mention we're coming to his office."

Jeopardy nodded. "What else can I do?"

"Nothing right now. We need to talk to Barker as well. We need his permission to discuss his stay at River Bluffs."

She nodded, the "I'll do anything to help" expression pasted to her pretty face. I was hoping she would volunteer why Barker excluded her from the list to release medical information.

"And speaking of, what was that called?" I asked Bobo. "A release of medical information."

"You mean the HIPAA stuff?"

"Yeah, that. Speaking of HIPAA, why would you, Ms. DuPree, be on the do not give her any information list?"

Her eyes widened. She stiffened. "Barker said that?"

"No. The facility said that Barker specifically told them not to give you any information about his treatment."

"Why would Barker do that? He knows I love him dearly."

"We don't know. You tell us."

Her eyes clouded over. She looked away, then got up and paced around the room once. When she returned to the sofa, she said, "Daddy and I were close. And I think Barker resented that. Barker was ... well, he was weak. And Daddy wanted a strong son to take over for him." She perched on the edge again. "You see, since Barker wasn't that person, Daddy groomed me to take over. He made me strong."

Her gaze became vacant. She dipped her head. Her hands were clasped together, cradled in the fabric between her legs. Her head came up quickly, eyes blazing. "And that's why he had to—" She put both hands over her mouth, jumped up, and turned away. Her shoulders shook.

Bobo looked at me, eyebrows raised. I shrugged.

Jeopardy turned around, then sat. She smiled sadly. Gentleness had returned to her eyes.

"You were saying?" I asked. "That's why your dad had to what?"

"Oh?" She looked around the room. "Oh, yes. That's why he wanted to make me strong. Because of his health, he stepped down. I had to take over."

"Okay?"

"And Barker was in the facility by then. No real choice."

"Then why did you kill your dad?"

She jumped up again. I checked her hands. No weapon.

"I didn't, Mr. Sledge. Please, it was Connie. And she is gone. And believe me, I paid for her crime."

"Tell us about that, would you? How is Connie gone?"

Jeopardy collapsed onto the sofa. "Three years of intensive treatment, Mr. Sledge. I even had to, had to go through electro-shock therapy."

"Really?"

"They said it would help erase some of my memories. The ones that caused Connie to appear."

"And you're sure she's gone?"

Jeopardy nodded. She dropped her head and rubbed her hands together.

I started to ask something else, but Bobo interrupted me.

"Thank you, ma'am, for the information. We need to go see Mr. Jorgenson, now." He stood. "Don't we, Jake?"

When Bobo asks a question with the tone he used, there is only one correct answer. I nodded and stood as well.

"Thank you, Ms. DuPree. We'll keep you informed of our progress. There's no need to come to Barker's arraignment. At least one of us will attend. And if he needs bail money, we'll let you know."

Jeopardy rose and led us into the foyer. Before we could leave, she asked, "How about I buy you both dinner tonight, and we can go over what Mr. Jorgenson says?"

I wanted to get out of there and continue working on the case, so I said something I should not have and would regret later.

"Thank you for the offer, but I have a date tonight. We'll catch up with you on Monday."

Jeopardy opened the door and watched us leave with an unreadable expression. When we hit the bottom step of the portico, she slammed the door.

Seven

Before Bobo and I entered the office building where Theodore Jorgenson worked, I stopped on the sidewalk and gazed around. Mini cement columns sprouted in a concrete plaza narrowing to a thoroughfare running between two tinted glass towers. People sat on the columns, having conversations, eating lunch, staring into space. Not even a month ago, William J. Abernathy, another lawyer, was found dead on this same sidewalk. I shuddered and blinked, feeling a sensation like an old-fashioned slide projector changing slides. Sitting on one of the closer columns was a young man in a black T-shirt glaring at me. A swastika tattoo wrapped around his bicep. His beady eyes shot daggers from below his shaved head. I reached for my gun under my jacket.

Bobo grabbed my arm. "Jake, you okay, man?"

I blinked again. New slide. A young man sat on the column. He had long brown hair tied into a short ponytail, not a shaved head. And he wore a suit, not a black T-shirt. Instead of glaring at me, he was talking to a young woman in a dark blue pantsuit.

"Yeah, fine. Let's go see Theodore Jorgenson."

Talk about a leather explosion. The outside lobby of Jorgenson and Jenkins had no less than ten leather armchairs, gold-colored studs around the edges. Bookcases lined two of the walls, filled with leather-bound editions. A glass-walled conference room comprised the third. Dark wood paneling surrounded the double doors we entered. A hallway disappeared past the conference room. We stopped at the desk halfway into the cavernous lobby. A curt woman with short black hair peered up at us through horn-rimmed glasses.

"May I help you, gentlemen?"

I made a big show searching for said gentlemen. It's my schtick. What can I say? But the young woman either didn't appreciate the joke or ignored it, thinking it was stupid. Which it is. But that's the point.

Before either of us could state our business, the young woman said, "I recognize you." And of course, she was looking at Bobo. She flashed a huge smile. Everyone smiles at Bobo

"You're Bobo Johnson. Hall of fame defensive tackle for the Bengals. I used to watch you when I was a kid."

Bobo's face lit up like a Christmas tree. Me, I just felt old. *When she was a kid?*

"Yes, ma'am. We're here to see Mr. Jorgenson."

"Let me check. That's so cool. You coming in here. My dad is going to freak when I tell him I met you." She looked at me. "And your name?"

Before I could answer, Theodore Jorgenson entered the lobby from the hallway. "Mr. Jake Sledge. Welcome to my humble place of business. Mr. Johnson, good to see you again."

Humble?

"It's okay, Brittany. I'll talk with them. Ms. Dupree told me to expect them."

At least Jeopardy wasn't mad enough that she forgot to do her part in helping her brother.

"Come into my office, please, gentlemen."

I couldn't resist. I made another big show looking around for said gentlemen. But they ignored me. Bobo followed Jorgenson. With head hung, I tagged along. Tough crowd.

I expected a mini-lobby-type office, all leather, dark wood, that kind of thing. But Jorgenson surprised me. A modern glass desk, on which sat a computer, a legal pad, and a couple of files. Three chrome-framed, modern chairs with black vinyl seats flanked the desk. Glass-shelved bookcases lined two of the walls. And floor-to-ceiling windows on the back wall revealed downtown River City in all its non-glory.

"Sit, gentlemen."

I didn't bother with the schtick the third time. We all sat.

"Mr. Sledge, though I admire your outfit, I don't think you and I should walk too close together today."

I smiled. He wore a lime-green suit with a pastel purple shirt. I wondered about one more item, so I swept my gaze around his office. Yup, he had one. A lime-green fedora hung on a coat rack in the corner past the door. Sweet.

"Where shall we start?" Jorgenson asked.

"We need a copy of Barker's case file from River City PD."

"Done. I'll have a copy delivered to your office Monday morning."

"And we need to get permission from Barker to get his medical records from the facility. Some regulation. Hippo something. What was that, Bobo?"

Both Bobo and Jorgenson said, "HIPAA."

"Yeah, that one."

Jorgenson glanced at his watch. "How about you two gentlemen accompany me to the courthouse for Mr. Dupree's arraignment?"

"Um, sure. We can do that. What time?" I assumed he meant Monday.

"About an hour from now."

Both Bobo and I said, "What?"

Jorgenson smiled. "His arraignment is in an hour."

"But we were told the judge was out until Monday."

Another smile from Jorgenson. "Judge Howell is out until Monday. When I called his office and pointed out the inappropriateness of having no one to cover, voila, they found someone. Judge Gilmore will hold an afternoon arraignment session."

This dude had pull. I liked it. Finally, some things were going right in our case.

He got up and grabbed his fedora.

"Want to switch for the walk to the courthouse?" I asked.

Jorgenson nodded. I put on his lime green fedora. He donned my light tan one. We followed him out of his office and walked two blocks to the courthouse. I kept Bobo between us to avoid fashion clashing with the dapper lawyer.

Before entering the courthouse, Jorgenson and I swapped fedoras. I made a mental note to hunt one down that color.

Nothing exciting or unusual about the courthouse in downtown River City. There was a gallery of wooden seats. A couple tables, one for the defense and one for the prosecutor. An elevated bench for the judge. However, that day, there was one spectacular addition to the courtroom in which Barker was to be arraigned. Especially in Bobo's eyes. Assistant Prosecutor Liliana Goodhue. Tall, chocolate brown skin, glossy black hair, and delicate, Asian-accented features. A gorgeous woman whom Bobo was madly in love with.

We sat in the row immediately behind Jorgenson. He and Liliana shook hands. She then glanced at us.

"Mr. Johnson. Nice to see you. What brings you here?"

"Mr. Dupree is our client."

To my amazement, Bobo didn't drool when he spoke.

Liliana nodded and returned to her table, joining a man and a woman. Both wore suits. Both were in their late twenties to early thirties. I assumed one was a clerk and one a junior prosecutor.

I glanced at Bobo, expecting him to be staring at the prosecution table and the lovely queen of the law. Instead, he faced the door behind the judge's bench where a county deputy led Barker Dupree into the courtroom. Not watching Liliana? Something was up. I'd ask him later.

Barker wore an orange jumpsuit. His eyes darted all over, his gaze passing over us, like he didn't recognize us. The deputy deposited him in the chair next to Jorgenson. A blond woman in her early thirties walked down the aisle and sat on the other side of Jorgenson. His assistant, I assumed.

Barker looked back at us. His vacant eyes finally registered our presence.

"Oh, hey, Mr. Sledge. Mr. Johnson. Thanks for coming."

I shrugged. "No problem." No judge yet, so I leaned over and tapped Jorgenson on the shoulder.

He swiveled the wooden chair, making an awful screech on the tile floor.

"Yes, Mr. Sledge?"

"Do you think Ms. Goodhue is going to allow bail?"

"I'm sure she'll ask for no bail, given the severity of the charges. However, I believe our compromise will be sufficient to get him out of jail."

"And what compromise is that?"

"All rise for the honorable Judge Gilmore," the bailiff intoned.

We rose. The bailiff and judge took us through the preliminaries. My eyes grew heavy, but I forced them to stay open. While the judge droned on, I examined the courtroom. Only four other people. Two of the moron rookie cops who nearly shot me and arrested Barker sat a couple rows back on the prosecution side. In the far back corner behind the defense table sat a woman with short dark hair, wearing rose-tinted glasses and a bulky denim dress. She had a round, puffy face. Next to her sat a thin man with a baseball cap pulled down low, hiding his eyes. He wore jeans, a plain white T-shirt, and a brown sports coat. Both stared in the direction of the judge.

We finally got to the part where the two lawyers argued about bail. As predicted, Liliana wanted no bail, claiming Barker was a flight risk. Jorgenson argued that Barker had nowhere to go. His home was here. He knew no one outside of River City. The two went back and forth, a polite but firm tennis match of legal arguments. Neither lawyer raised their voice or sharpened their tone. Both nodded to the other after speaking. They both showed hints of a smile.

Their interaction blew my mind. I'd been in a courtroom with the queen of the law several times. Liliana Goodhue usually shredded the defense. I knew of public defenders who changed careers after an encounter with her. But with Jorgenson, she remained calm, even pleasant.

A short, stocky, thirtyish woman walked into the courtroom, down the aisle, and to the defense table. She leaned over and whispered into Jorgenson's ear. To my surprise, neither the judge nor Liliana made any protest. They both waited patiently. The woman stood and left the same way she came.

Jorgenson stood. "Your honor, before you rule on bail, may I make a proposal?"

"By all means, counselor."

"Thank you, your honor. My client will not do well in jail. He's schizophrenic, and he needs his medication. We propose he go back to River Bluffs Residential Treatment Center."

"Your honor." Liliana stood. "He walked away from there already. What's to keep him from doing the same?"

The judge looked at Jorgenson.

"We've arranged, your honor, on your approval, for him to go into the locked unit at River Bluffs."

Barker looked up at Jorgenson, frowning, his eyes narrowed. Jorgenson must have felt the gaze, for he looked down, leaned over, and told Barker that River Bluffs was better than prison. Barker nodded, then stared down at the table.

The judge addressed Liliana. "Counselor, does the county agree?"

Liliana pursed her lips then scratched her chiseled chin. "Yes, your honor. The county agrees as long as he remains in the locked unit until and throughout the trial."

And that was that. We went into the lobby and waited for Barker. I pulled out my cell phone and called Jeopardy.

"Mr. Sledge. What a pleasant surprise. I hope you have some good news for me."

I told her about Barker and where he was going next.

"That's good, right?"

"Better than jail."

"And what's your next move, Mr. Sledge? What can I do to help?"

A car horn sounded through the phone. "Are you driving somewhere, Ms. Dupree?"

"Finishing some errands."

"We're waiting for Barker. We're going to the facility to have him sign the HIPAA paperwork." Ha, I remembered. "That should allow us to get information about his treatment and his previous stay."

"Do you think I should come out as well?"

I had the phone on speaker. Bobo and Jorgenson listened. Jorgenson vigorously shook his head.

"That's not necessary," I said. "You can arrange a visit with him later after he's settled in."

Jorgenson nodded.

"That sounds fine, Mr. Sledge. Thank you for the call." She disconnected.

I looked at Jorgenson. "And why were you against Jeopardy going with us?"

"The two of them have a precarious relationship. For now, let's allow her to think she's helping by footing the bill. But I suggest we keep them separated."

I shrugged. Fine by me. The less I had to personally interact with Jeopardy Dupree, the better.

An hour later, a county deputy escorted Barker outside the courthouse and put him in a squad car to take him to River Bluffs. Jorgenson told us he'd meet us there in thirty minutes and walked back to his office. I vowed if I ever needed a defense attorney, Theodore Jorgenson would be that person. We headed to River Bluffs, hoping to get more information from the staff about Barker's last days before he walked out.

What should have been an uneventful ride was anything but.

Eight

I turned onto Marian Road and headed north. After about a mile, an older four-door sedan hurtled toward us, going well over the forty-five-mph speed limit. As the car passed, I glimpsed a male driver. Long hair blew across his face. He held a cell phone to his left ear. I had no idea why he was in such a hurry, nor did I care—until I noticed in my rearview mirror the car skid to a halt, make a Y-turn, and careen back toward us. I braced for an impact that never happened.

The driver stayed close but swung partially out into the other lane. A loud crack, then the back window of the rental Mazda shattered. The man behind us had fired a gun. Bobo stuck his head out the window. Through my driver's side mirror, I saw a short-barreled revolver in the guy's left hand, hanging out of the window. Another crack followed by a whine. The slug hit the back door on my side.

"Ideas?" I yelled at Bobo.

"Give me your gun."

"Aren't you carrying?"

"Yours will do more damage."

I slipped my .45 out and handed it to Bobo, then accelerated to put some distance between us. The car behind matched our speed.

Another crack. A plunk. The slug must have hit the back of the rental.

Bobo leaned out again, aimed, and fired four rapid shots. I flinched four times. My vision wavered. I shook my head, trying to clear the fuzziness and keep us on the road. Through my side mirror, I saw steam rising from the front end of the sedan. We pulled away. I slowed to a stop and started to do my own Y-turn. The sedan veered to the opposite side of the road onto the shoulder. The driver's side door opened, and a tall, lanky, long-haired man sprinted into the woods.

"Call it in." I forced the words out. My heart hammered in my chest and my throat felt gritty. "Let the cops deal with it." My voice wavered. I gulped air, unable to get enough. Turning the car back toward the facility, I choked out, "Tell them we'll stop by and give our statement later."

I sped up. Moments later, I felt Bobo staring at me.

"What?"

"You okay?"

I realized I was gripping the steering wheel so hard my knuckles were white, and my arms and shoulders shook.

"Fine."

"Want me to drive the rest of the way?"

Before I answered, the River Bluffs driveway came into view.

"I think I can make it." And I did. But about halfway up the long driveway, I heard a siren. A cop car barreled toward us. I pulled onto the shoulder. It zipped by.

"That was fast," I said.

"Not River City. County sheriff."

As I started to pull back onto the road, more red and blue lights approached. An ambulance passed us. I checked. Nothing else coming. I took the outside drive to the parking lot as the county cop car and the ambulance blocked the driveway under the porte cochere. We parked and walked into the facility.

Two EMTs worked on someone behind the reception desk. Dr. Charnow stood by the corner. She glanced our way. Worry lines creased her forehead. A heavyset, nearly bald deputy turned toward us.

"And who are you?"

My heartrate finally slowed to normal and my breathing steadied. "Jake Sledge and Bobo Johnson. We're private eyes. Used to work for River City PD."

"Bobo Johnson? The football player?"

Bobo nodded.

Before the deputy launched into how great a player Bobo was, I cut him off. "What happened here? Some dude took potshots at us on the road back there."

The deputy raised his eyebrows. "We got a report of a shooting here at the facility. What did the guy look like that shot at you?"

I described the older sedan and as much about the guy as I could. Bobo added a little more to the description.

"That's the man who shot Marcellyn." Dr. Charnow joined our party. "He came in demanding to see the patient who killed his sister. When we told him he wasn't here, he screamed at Marcellyn and pulled a gun."

"I'm assuming the man was talking about Sandy Akins and was asking for Barker DuPree?"

Dr. Charnow remained mute. Another cop came out of the hallway off to the right of the main room beyond the desk and walked toward us. I recognized him and pointed. "That's the deputy who brought Barker here after his arraignment. How long has he been here?"

Dr. Charnow sighed. "About twenty minutes."

From behind me, someone asked, "What is going on?"

I turned. Theodore Jorgenson walked up to us. We all stared at the facility's director.

"Please, Dr. Charnow, tell us what happened," the heavyset deputy said.

The officer who'd brought Barker joined us. "I thought I heard a gunshot."

"Can we go to my office?" Dr. Charnow glanced at the woman being attended to. "For some privacy?"

One of the EMTs ran out from behind the desk and out to the ambulance. Charnow leaned over the corner. "Is Marcellyn going to be okay?"

The other EMT answered, "The bullet went clean through her just below her collarbone. We've stopped the bleeding."

"I'll be fine, Dr. Charnow." Marcellyn's voice came out weak, slow.

The doctor's shoulders relaxed. She turned back to us. "Follow me, gentlemen."

Given the gravity of the situation—and the presence of Jorgenson, a true gentleman—I skipped my usual schtick of looking around. We all followed her down a hall off the right of the lobby and into her office. Two certificates hung on the wall. Floor plants occupied two corners. A window looked out onto the parking lot. Dr. Charnow sat in her high-backed office chair behind her modest, oak desk. Only two other chairs were in the office. Jorgenson sat in one of the chairs. The two deputies, Bobo and I, all stared at each other. I waved to the overweight deputy. He nodded and sat, then took the lead.

"Dr. Charnow, please tell us what happened."

"I wasn't out there when that man came in. I heard some yelling and walked into the hallway to see who it was." She straightened a pen on her desk. "And this thin man with long hair was waving his arms and yelling at Marcellyn."

"Go on."

"I noticed he had a gun in his left hand. I hadn't seen it at first. Then the man yelled again, asking where the patient was that killed his sister. He never said a name, just said 'the patient.'"

"And who was his sister?" asked the deputy.

I chimed in. "I'm assuming he was talking about Sandy Akins, the nurse's aide who was murdered a week or so ago."

"That was my assumption," Dr. Charnow said. "But I didn't know Sandy had a brother. At least she never spoke of him."

The deputy was about to ask another question, but I cut him off. "Do you have surveillance cameras?"

The chunky deputy swiveled in his chair. "And what exactly is your interest in this again?"

"You mean besides the same man taking shots at us?"

He nodded.

"Barker DuPree's sister hired us to help prove Barker's innocence in the murder of Sandy Akins."

"I guess since this guy shot at you, I'm okay if you stick around."

"Can we see the surveillance?"

We followed Dr. Charnow to a small room at the back of the facility. No security personnel, at least no one in uniform. When I mentioned that fact, Charnow said they had several large, strong orderlies, but they didn't want a uniformed presence as that would intimidate the residents.

All of us except Jorgenson squeezed into the room. He said he was going to talk with his client. Charnow picked up the receiver on a desk phone and called for an escort.

"He's in the locked unit, so you'll need someone to let you in."

Jorgenson nodded and waited in the hall.

The two deputies positioned themselves closest to the monitors. No big deal. They were both shorter than me and considerably shorter than Bobo. Dr. Charnow hit some buttons on a keyboard and the feed played rapidly backwards. She stopped it and allowed it to play forward at normal speed. For several minutes, nothing. Then a car pulled into and through the porte cochere. It was the four-door sedan that had come after us. A minute later, a thin man with long hair, the same dude we'd seen run into the woods, entered the facility.

I asked her to rewind to watch the car pull through again.

"Slow it down."

She did. It was hard to tell, but it appeared no one else was in the car. The deputy asked her to stop it when the license plate came into view. Charnow zoomed in. The deputy noted the plate number. I also wrote it down. Bobo and I still had enough contacts at River City that getting a plate run was no big deal.

"Anything else?" Dr. Charnow leaned back.

The two deputies said no. The heavier one asked me if I wanted to file a report on my car. I said we'd need to do that, so he gave me the address of their sub-station. Bobo and I would stop there on the way back to River City. The two deputies left the video room, saying they were going to go talk with the other staff. One of the deputies' radios blared as they left the room.

Someone said they'd found the perp's car and were waiting on forensics.

I closed the door to the room. "How far back do you save the video?"

Dr. Charnow answered, "About a month live. Then we archive it for several years. Sometimes it's needed for litigation."

"Can we see the video from July 28?"

"Why?"

"We'd like to see when Barker walked out. Was he picked up? Did anyone else leave after him? That kind of thing."

The director hesitated. As she was about to speak, the door opened. Theodore Jorgenson walked in.

"I heard the request, Dr. Charnow. And I have signed HIPAA documents from Barker that names Mr. Sledge and Mr. Johnson as people with whom you can share details of the patient." He handed a few sheets of paper to the facility director.

I really liked that lawyer. And that's not something I say often.

Dr. Charnow moved the mouse around and selected a folder labeled "July 28", then started another video. She fast-forwarded until early afternoon. Barker walked out and turned toward the parking lot. We watched him until he disappeared. A couple minutes later, a Toyota Prius drove out the driveway, but not through the porte cochere.

"Do you recognize the car?" I asked the doctor.

"Yes. That's the same type of car Sandy Akins drove. She was off that day."

Sandy Akins had picked Barker up. She knew about his wish to leave the facility. And probably knew she was the reason. Therefore, why would he kill her?

"Please keep the video going, but fast forward."

Forty minutes later, in video time, a vehicle appeared.

"Slow it down."

Dr. Charnow did.

An SUV drove to the parking lot, bypassing the porte cochere.

"Stop the feed." She did. "Back it up a bit, please. Stop on the SUV." She did. "What do you think, big guy?"

Bobo leaned in. "Could be the same vehicle that tried to run us down yesterday."

"Someone tried to run you down?" Jorgenson asked.

Bobo gave him a quick synopsis.

With the tinted windows, we could not make out any physical aspects of the driver. And due to the angles, we had no view of the back plate. Five minutes after the vehicle drove out of view of the camera, a man exited the facility and walked toward the parking lot. He was tall and thin, had a buzz cut and wore a T-shirt and jeans. A minute later, the SUV left, presumably with the man in it.

"Who was that?" I asked.

Dr. Charnow again hesitated. "Mr. Sledge, I can't divulge resident information."

"That was another patient, then. Can you tell us anything about him?"

"He has a violent nature." She looked at each of us. "He and Barker didn't get along."

Jorgenson spoke up. "I think, Dr. Charnow, considering the gravity of the situation, Barker being accused of murder, Mr. Sledge and Mr. Johnson being attacked possibly by that vehicle, and the shooting today, you need to divulge the name of that patient." He paused. "I can get a court order, if necessary."

Did I mention I liked Jorgenson?

The doctor furrowed her brows, frowned, and sighed. "Braxton Anderson."

"Thank you, Dr. Charnow. We will make sure he never knows where we got his name."

Jorgenson's point became moot, however, as the thinner deputy entered the video room.

"You're still here. Watching movies?"

"We are," I said. "Interesting movies. What's up, deputy?"

"Braxton Anderson is the owner of the car that came after you. And we believe he was the driver."

"Thank you, deputy. But I'm curious why you're sharing that with us civilians?"

"A lieutenant Kazminsky from River City said we should let you know."

I almost fell over.

"He said it would be in the report anyway, and with your lawyer, you'd get a copy, so might as well give you a head start."

I nodded. Sometimes the lieutenant came through. Nice.

"But that wasn't...wait a minute." Dr. Charnow clicked her mouse and pulled up that day's video. She paused it. In view was the tall, thin man with long scraggly hair who had walked into her facility demanding to know where Barker was, pretending to be Sandy Akin's brother. "Oh my gosh. I didn't see it. But I do now. That's Braxton Anderson."

Nine

Between filing our report at the county sheriff's office and waiting on a new rental car, we made no more progress on Barker's case that afternoon. At four-thirty, an Enterprise representative dropped off a new, red Mazda SUV at our offices. I took Bobo to his house, then drove home, which left me one hour to get ready and go to Mama Leona's for my date with Allison.

Mama Sledge watched me from her porch swing, an evening ritual. Often, I'd visit her, and we'd tell each other about the events of our day.

I shouted, "I have a date. Got to get going."

She continued swinging. "A date? That's nice. I want to hear all about this date and the girl tomorrow. Promise?"

"Sure, Ma. See you tomorrow."

Fresh deodorant, a spritz of cologne, a mint, and I was ready. I arrived at Mama Leona's on Front Street at five-forty-eight.

Twelve minutes early. I walked in and glanced around the medium-sized Italian restaurant, one of three in River City. No gorgeous brunette sitting by herself. And no gorgeous brunette sitting with anyone else. Most of the women had gray hair and the men had either gray or no hair. Nearly all the tables were occupied. A pair of unoccupied tables awaited cleanup. Two older couples sat on benches inside the door, waiting, I assumed, to be seated.

"How many, sir?" asked a girl of about seventeen, thin in a tight, black shirt and short skirt.

"Two. Reservation under Sledge."

She looked at her screen. "I don't have that reservation, sir."

My stomach fell. The reservation I had made was for yesterday, and I'd forgotten to make a new one. I slapped myself on the head.

"Do you always beat yourself in public?" Allison Rogers walked into the restaurant. Though tall, she still came up seven inches shorter than my six-foot-four. But with her spiked heels, she made up half the difference. Like the day I met her, she wore a red knee-length dress. Tight, but not overly so. Gold buttons on the front. The last one was open at her throat. A gold cross hung on a gold chain. Her radiant brown hair was swept into a bun, her wide brown eyes twinkled, and her full lips curled into a mischievous smile.

"I ... I forgot—"

"Please check under Rogers," she said to the hostess.

"Yes, Ms. Rogers. I have a reservation for two."

Allison smiled at me. "I figured you'd forget, having been arrested and all. I called and moved the reservation."

Maybe Bobo was right; this woman was too smart for me. Too nice for me. Probably, too everything for me. But for some reason, she still agreed to a second date.

We followed the hostess to a table in the center of the room. I pulled her chair out. After she sat, I took off my sports coat and hung it on the back of my chair. I'd left the shoulder holster in the trunk of the rental car.

A waitress, looking no older than sixteen, slightly heavy-set but with a wide smile, dropped two menus on the table.

"You look fantastic," I winked at Allison.

"And you. I love that jacket. Purple is my favorite color." She got that mischievous smile again. "But that shirt is a bit tight, isn't it?"

"Hard to find something that fits this incredible physique."

She shook her head. "I'll bet Bobo doesn't wear such tight shirts."

"That's because he buys family-sized tents to wear."

She chuckled. The waitress returned and asked us what we'd like to drink. We ordered two Dr Peppers. I wanted something stronger, but Allison didn't drink alcohol, and I didn't want to make her uncomfortable. Okay, I'd have been the one feeling uncomfortable, afraid she'd be judging me. Completely idiotic, of course, as she didn't have a judgmental bone in her body. Guilt, I guess. Whatever. I liked Dr Pepper, anyway.

"How was your day, today?" she asked.

"Interesting to say the least. Once again, someone tried to kill me."

"What?" She leaned forward, eyes wide. "Tell me about it."

I was about to when I felt the presence of someone standing behind me. Allison looked up at the person as well and gave a half-smile.

I didn't look behind me. "We're not quite ready to order."

"Mr. Sledge, how nice to see you again." The thick Southern drawl could belong to no one else but Jeopardy Dupree.

I swiveled. "Ms. Dupree, what brings you here?" Dumb question, I know, since we were in a restaurant. But my question was more why *that* restaurant. River City had more than twenty others and at least one other nice one.

"For dinner, of course, Mr. Sledge." Behind her hovered an older man. Thick head of gray hair. Cleanshaven. Wearing an expensive suit. Jeopardy wore a jade-green dress that ended above the knees. Unlike Allison, Jeopardy's dress had a low collar and a couple of buttons undone.

She leaned over and extended her hand to Allison. "I don't believe we've met. I'm Jeopardy Dupree. And you are?"

Allison took her hand. "Allison Rogers."

"And how long have you and Mr. Sledge been an item?"

"Item, well, it's our second official date." She shot me a glance and flashed her mischievous grin. "Though he stayed over one night in between our dates."

Wow. I didn't expect that.

Jeopardy gave a plastic smile and nodded. "That's nice. I hope you two enjoy your dinner. Mr. Sledge." She nodded at me. "Ms. Rogers, so nice to meet you."

"Likewise, Ms. Dupree. I do like your first name. Seems quite appropriate."

Another fake smile from Jeopardy. Our client and her older date left and sat at a table diagonally from us.

I stared at Allison. "That was amazing. Especially that last little dig. Nice."

She smiled. "And just who is Jeopardy Dupree?"

Was there a hint of jealousy in her voice? Maybe. I hoped so.

"She's our client. Hired us to prove her brother innocent of murder."

"Hmm. Interesting."

The waitress approached. I was about to dismiss her, but Allison ordered lasagna. I went ahead and ordered the manicotti.

"You were telling me about someone trying to kill you."

And I did. She never interrupted me during my tale about Braxton Anderson, though I kept his name out of it. She repeatedly glanced over my shoulder. I finished my tale of woe.

"I'm very glad that man didn't shoot you. Sorry about the car. And speaking of cars, when will you get your classic ride back?"

My 1975 red convertible Delta 88 had gone through purgatory the last month. For the second time, I had to take it to CS Auto, this time to have bullet holes patched up.

"Perkins says I should get it back Monday afternoon."

"Great. If it's not too hot, let's go for a drive with the top down."

"Deal."

A server came and deposited our food on the table. I was about to take a bite of the Italian salad, when Allison gently laid her hand on my arm and pushed it down.

"May I pray for our meal?"

Bobo did that as well, so I was used to it. Besides, anything Allison asked, I would agree to. I nodded. She watched me for a bit.

"Aren't you going to pray with me?"

"Oh, yeah. Sorry." I bowed my head and closed my eyes. Though that made me nervous with Jeopardy Dupree so close by. Allison prayed for the blessing of the food, for my safety, and for quick resolution of our case. After she closed with "Amen," I thanked her and took a bite of salad.

Allison raised her head and narrowed her eyes. "Ms. Dupree has a thing for you."

Mouth still full, I asked, "Why do you say that?"

"She's been staring at you nearly the entire time with a far-away dreamy look. But when I look at her, she glares at me."

"The faraway dreamy look pretty much describes every woman in River City when I'm around."

She laughed. "Your head gets a little too big sometimes."

"And that's why I like you. You're so sweet."

She arched her brows.

"Anybody else would have said my head is too big *all* the time. You gave me some credit."

She nodded. "You can be very sweet as well."

We ate in silence for a few minutes.

"What did you have planned for after dinner?" Allison sipped her Dr Pepper. "Are we going to chase some junkies again in the park?"

On our last date, we'd walked through River City's downtown park and had, as she said, chased junkies out of the park.

"We can, though that wasn't what I had planned."

"And what do you have planned?"

"I thought I'd come over. We could watch a movie. And I'd stay the night."

She shook her head, though the smile remained. I knew what was coming next.

"The movie part is okay. But not the staying overnight."

"But last time someone was trying to kill me, you let me stay."

"Jake, you're incorrigible. From your story, I don't get the impression you need to hide out again."

"Busted." On our last date, Allison told me about her pledge of purity she'd made as a young teenager and how she had not yet broken that, nor would she until married. "I heard Bobo's church has an opening tomorrow."

"Opening for what?"

"For our wedding, of course."

She blushed, but flashed the biggest smile yet, then shook her head. "Movie night it is. I have just the flick."

"A chick flick?"

"No. Action. New spy thriller."

I pulled out my cell phone. "I'm definitely calling that pastor."

Her wide smile disappeared, and she looked up over my shoulder. I felt a tap and turned slightly.

"Will you be coming over tomorrow, Mr. Sledge, to review the case?" Jeopardy smiled and blinked her eyes. Her companion walked away toward the door.

"I'll call you if anything new comes up. Not sure how much we'll get accomplished tomorrow."

"Call me? I thought we'd have lunch and catch up."

"Catch up?"

She nodded and looked at Allison. "It's been a while. I want to know what's been going on in your life, Mr. Sledge."

"You mean since you tried to kill me?"

She scrunched her eyebrows. "Now, Mr. Sledge, I keep telling you, that wasn't me. It was—"

"Yeah, I know, it was Connie. Have a good night, Ms. Dupree, and I'll let you know if anything breaks with Barker's case."

Jeopardy remained standing by me for a bit. She shifted her gaze from me to Allison, who had her head resting in her hands, elbows on the table, giving Jeopardy a wan smile.

"Goodnight, Mr. Sledge. Enjoy the rest of your evening."

The nice words were laced with venom. Jeopardy joined her companion and they left the restaurant.

"Who is Connie?" Allison straightened and stared at the restaurant entrance as if she expected Jeopardy to return. Not a bad assumption. But she didn't.

I explained to her what happened the last time Jeopardy Dupree had hired me to investigate her sister. "Jeopardy thought her sister was trying to kill her daddy."

"Was she?"

"Not only was she planning, but she already had killed her daddy. And then she tried to kill me."

"That's awful. Were you okay?"

"Yes, I was able to subdue Connie. But here's the kicker. Connie was Jeopardy's alter ego. Or other personality."

"Jeopardy Dupree has dissociative disorder?"

Did everybody already know what that was but me? "Yes, that's what she supposedly had. She stayed a couple years in a locked mental facility but apparently is now cured."

"Wow. Only a couple of years for murder and attempted murder?"

"Insanity plea. And now cured. So, she says."

"You don't buy it?"

I shrugged. "She hasn't tried to kill me the couple times we've met."

Allison chuckled.

"What?"

"She likes you, Jake. That's why she hasn't tried to kill you."

Before I could come back with anything, the waitress appeared and asked if we wanted dessert. We hadn't even finished our main course, so we dug into our pasta, which had grown cold. But it was the best cold manicotti I'd ever had.

After dinner, at Allison's house, we watched a poorly acted, beyond-belief spy thriller. It was the best movie I'd ever seen. I couldn't remember a single part of the plotline, but I could remember every word Allison said and every facial expression she made.

Ten

Saturday, around eleven-forty-five, Bobo and I drove to my sister Alicia's house. She'd invited us for lunch.

"You had a date last night, too, didn't you?" I turned north onto Riverview Road.

Bobo smiled. "With Liliana."

"Where'd you take her?"

"Chez Martins, where I took Jackson last week."

Jackson was Bobo's hacker friend. Though the man insisted on adding "white hat" in front of hacker when describing what he did. He'd been invaluable in our last case.

"Do me a favor, would you?"

Bobo nodded. "Probably."

I grinned. Good answer. I had been known to ask for some outrageous things. "Don't tell Alicia about the date."

"Why not?"

"You know." I slowed below the speed limit to delay reaching Alicia's, wanting to finish the conversation before we arrived. A gray-haired lady following in a newer Bug glared through her windshield. Tough. "With Myron out of the picture, she might have her sights set on you."

Bobo shook his head. "Not likely. We're friends, Jake. And that's how it will remain. And besides, I won't date a married woman. The divorce isn't final."

I swung the rental into Alicia's driveway. "Just don't mention it, okay?"

Bobo nodded. "Sure."

Mom had arrived before us, since I had to drive the opposite way to pick up Bobo first. He lived in an older subdivision with decent-sized two-story homes. A couple of blocks north of him were huge estates with multiacre lots. I'd asked him several times why he didn't move into a bigger place. The man was loaded from his NFL days. He always answered the same way: He had all he needed.

I'd called Mom earlier and asked if she wanted to ride along with us. Nope. Her comment was, "I ain't riding with you in no SUV. If it's not the Delta, I'll drive myself." And she did. In her light blue 1985 Impala, a car the size of a small house.

Bobo and I exited the Mazda. I frowned at the grass growing between the cracks in the driveway.

The screen door flew open and my four, soon-to-be-five-year-old niece, Julia, flew down the concrete steps and jumped into the arms of Bobo, who'd knelt. Not me, who was also waiting. Bobo.

"Uncle Bobo!" She buried her head into his chest, then wiggled out of his arms and ran to me. "Uncle Jake!" I picked her up and threw her in the air.

"Jake! Stop that. You're on the driveway." Alicia stepped out onto the porch.

I caught Julia, then turned her upside down, grabbed her ankles, and swung her around. She screamed and laughed. When I stopped, she yelled for more.

"Julia, come on in," Alicia said. "Wash your hands for lunch."

Alicia and Julia were a matched set. Often, they dressed alike. And that day was one of them. They both wore white dresses patterned with red and purple roses that fell to their shins. Alicia had even done both of their hair. Hers was pulled up into a bun with a red bow, and Julia's was tied into pigtails with red bows. I doubted Alicia's attraction to Bobo had waned. She never dressed up for me. And that day she wore makeup. I hadn't seen her with makeup in years.

I put Julia down, who ran back to the house and squeezed past Alicia. My sister walked toward us.

"Hi, Bobo. Good to see you." She looked down, and I swore she blushed.

"Alicia. You look great. And something smells wonderful."

A smile bloomed on Alicia's face. She glanced at me, lost most of the smile, waved, turned, and walked toward the house. We followed her inside.

"Bobo!" Mama rose from the easy chair. She wore her usual jeans and a button-down, plaid short-sleeved shirt. Farm wear, she always called it. And though she hadn't lived on their farm for several years, she still dressed like she did.

"Mrs. Sledge. You look great, too. Have you lost weight?"

A wide smile spread across her face, and she blushed. Did I mention everyone smiles at Bobo? They hugged. My mom was not small. About five-eight and one-fifty, but in a hug from Bobo, she disappeared.

Alicia called me into the kitchen. Bobo sat on the sofa, and Mom returned to her easy chair. I heard small feet pounding down the hall toward us. When Julia burst into the kitchen, Alicia directed her to the living room.

"Okay, Sis, what's up?"

I stood six feet four inches tall. My mom was five feet eight, and my dad had been six feet three. I often wondered if Alicia was really my completely biological sister, being only five-two and maybe ninety pounds. But in her case, size mattered little when it came to spunk and determination.

"Just what is going on with you, Jacob?"

She called me "Jacob." I was in trouble. Wasn't sure why, but I knew I'd soon find out. "A lot has happened in the last couple of days. What are you talking about?"

She put her hands on her hips and tapped one bare foot. "To start, I heard you were in jail. Because you almost shot a cop?"

I shook my head. "Wrong place at the wrong time without sufficient information." I then explained why River City PD had arrested me. "See, I did nothing wrong."

"But you almost pulled your gun on the officers."

"Reaction, Sis. But I didn't."

"And someone tried to kill you again. Twice!"

I sighed. "Hazards of the job."

"Was it them neo-Nazi's again?"

I shook my head. "We don't think so. Probably connected with the case we're working or some previous case."

Her turn to sigh. "You need to be more careful."

"Yes, Mama."

She glared at me. "By the way, where did you hear all this?" She started to answer. "Never mind. I know. Bobo has a big mouth."

She shook her head. "He just knows there's people who love you and are interested in what's going on in your life. Since you never bother to tell anyone."

"Been talking a lot to Bobo since Myron left, have you?"

She relaxed a little, done with chiding me. "No more than usual. Why?"

I raised my brows and tilted my head, then waved a hand from her head to her feet. "Mighty dressed up for a Saturday lunch."

"What?" She raised her hands. "Wait a minute. You think Bobo and me? No. We're friends, Jake. And that's all we'll ever be."

"Then why the fancy dress?"

"You're such an idiot."

"Then enlighten me."

"Did you happen to notice what Julia was wearing?"

I glanced into the living room. Julia was tossing a small ball back and forth with Bobo. "Yes. A matching dress. After all, I am a crack detective."

Alicia widened her eyes and nodded. "Cracked, maybe. And do you know whose idea it was to dress up for Uncle Jake and Uncle Bobo?"

"I'm assuming Julia, since you don't call us uncle." This was why I was a private detective. Extremely observant.

"Duh." Alicia shook her head and brushed past me. When she got to the doorway, she said, "Lunch will be ready in about ten minutes."

I leaned back in my chair and sighed with pleasure. Alicia had made a tuna casserole. The recipe had been handed down from Grandma Sledge to Mama Sledge to Alicia. And probably me, but I rarely cooked anything. After Alicia cleared the dishes, she pulled a banana cream pie from the refrigerator and started slicing pieces.

Julia's dish, face, and bib (smart call by Alicia on that) looked like someone had set an M-80 off on her plate. Mama got up and fetched a rag and cleaned Julia's face. Alicia placed a plate of pie in front of each of us. Just as she was about to sit down, someone knocked on the front door.

A shadow crossed Alicia's face. She frowned and scrunched her brows. "Dang it, I hope that isn't who I think it is." She got up and walked into the living room.

The door opened. "Hey, Alicia. I got off work early, so thought I'd swing by now."

Myron. What was that slimeball doing here?

"You shouldn't have come early. I told you four, and that's what I meant."

Bobo pushed his chair back. So did I, faster. And I stood. Bobo got up and started toward the living room. I pointed at him. "Stay." If that big dog decided not to obey my command, there wasn't anything I could have done about it. He took a deep breath and returned to his chair, surprisingly calm.

Mama also got up, fire in her eyes. She clenched her fists and started toward the living room.

"Not a good idea, Ma."

"Why not?"

"I'll go talk to them."

"Last time you were with Myron, you knocked him out."

"Lot of good it did."

Mama returned to her chair.

"Since I'm here, can't we talk now?" Myron asked.

I entered the living room. "What are you doing here, Myron?"

"Jake." He was standing on the little rug in the doorway landing. Alicia blocked his way. And mine, unless I moved her. "Alicia and me are going to talk about some things."

"What's there to talk about?"

"Myron, please leave," Alicia said. "Come back at four."

"Maybe Jake should hear what we have to say."

"Bobo's here," I said. "Should he hear as well?"

Myron's eyes widened. He turned and opened the door. "See you at four, Alicia." He left.

Alicia slowly closed the door and even more slowly turned around. She hung her head. "I was going to tell you and Mom tomorrow. After Myron and I had talked."

With a louder voice than I should have used, I asked, "What is there to talk about? You're divorcing him. He's got to go."

Alicia shook her head. Bobo walked up beside me.

"Explain, Alicia," I said. "What is there to talk about?"

She looked up, but at Bobo first. "He's never been unfaithful to me. You understand, don't you, Bobo? I can't divorce him."

"What?"

Alicia jerked back at my loud question.

"That's ludicrous. He gave you and Julia up to the skinheads. Julia could have been killed."

"Please, Jake, lower your voice."

Julia joined the party. "Mommy, why is Uncle Jake yelling?"

I turned and squatted. "Sorry, baby. I won't yell anymore. Go back and eat your pie." An activity she'd already started, judging by the yellow goo all around her mouth.

Mama came out and took Julia by the hand, leading her back to the kitchen. The look on Ma's face could have melted butter. Not sure who it was directed at, as she looked first at me, then at Alicia.

I straightened.

Bobo said, "You know your sister's a Christian, right?"

"Yeah, so?"

"She's right. She shouldn't divorce him."

"Oh, for God's sake."

"Exactly," Bobo said. "For God's sake, she should not divorce him."

I felt a small hand on my arm. I looked down at Alicia and my heart fell to my knees. Her sad eyes pleaded with me.

"Julia needs a father. I need a husband."

I lowered my voice to just above a whisper. "A husband, not a man who beats you."

"He's promised never to hit me again."

"And if he does?"

"I'll tell Bobo."

I glanced at the big guy.

Alicia continued, "And you, Jake. I promise. He knows he screwed up. He's sorry. We're going to go to counseling."

I hugged Alicia. She squeezed me and started crying into my chest.

I looked over the top of her. "You knew about this, didn't you?"

Bobo nodded. "She asked me for my Christian advice. She couldn't very well ask *you* for that."

He had a point. Didn't make me any less angry. I put my mouth down to Alicia's ear.

"He's on strike two. One more strike and he's out."

She nodded against my chest.

Eleven

The look on Bobo's face as I strode toward him at the First Baptist Church of River City wasn't the expression of happy surprise I'd hoped for. He studied me like a curiosity in a museum. When I reached him, he arched a brow.

"Morning." Bobo put out his hand, and I shook it.

"Hey, big guy. Beautiful day for church, isn't it?"

"Any day is a beautiful day for church, if you're here for the right reasons."

"I agree."

No one lingered outside because the temperature had already climbed to over eighty at eight-forty-five in the morning. Bobo wore a pin-striped suit. All he needed was a black pin-striped fedora and he would have made a great gangster. I wore my blue plaid sports coat, a light blue twill grid dress shirt, dark blue pants, and—of course—my dark blue fedora. I never leave home without the fedora. At least if I'm going somewhere other than the gym.

I followed Bobo inside.

A blast of frigid air conditioning hit us as we entered the church lobby. Bobo stopped before heading into the worship center.

"What about our case involves the need for you to come to church?"

"Ouch. That hurts."

Before I could explain why I was there, the queen of the law, our distinguished assistant prosecuting attorney, Liliana Goodhue, and her deputy mayor father Arthur Goodhue approached us.

"Mr. Sledge. What a surprise seeing you here." Liliana put her hand on Bobo's shoulder, leaned in, and gave an air kiss. How chaste. But then daddy was there, so I guessed that was appropriate.

"Liliana. How are you?" I stuck out my hand. She took it, pumped once, and dropped it. At least she kept her expression neutral. It beat disgusted.

"Mr. Sledge, Mr. Johnson, so good to see you." Deputy Mayor Goodhue eased his daughter out of the way and shook both our hands. "I haven't had the opportunity to thank you for ridding River City of that menace, Roth."

I smiled. "It's what we do."

"And what brings you to our lovely church, Mr. Sledge?"

Liliana glared at me from behind daddy. "Yes, what *does* bring you here?"

Bobo looked at me with both brows raised and nodded.

Tough crowd. I started to answer.

"Jake. I didn't expect to see you here."

I turned. My knees quivered. "Wow," I said under my breath. Out loud, I added, "Good morning, Allie. I didn't know you went to this church."

Allison Rogers gave me a big hug. She wore an ankle-length dark blue dress with a slit on one side to the knee. High collar. Slim fit. Coiffed hair. A white pearl necklace adorned her neck. Beautiful. "I don't normally. But I've heard good things about it. I thought I'd come and see for myself. You never told me you go here."

Deputy Mayor Goodhue stepped in front of me. "Ms. Rogers, nice to see you."

"Deputy Mayor." They shook hands.

"You know her?" I asked the deputy mayor.

"Of course. She works for me."

Duh. Allison worked in the commissions office. I hadn't put together that the commissions office worked for the mayor's office. And the city council. And eighty-thousand other bureaucrats. Exaggeration. But not by much. I squeezed in front of the deputy mayor. He took the hint and joined his daughter.

"I also don't normally come to church, but—"

"Mr. Sledge? How nice to see you." A deep Southern drawl. I turned around again. And as I suspected, Jeopardy Dupree walked toward our party. She wore an emerald-green dress that kissed the tops of her knees. Thin straps, shoulders bare. Her blond hair flowing behind her like a train on a wedding dress. "Mr. Johnson. So good to see you again."

Bobo answered, "Ms. Dupree. You look lovely as always."

"Thank you, kind sir." She curtsied.

I nearly threw up.

Jeopardy turned to me. "I didn't know you went to church here."

"It's my second time. Do you normally come here?"

"I usually go to Shepherd's Baptist Church. But I thought I'd see what this one was all about."

Shepherd's was near the subdivision west of The Heights, where Allison lived, and where the houses were even bigger and the lots larger. A gated community, though the church sat outside the gates.

I glanced at Allison. She studied Jeopardy with narrowed eyes and her head slightly cocked.

"Where do you normally go, Allie?" I asked.

"Shepherd's." She hooked her arm under mine. "I don't remember seeing you there, Ms. Dupree."

Jeopardy smiled big. I wished I had my sunglasses on. "It's been some time since I went to church. I wasn't in a position to attend for a couple of years."

I whispered to Allison. "She was in the funny farm, remember?"

Allison nodded.

Liliana stepped near Jeopardy. "Dupree? Any relation to Barker Dupree?"

"Why yes. He's my brother. And you are?"

"Liliana Goodhue. I'm prosecuting your brother's case."

Her smile never faltered. "Ah, yes, well. I'm confident Mr. Sledge and Mr. Johnson will prove Barker's innocence before you have that chance." The two women locked gazes.

That was a cage match I'd love to witness.

"It was nice meeting you, Ms. Dupree. Honestly, I hope Mr. Sledge and Mr. Johnson do just that. Provided he is indeed innocent." And on that note, the Goodhues left our little party and headed into the worship center.

Bobo stayed with Allison and me. We three stared at Jeopardy.

"Where's your companion?" I asked. "Doesn't he attend church?"

"Companion?" She paused. "Oh, you mean Derrick. He's my accountant. I took him to dinner to reward him for the excellent job he did on cleaning up daddy's books. They were a mess."

"Okay. Enjoy the service, Ms. Dupree. I'm sure we'll talk Monday." I turned and led Allison to the worship center. Bobo said something that made me cringe.

"Would you like to join us, Ms. Dupree?"

"Why, Mr. Johnson, that is so kind of you. I'd be delighted."

I inched along. Allison tugged to speed me up, not understanding my motivation. But she had as much effect as a chihuahua tugging on a St. Bernard. Bobo and Jeopardy passed us, Jeopardy's arm hooked under Bobo's. Such the gentleman.

When they were far enough ahead, I whispered to Allison. "Did she follow you here?"

Allison stopped and stared at me. "Followed me? Why would she do that?"

"No idea, but her being here is strange."

"I don't think so. But to be honest, I didn't really look."

I shrugged and entered the worship center. To be honest, I hadn't checked if Jeopardy had followed me, either.

We sat in seats directly behind Bobo and Jeopardy. A timer on the screen showed a little over two minutes. I assumed that meant before the service started. Or the church would blow up. I wasn't sure.

I leaned forward. "Does Alicia go here?"

Bobo shook his head. "She goes to a small community church near her house."

"When did she start going to church?"

"Several months ago."

"I didn't know that."

"If you'd bother to talk to your family about their lives, you might learn something."

Harsh. But unfortunately, true.

"Is that why you're here? You thought you'd find Alicia?"

"No. Though I am here because of Alicia."

The band on the stage took their positions.

Bobo turned. "Why?" An expression of tenderness? Maybe. Bobo has those occasionally. Not usually for me, though.

"She got me thinking. Maybe I'm missing something. You know, that last time I was here wasn't all that bad."

Two guitars and a drum sounded. Conversation ended. We all stood and listened to rock-style worship music. It wasn't country, but I got into it.

Like the last time I'd attended church, I felt the pastor, a young guy with great hair, spoke right at me. I swear he even looked at me a couple of times, especially when talking about living for the world, living to please others rather than God. Living to please myself. What was it with this guy? Did he reserve talks about selfishness for every time I came to his church?

Afterwards, we lingered around the seats for a bit. The pastor did a kind of receiving line outside in the lobby, but Bobo's receiving line was twice as long. Everyone wanted to say hi to the Hall of Fame football legend that was Maurice "Bobo" Johnson. A few acknowledged me. All the men stared at Jeopardy and Allison. Jeopardy basked in the attention, introducing herself to everyone Bobo spoke to.

Until Liliana came by and leveled a harsh stare at Jeopardy. Our favorite gameshow-named blonde said nothing.

Liliana moved in beside Bobo and turned her back to Jeopardy. "Dad wants to know if you'd like to join us for lunch. His treat, of course."

Before he could say anything, I said, "We're in."

I expected the queen of law to shoot daggers at me with her gaze, possibly even stab me with a real dagger. Instead, she offered a thin smile and nodded. She punched Bobo on the shoulder. "You good, too?"

"Yes'm, I's be coming."

Liliana shook her head. I wondered what she thought of Bobo's sometimes lapses into a street dialect. Alicia loved it. Liliana, though, having lived it, I wondered. She turned away, nearly shoving Jeopardy into the seat, and walked to her dad.

Jeopardy shook herself as if she were a dog who'd been petted against the grain. "I would love to join y'all for lunch as well, Mr. Johnson, but I have pressing business this afternoon. Give my regards to Ms. Goodhue and the deputy mayor."

Bobo nodded. "We'll miss your company, Ms. Dupree."

We? I was not included in Bobo's generalization.

"So kind of you." She turned to me. "Mr. Sledge. I do hope to see you Monday."

I didn't. If she wasn't paying the fees, I'd never see her again and deal directly with Barker. But she was the client. I nodded to her.

Jeopardy left. She sashayed up the aisle, head held high. Eyes straight ahead. Every remaining male ogled her as she passed.

Allison took my arm. "That woman is madly in love with you. Maybe she followed *you* here."

"I think I would have noticed." Maybe? Was I being stalked? I decided to keep better tabs of who was behind me when I drive somewhere.

Twelve

I'm a light sleeper. Any little noise wakes me, especially when I'm sleeping in the easy chair. Sunday night I fell asleep watching *SportsCenter*. I awoke around midnight, turned the television off, and fell back to sleep. A little later, I was startled awake. A metal-on-metal sound came from outside. I eased the lever of the chair down and sat up. Three rapid clacks sounded near my kitchen door, which led into my carport. I slipped out of the chair and snuck through the kitchen, stopping at the door to listen. A faint hissing sound. I slid the dark brown curtain to the side and peeked out. My rental car. Nothing else. I unlocked the deadbolt. The click it made probably woke the dead. I froze and peeked out again. Nothing. I turned the knob and inched the door open, then stepped onto the concrete stoop. All I wore was boxers and a T-shirt. Barefoot. But the early morning was warm and sticky. I looked toward the front of the rental car, then the back. Nothing. I stepped down and scanned beyond the carport, trying to detect any movement.

A single clack, then a crunch as something hard hit me in the back of the head. My knees wobbled. Someone shoved me toward the concrete steps. I tripped on the bottom one and landed hard on my elbow. Footsteps faded. My vision clouded, but I thought I saw a tall person running down the driveway. *Was he alone?* I rolled over. Faces crowded above me. I curled up, expecting to be kicked or punched. Voices, mostly with German accents, flooded my ears. I waved my arm, trying to ward them off. Nothing. No one was there. My vision cleared. The noise in my head subsided. I sat on the first step, alone, angry at my weakness, my inability to give chase. A car engine started, probably a block away. I waited and watched, but nothing drove past. In my boxers, bare feet, and T-shirt, I would not have run after it, anyway.

Around six, after a fitful sleep, I limped to the kitchen, pulled down the aspirin bottle, and downed three, chasing them with orange juice. The back of my head throbbed. The bump was still tender to the touch. I couldn't see it in the mirror, but when I showered, dark blood ran off my head and down the drain.

A quick breakfast of a toasted bagel, cream cheese, and more orange juice. I put on my light tan linen blend sports coat, white shirt with dark green palm leaves, blue chinos, and the light brown fedora.

"Ouch!"

The back edge of the fedora settled right on the head wound. I adjusted it to relieve the pain and left the house.

Outside, I surveyed the carport area. Nothing looked disturbed. I couldn't figure out what the intruder had hit me with or what they had been doing in my carport. I walked around to the driver's side of my rental and discovered the answer to both questions.

"Oh, come on."

The intruder had hit me with a spray-paint can. That explained the clacking I'd heard, as they shook it. The person had painted "Barker killed her" in bright yellow on the side of my rental.

I could already picture my auto insurance rates skyrocketing, or the company dropping me completely. My own car, twice, and two rentals had been damaged in less than two months. Just wonderful.

There was no point in trying to wash the paint off. It would take chemicals I did not possess. Before going to the office, I would swing by CS Auto, hoping Riley had my Delta 88 ready. And maybe he could help me out with the rental before I called it in.

I parked the rental in CS Auto's one guest parking spot and walked into the shack that served as the office. One mechanic I didn't know, and Riley Perkins were looking over some paperwork and talking.

Riley looked up.

"Sledge. You're early. But I have your baby ready."

Riley Perkins was in his mid-fifties, about five-eight, but pushing two-hundred pounds. He had a shock of gray and brown hair that spewed out at all angles. A rare hair sighting, as Perkins usually wore a greasy gray and black baseball cap. A Yankees fan in the middle of Royals territory. He never missed an opportunity to gloat when his team was having a good season.

"Did you see the game last night?"

"A few innings." The Yankees played the Royals and pounded them. I gave up after about five innings.

"Looking good, aren't they?"

I crossed my arms. "The car?"

"Yeah, hold tight. By the way, love the hat." He shoved the paperwork at his employee and hustled out the back door of the shed. Amazing. That popsicle stand had two doors.

I went out the front door and waited. Riley pulled my baby around and parked by me. He jumped out, leaving the engine purring. The top was up so he could show off the new back window. Clear plastic. Better than what I had before it was shot to pieces. I walked around the 1975 Oldsmobile Delta 88 and failed to find any evidence of bullet holes. Perkins and his crew did incredible work, though I was convinced the CS in CS Auto stood for "Chop Shop."

"I need another favor."

Riley raised his eyebrows. "What?"

"Over here." I led him to my rental.

"Who's Barker?"

"Can you clean it off, or not?"

"Wait a minute. Barker. I saw something on the news a little bit back. Didn't he kill some nurse or something?"

"Nurse's aide. And I don't believe he killed her."

"Someone does."

"Brilliant deduction, Sherlock. You should be the detective."

Riley grinned. "Yeah, I can clean it up. Should be done before we close."

I slapped Riley on the back. "Thanks, buddy. Call me when it's done, and I'll let Enterprise know so they can pick it up."

Riley walked back to the office, shaking his head the entire way. I climbed into the Delta 88 and headed for work, hoping no one would attack or accidentally hit my car on the way.

Thirteen

Of course, Bobo beat me to the office. No matter what time I arrived, he was already there. That day I got there around eight-twenty—early for me. Bobo pecked away on his computer.

"What's up, big guy?" I hung my fedora on one coat rack hook and my sports jacket on another.

"That don't look so good. What happened?"

I assumed he was referring to my head wound. That's why I'm a crack detective. Phenomenal deduction skills. I explained about the intruder, but I left out the hallucination. Bobo already thought I was losing it. If I told him I saw a bunch of skinheads surrounding me, waiting to finish me off, he'd leave me at River Bluffs next time we visited.

"The same guy that attacked us Friday, you think?"

"Could have been. Seemed about the same size. Never saw a face, though. Or a vehicle. Parked down the street and didn't drive by my house."

"You give chase?"

I shook my head. "I was barefoot and in my skivvies."

The door opened. In walked Theodore Jorgenson, carrying a briefcase and dressed remarkably like me. Only he wore a full suit, dark green, with a light green dress shirt, a black and dark green patterned tie, and a dark green fedora.

Nice.

"Good morning, gentlemen." He put his briefcase on my desk and opened it.

"Nice hat. Love that color."

"Thank you. Love that shirt."

I gave him a thumbs-up.

"I have a gift for you." He handed me a thick nine-by-twelve envelope. "A copy of Barker's case file."

"Hand delivered. I'm impressed."

Bobo shook his hand. "Good to see you, Mr. Jorgenson."

"You, too, Mr. Johnson. Oh, I have a favor to ask." He pulled out a card from his briefcase. "It's for my nephew, but would you sign this card?" He handed it to Bobo.

"This is my rookie card. Haven't seen one of these in a while. Jake, throw me a Sharpie, would you?"

"To sign your card? You nuts? That'll ruin it."

Bobo walked over to the file cabinet and opened the bottom drawer. He rummaged around and pulled out a couple of things. One was a football, still in the box. The other, a piece of plastic he placed on the desk. He took the card and slid it into the plastic football card holder.

Ah, I got it. I tossed him a black Sharpie from the Northwestern University pencil holder I had on my desk.

Bobo signed the plastic. "What's your nephew's name?"

"Jeremy."

Bobo wrote on the football. When he was done, he turned it around so Jorgenson and I could see what he'd written. It read, "God bless you, Jeremy. Stay strong. Bobo Johnson."

Show off.

"Why didn't you sign the card directly?" Jorgenson asked.

"A signed card that doesn't have a factory signature on it can be devalued. Especially a rookie card in near-mint condition like this one. The signature on the plastic won't make it more valuable, but it keeps the card from losing its value." Bobo handed the football to Jorgenson.

"Jeremy is going to love this. Mr. Johnson, you just made me uncle of the year. Thank you so much."

"My pleasure. Would love to meet your nephew sometime."

"He'd flip over that." Jorgenson closed his briefcase. "Gentlemen, I have to go. Please keep me informed of your progress."

I stood. "Before you do, I have a question."

Jorgenson nodded.

"Would it be better if you hired us for Ms. Dupree? Do you think we'd have more pull with the authorities?"

"If it were any other lawyer, I'd probably say yes. But, if you need cooperation from River City's finest, just say the word. The chief and I play golf nearly every Saturday morning."

Did I mention how much I liked this guy? And small-town politics. Sometimes it works to your advantage. "Just don't mention my name. Tell him Bobo is working a case for you."

Jorgenson gave a wry smile. "I won't ask. And sure, I'll drop Mr. Johnson's name." He tipped his hat to us and left the office.

I tore open the envelope and put the case file on the desk, then started flipping through it. "Here." I handed Bobo the written reports and I looked at the crime scene photos. And no, that wasn't unfair, as Bobo reads ten times faster than I do. He actually paid attention in school—a fact he often reminds me about. And he reads books all the time. I read the occasional sports magazine but tend to spend more time watching television.

"By the way, what were you looking into when I got here?"

"Braxton Anderson. Didn't find much, so I sent his name to Jackson."

Jackson, the white-hat hacker, as he insisted on being called, played a crucial role for our agency. And he came cheap. For the last case, Bobo took him to dinner.

"How come Jackson doesn't bill us?"

"I'm helping his two kids learn to play football."

"A computer nerd has kids that want to play football?"

"Yup. His oldest is already big for his age. He's a ninth grader. The younger one is seventh grade and decent sized."

"Big, like you were big at that age?"

Bobo shook his head. "More like *you* were big at that age. But they're both smarter."

"Yeah, whatever." That didn't really say much about their intelligence. As Mom used to tell me, I was about as smart as a box of rocks. Usually after some parent or some authority called her about the trouble I'd been in.

I focused on the crime scene photo of Sandy Akins's body. She was face down. Her left hand was at her side, splayed open. Her right hand was raised above her shoulders, with her index finger curled under and the other fingers out. A pool of blood spread from her neck and from her torso. Other photos showed bloody handprints on the kitchen counter. Unfortunately, they were hers, not the killer's.

"Any DNA results?"

Bobo nodded. "They found a lot of DNA and fingerprints in the apartment belonging to Barker. Oh, and a couple bloody fingerprints on the inside doorknob. They also belonged to Barker."

"That's great. We need to talk to Barker about when he was there."

Bobo nodded again. "A couple strands of blond hair, five inches or so in length, that did not belong to the victim. But nothing on file, either."

"Cause of death?"

"Exsanguination."

"Manner of death?"

"Multiple stab wounds. Back, abdomen, throat. Missed the carotid artery, though."

I examined a couple more of the crime scene photos. "Bleeding to death is a terrible way to die."

Bobo nodded. "No murder weapon found at the scene or in the trash bins outside the apartment building."

"I'm hungry."

Bobo shook his head. "No breakfast?"

"Light one a long time ago."

"How early did you get up?"

"Six."

Bobo slid the paperwork back into the envelope and stood. "For you, that's early. We're going to River Bluffs, right?"

My turn to nod.

"Then let's stop at the Denny's on the way."

I wasn't about to argue with that. A Grand Slam breakfast, or two. That's what I needed to refill my already draining energy. I added the photos to the envelope and decided we'd take it with us. Might help to show Barker some of the graphic images. Shake him up a bit to loosen his tongue. I was convinced he didn't kill her, but the evidence wasn't pointing at anyone else yet.

After I put on my jacket and gingerly set the fedora on my head, my cell phone played "She's Not There". I started belting out the tune along with Greg Walker, the vocalist for Santana.

"Are you going to answer that?"

I shrugged. "I might just sing along with it."

"Please, spare me and answer our client."

The big dude was a major killjoy.

I pressed the green button, then the speaker button so the killjoy could listen in. "Ms. Dupree. How are you this lovely morning?"

"Lovely? Did you prove Barker innocent yet?" Curt, to the point, her accent not quite as pronounced.

"Working on it."

A long pause. Then the accent returned in full force. "Would you and your wonderful partner like to join me for lunch today? We can talk about what's next."

I looked at Bobo who shrugged. Good, he was leaving it up to me. "While that is a generous and tempting offer, our calendar is full."

Bobo lifted his brows.

"We're going to go spend some time at River Bluffs. Talk with Barker and the staff there."

"Oh. And when do you think you'll be there?"

"Probably about an hour or so. Making a stop or two on the way." I wasn't sure what the second stop would be, but just in case.

A long, exaggerated sigh. "Maybe tomorrow, then. Hopefully, you'll have some good news."

"Maybe. I'll check in with you either later this afternoon or tomorrow morning. Have a great day, Ms. Dupree."

"You too, Mr. Sledge. And tell Mr. Johnson how much I appreciated his company yesterday."

I decided not to let on that he was listening, though the big lug was grinning from ear to ear. "Will do. Goodbye." I hung up. "She likes you."

Bobo turned to leave. "Not as much as she likes you, though."

We left the building in silence. Loose ends whirled around in my brain. Like in so many cases, we were at the point where we had a lot of links but no chain. The two attacks on me or us. Were they the same person? Braxton Anderson. What was his connection to Sandy Akins? Clearly not her brother. Was he the person who spray-painted the rental? The crime scene evidence. It pointed to Barker. Two strands of hair. Who did they belong to? Where was the murder weapon? It wasn't among Barker's possessions. At least not what he had with him, as the residential facility thoroughly went through that stuff. Why was Sandy Akins killed? Was our client stalking me? All of us showing up at church the same day seemed too much of a coincidence, and I didn't really believe in coincidences.

Time to get some background on Sandy Akins and the relationship with Barker. Hopefully, we could also get some information from the staff and other patients at River Bluffs. It turned out we'd get a few more random links that still would not complete the chain or even fit together.

Fourteen

I restrained myself and ate only one Grand Slam breakfast. Bobo had lighter fare, avoiding carbs, sticking with eggs and bacon. I figured I could grab lunch after our visit to River Bluffs.

Inside the residential facility, we asked for Director Charnow. The new receptionist, a redhead with a face full of freckles, punched a button on her phone and told Dr. Charnow she had visitors. When asked who, the redhead looked at us.

"Jake Sledge and Bobo Johnson."

The receptionist started to repeat our names, but Dr. Charnow said she heard and hung up. She appeared at the end of the hall that led into the lobby and waved at us to follow her. We did.

Dr. Charnow sat behind her desk. We took the two chairs opposite her.

"How is the other receptionist?" I couldn't remember her name.

"She's going to live. Another couple of weeks, and hopefully she'll return to work. If she wants to, of course."

"We'd like to talk with some patients about both Barker and Braxton Anderson."

She stared at us, lips in a straight line. Both hands rested on her desk. After a bit, she nodded. "Let's start in the unlocked area, as both of them were there before they left." She punched a phone button. Another woman answered. "It's Lila. Please bring Davis, Anton, and Ophelia to the main room." The other woman acknowledged. "Follow me." She led us out of her office and into the large open area behind the receptionist's desk.

We sat on one of the long sofas. Dr. Charnow sat on a perpendicular couch. A tall, thin woman with short, black hair led three other people into the room. The three patients sat on the sofa opposite Dr. Charnow.

"This is Davis." A stocky, pimply-faced man nodded to us. He was probably in his thirties.

"And Anton," Dr. Charnow continued. A darker-skinned man with tight-curled black hair gave a quick wave.

"And Ophelia." The woman had sandy hair that fell to her shoulders and darting eyes that never settled on anything for more than a second.

"Thank you for giving us some of your time. I'm Jake Sledge, and this is my partner, Bobo Johnson. We work for Sledge Hammer Detective Agency. I believe you all know Barker Dupree?"

They nodded, though Ophelia's nod was barely perceptible.

"We're helping him out." I stopped and let Bobo continue.

"We'd like to ask you some questions about Barker and another former resident here."

Bobo used "resident." I would have said "patient" and risked the ire of Dr. Charnow. The three patients—I mean residents—stared at us.

"What can you tell us about Barker?" Bobo asked. "What was his mood like before he left here?"

Nothing.

"Anything you tell us is strictly confidential," Bobo added. "We won't tell Barker or anyone else."

Still nothing.

I looked at Dr. Charnow. I'm not sure if she read something in my look or knew how things would work better, but she stood and addressed the three. "I'll leave you alone to talk. Please be cooperative. We're trying to help Barker, who is in a serious situation. I'm sure he'd do the same for you." She started to leave. "And you don't have to disclose anything about yourselves or your reason for being here. But Barker has given us permission to share details of his stay with these two." She left.

"Barker was in love with Ms. Akins," Anton said. "We all knew that. Not like they hid it or anything. And she liked him, too."

I started to ask something, but Bobo cut me off.

"Was their behavior that obvious, or did Barker confide in you?"

"I'd say both." Davis scratched his face. "He even told me they were going to date when he got out."

"Did this cause any issues with the other residents?"

I'd have said "patients," which was why I was letting Bobo ask the questions. He put other people at ease much better than I did.

Ophelia nodded almost imperceptibly.

Bobo spoke in a soft, comforting tone. "Ophelia, is there something you'd like to share?"

Maybe Bobo should have been a counselor.

We waited. Then Anton prodded Ophelia. "Go ahead, O, tell them what you know. It's Barker's life here."

Ophelia spoke softly. Her eyes darted everywhere but never made eye contact. "There were two other guys who really liked Ms. Akins."

"Was one of them Braxton Anderson?" I asked, probably a little harsher than necessary.

Her eyes widened, and she hung her head, nodding.

Bingo. We had a connection. But why would he kill Sandy Akins instead of Barker? I didn't bother to ask who the other one was. Besides, I didn't think we'd get much more out of Ophelia. She had her head down. Both legs bounced up and down, and she started muttering to herself. I hadn't meant to scare her.

Bobo came to my rescue. "Ms. Ophelia, thank you so much for the information. If you have elsewhere to be, we understand."

She leapt from the sofa and ran to the hallway. I didn't think she could move that fast.

The guy who'd told us where to find Barker during our first visit joined our little party.

"Hey, guys. I saw you found Barker."

The other two looked at him and frowned. Then they both left.

"Thank you, guys," Bobo said to their departing backs. They both put a hand up but didn't turn around.

"Tough crowd," I said. "They don't seem to like you."

Connors shrugged. I remembered his name. Probably because he scared the you-know-what out of me by pounding on my window that day. Not that I'd admit to anyone it frightened me.

"I'm not real popular around here."

"Was Barker Dupree popular?" Bobo asked.

"He was a nice ... or is, a nice guy. It's too bad they're accusing him of Ms. Akins's murder. They were a thing. It started in the locked unit, you know." Connors sat about two feet from me. "Barker, he was in a bad place. And Ms. Akins always took extra time to help him out."

"Don't you think a nurse-patient relationship is inappropriate?" I asked.

"She wasn't a nurse."

"Okay, nurse's aide and patient. Still."

Connors shrugged. "It wouldn't have been an issue except for Braxton Anderson. He was insanely crazy about Ms. Akins."

Connor looked around the room, then leaned in, lowering his voice. "And just plain insanely crazy."

"We noticed."

Bobo asked, "Did they ever have a confrontation?"

Connors shook his head. "Naw, they both kept to themselves." He straightened. "Besides, on the locked unit we are watched carefully. And if Braxton had done anything, he'd have been transferred to the state forensic psych hospital."

"You were on the locked unit?" I shifted away from him a little.

"Suicidal for a bit."

"I'm sorry to hear that."

"Hey, I'm still here." He scooted closer to me.

"Yes, you are. You're right here. Anything else you can tell us that might be useful?"

Connors started to say something, but Dr. Charnow cut him off. "Mr. Connors, aren't you supposed to be in group right now?"

He shot off the couch and hurried toward the hall. "Sorry, Dr. Charnow. On my way."

She came over to us. "Find out anything?"

Both of us stood.

"We did," I said. "Now, we need to talk to Barker. How does that work?"

Dr. Charnow studied me. "You open your mouth. Words come out. And hopefully, he says things."

I shook my head. Bobo laughed.

"I mean, since he's on the locked unit. How do we get in there to talk to him? Or is there a room or something he comes out to?"

"We'll consider you both trusted visitors, so you can go in. We do have visitation rooms for people who are either nervous about being on the ward or we don't know them yet."

I nodded. "Makes sense."

"Follow me, gentlemen."

We both got in on that gag. Neither one of us moved. Dr. Charnow started walking away but only made it about five steps. She turned around. "What are you waiting for?"

"Oh, you were talking to us?" I pointed to the two of us.

She frowned, turned around, and walked toward the left hallway. We followed her to the elevator, where we took a short ride up one floor. After exiting the elevator, we waited outside a locked door.

"Any guns?"

"I have lots of guns."

"On you?"

"We left them in the car."

"Good. You can hang your jacket and hat up out here."

I did.

She swiped her badge. A loud buzz, and she opened the door.

I expected the usual hospital smell. Stale urine, strong disinfectant. But the air smelled pleasant, almost perfumy, but subtle. At the halfway point down the hall on the left was a long desk. A couple of women and four good-sized men hovered around it. The men all wore dark blue polo shirts with the facility's logo and khaki pants. The women wore light blue polos and various shades of dress pants. No white coats. Shattered my image of a funny farm. So disappointed.

"You told us the first time we visited that the patients were free to leave anytime. And yet you have a locked unit." We walked down the corridor. Rooms on both sides, most of them with doors closed.

"And that's the truth. But residents can get into a state where they are a danger to themselves or others, thus require more monitoring. Or other people are a danger to them."

We passed a room with an open door. A scrawny man with wispy gray hair stood just inside. We locked eyes. His eyes widened like an owl's. He gasped. Not the usual effect I have on people. Maybe he had wandering eyes and was really looking at Bobo.

Dr. Charnow continued. "In many cases the lock is to keep others out, not necessarily residents in. It's between the resident and their doctor on how long they are here." She emphasized "resident" both times. I needed to stop referring to them as patients.

"Here's Barker's room." She knocked on the closed door.

A sound like a Celtic warrior entering battle rose behind me. Then something jumped on my back. I shook myself, and whatever it was fell off. I turned around. A skinhead with a leering grin and a metal pipe glared at me. He stepped forward. I brought my fist back and was ready to slam him in the face. But

I couldn't move my arm. I tried to move toward the guy, but I was stuck. I thrashed, but I remained stuck.

"Jake, cool down, man."

Bobo's shout penetrated the fog in my brain. The skinhead in front of me dissolved into the scrawny man from across the hallway, now flanked by two of the guys in dark blue polos. They pulled him away, toward his room.

"Are you okay, Mr. Sledge?" Dr. Charnow asked before turning to the two staff members. "Call his doctor. What the heck was that?"

One man shrugged. They dragged him into his room and closed the door.

"I'm so sorry, Mr. Sledge. I don't know what came over Mr. Katsaros. He's been doing so well for several months."

Bobo narrowed his eyes.

"What?"

"Exactly. What came over you? Why were you going to punch that guy? He couldn't weigh any more than your leg."

"I thought ... he had something in his hand. He was going to hit me with it."

"He didn't have anything. He jumped on your back, and you shook him off. Then, you started toward him. Good thing I held you back. No telling what you might have done." Bobo turned to Dr. Charnow. "See, this is what I told you before. I think he has PTSD."

Dr. Charnow nodded. She put a hand on my shoulder. "We can help you with that."

I shook her hand off. "We need to talk with Barker."

On cue, Barker opened the door. "Hey, Sledge, Bobo, come on in." He stepped aside. "What was that yelling about?"

"Please, Jake, you should consider Dr. Charnow's offer."

I stepped into Barker's room, ignoring Bobo. I felt fine, considering I had been attacked.

"I'm going to go check on Mr. Katsaros and try to find out what set him off." She left us with Barker.

"Sorry, only one chair." Barker sat on the edge of his twin bed. "What happened out there?"

"A patient wanted a piggyback ride." I surveyed the fifteen-by-fifteen-foot room. Desk, chair with a dark blue cloth-covered seat, bed, and a camera in the corner of the wall below the ceiling.

"They watch you?"

"We sign a release that says they can. That's the condition of staying in this unit."

"And what's the alternative?"

"We leave, and if someone is in a bad enough spot, they'll get committed to the state hospital."

"Like Jeopardy?'

Barker frowned.

Bobo motioned for me to sit. He closed the door and leaned against the wall next to it. With his arms crossed, he looked like a bouncer. A very big bouncer.

Barker scooted back on the bed to use the wall as a backrest. "Jeopardy was in the forensic psych unit for criminal behavior."

I sat. The cushion was sufficient. "How do you know this?"

"People talk. There's a lot of movement between the facilities. Depends on insurance, how many days left, all that fun stuff."

Barker looked okay. No deep circles under his eyes. He maintained eye contact. No nervous ticks. So far, he'd only talked to us, not to imaginary friends.

"You seem to be doing well."

"Back on my meds. They really help keep the voices away."

I glanced at Bobo.

"Tell us about Sandy Akins," Bobo said.

Barker twisted his head so fast to look at the big guy, I thought he'd strain something.

"I loved her." Then with more assertion, "I didn't kill her. Why would I kill the woman I was going to marry."

Bobo's brows shot up. "You asked her to marry you?"

"Not yet. I was going to, though."

My turn. "Tell us about the day she died. Were you there anytime that day?"

He looked at me, then bowed his head. "I ... I found her on the floor. I ... I checked her pulse, you know, at the neck, like they do on television." He raised his head. "But I panicked and ran out."

"Why didn't you call the police?"

"I did. But after I left. And anonymously."

Bobo asked, "How did you call anonymously? There ain't no more phone booths in River City."

"Burner phone. I had picked it up the day before."

"Dude, you're not helping yourself here," I said.

"You left bloody fingerprints on the doorknob."

Again, Barker's head snapped in Bobo's direction. "Oh, man. There was blood all over. On her neck. I … I must have got some on me when I felt her pulse."

I shifted in the chair. "You're really not helping yourself. What have you told the cops?"

Barker stared at me for a few seconds. "Pretty much what I've told you."

"Did Sandy have any enemies?" Bobo asked.

"No. She was the kindest, gentlest, sweetest person I've ever met."

"Ex-boyfriend?" I asked.

"Probably, but no one recent. She'd told me she hadn't dated anyone in over a year."

It was time to spring the big question on him. "What about Braxton Anderson?"

Barker jumped like I'd poked him with a cattle prod. "Nasty, nasty man. He hated me for some reason."

"Maybe because you and Ms. Akins were a thing?" Bobo pushed off the wall and paced to the other side.

I got up and let Bobo sit. He barely fit in the chair, but I knew his knees were bothering him. Too much standing caused him discomfort. My turn to lean against the wall and cross my arms. The understudy bouncer.

"Yeah, Braxton had a thing for Sandy. But she never encouraged it. I mean, she was nice to everyone. Cared about all the patients."

I pointed at Barker. "But she gave you more attention than the rest, right?"

"Only on her breaks. Never while working. She'd have lunch with me. Just that half hour each day."

Bobo shifted in the chair, which protested but held. "Was lunch in a cafeteria?"

Barker nodded.

"All the other patients, and all the men that had a crush on the cute nursing assistant, saw you two together every day." We weren't really doing good cop, bad cop, but we had to rile him up a bit to cover all the angles and make sure he wasn't hiding anything.

Barker shrugged. "I guess. But why would Braxton kill her? If anybody, he'd kill me."

He had a point. The same point I'd been mulling. And Braxton seemed to think Barker was guilty, or at least wanted us to think so.

Bobo said, "Maybe it's the 'if I can't have her, nobody can' thing."

This time I shrugged. "Could be. What else are you not telling us, Barker?"

He shook his head and stared past me. I wondered if he'd start having a conversation with unseen entities. "I just don't get why anyone would kill her. I miss her so much." He put his face in his hands. His shoulders shuddered.

Bobo stood and went to Barker. He laid a hand on the crying man's shoulder. "Let me pray for you." And he did. When he finished praying, he told Barker we'd find out who killed Ms. Akins.

I wished I shared Bobo's confidence.

Tears rolled down Barker's sunken face as we left his room. I looked both ways in the hallway but didn't see any crazies eyeing me or coming after me. One of the polo-shirted aids let us out, and we went to find Dr. Charnow.

The good doctor looked ready to cry when Bobo and I walked into her office. Probably worried about a lawsuit.

"Again, Mr. Sledge, I am so sorry about Mr. Katsaros."

I waved it off. "I'm fine. Any idea why I set him off?"

"Come look at this." She swung her computer monitor around so Bobo and I could see. She started a video showing the outside of the facility on the top of the screen and inside the door on the bottom. A woman walked into the facility. She wore a dark blue derby hat so none of her face was visible. Straight, brown hair hung down and curled under her cheeks. She also wore a dark suit. It was hard to tell how tall she was.

"Who is she?" I asked.

"No idea. She showed a license to Jenny with the name Mrs. Scarlett Hare."

"Seriously? Is she married to Rhett?"

Dr. Charnow shrugged.

Bobo leaned in to examine the video that was frozen on the woman. "What's so unusual about her coming to see Mr. Katsaros?"

"He hasn't had a visitor in nearly a year."

"Is she family?" I asked.

"Said she's his niece. And Mr. Katsaros had seven brothers and three sisters, so there are a lot of nieces and nephews."

I sat down in one of the chairs. "I'm still not seeing the connection between a visitor and his surprise attack."

Dr. Charnow swung the monitor back to facing her, did some typing, and then swung it back around. "Mr. Katsaros has this delusion that there are people walking around that eat a person's soul. And he's been terrified for years about losing his soul."

"Maybe he needs to give his life to Jesus," Bobo said.

Dr. Charnow nodded. "Probably. Anyway, we video visitations if a person is in the locked unit, but we don't record the sound. Watch."

Bobo and I moved to where we could see her monitor.

Katsaros sat back in his chair, arms crossed, and eyes narrowed. Suspicion to start. Did he really know that lady? The big hat still obscured her face. As the conversation progressed, Katsaros leaned forward. His eyes widened. He frowned. Then he shot backward with eyes wide and mouth forming what looked like a long "no." He put his hands out and shook his head. The lady nodded. She reached across the table, and Katsaros took her hand. It seemed to calm him. She stood, walked to his side of the table, and kissed him on the top of the head, then left, keeping her head bent so her face remained hidden.

Bobo and I retreated to the chairs. Dr. Charnow swung the monitor back to her.

"And about a half hour later, you two walk into the ward, and Mr. Katsaros attacks you."

I nodded and was about to say "coincidence," but I don't believe in coincidence, so I kept my mouth shut. Another weird link to add to our unlinked chain.

Bobo shifted in his chair. "Did anyone talk to Mr. Katsaros and ask him why he attacked Jake?"

"Yes. I spoke to the counselor assigned to him while you were talking with Mr. Dupree. The counselor said Mr. Katsaros acknowledged it was his niece but wouldn't say anything more about her. When asked why he attacked Mr. Sledge, he replied that he had to, or he'd lose his soul."

"Didn't know you were a soul eater." Bobo punched me on the shoulder.

"Private detective by day, soul eater by night. That dude is a whack job."

Dr. Charnow glared at me. I guess "whack job" is not an acceptable clinical term.

"Anything else?" I stood.

Dr. Charnow shook her head. "If I hear anything more, I'll let you know. So far, Mr. Dupree has been a model resident. He's kept to himself and stayed in his room. We're waiting for his doctor to let us know if we need to have him participate in the group activities or if this is just a holding cell for him."

I stuck out my hand and shook Dr. Charnow's. "Thank you for your help."

Bobo did the same and thanked her as well.

We left her office. On the way out of the facility, we stopped at the reception desk.

"Do you remember the derby lady in the hat that came to visit Mr. Katsaros?"

"Yes. Seemed pleasant enough."

I leaned on the desk. "What can you tell us about her?"

"She was tall."

"How tall?"

"I'd say at least six feet. Not too thin, but not too heavy. Had a pleasant, soft voice."

"Any type of accent?"

"Nope. Could have been from here. And she dressed nicely. The suit was an Armani. And the hat, had to be a thousand-dollar hat."

"Can you describe her face?"

"I don't know. Pretty. Nothing unusual. Sorry."

I pushed back from the desk. "No problem. Thank you so much." We left.

I started the car. "What do you make of this woman and that patient?"

"Not sure. We know Braxton Anderson has an accomplice. Someone picked him up here. But we have no clue if it's a woman. Just like we're not sure about the driver who tried to run you over."

"What's the end game, though? That's where I keep getting stuck. It seems it's more about putting Barker away than killing Sandy Akins."

Bobo nodded. "Agreed. But why?"

"Let's go visit Ms. Akins's apartment. Maybe there's security footage available. We can see who entered before Barker did."

Fifteen

A couple of miles north of downtown River City we pulled into the parking lot of the River Vale Apartments, which were probably built in the eighties. They still seemed well maintained. The few cars in the lot were three to five years old. The sparsity of vehicles indicated that most people who lived there worked day jobs. I know, once again, my brilliant detective skills.

I parked in a spot labeled "Visitors". We followed a sidewalk between buildings to a courtyard. One apartment had a sign that said "Office". Unlocked. We walked in. Bells mounted above the door rang. A middle-aged, larger woman parted floor-length curtains and came to the desk.

"Can I help you?" Neutral expression. Her eyes scanned both of us.

"Good afternoon. I'm Jake Sledge, and this is my partner, Bobo Johnson. We work for Sledge Hammer Detective Agency."

"Bobo Johnson? The football player?"

Was there anyone in River City who didn't know who he was? Doubtful.

"Yes, ma'am." Bobo stepped forward and put out his hand. "Pleasure to meet you. And you are?"

The lady smiled and held onto Bobo's hand. "Dixie. Dixie Thompson. The pleasure is all mine. And now you're a private detective?"

Bobo eased his hand out of Dixie's. "Yes, ma'am. And we wanted to talk to you about the murder of Sandy Akins."

Dixie pulled a stool over toward her and sat down. "Such a tragedy. Such a wonderful young lady. She lived here for a couple of years. Her death shook up many of the residents."

Bobo nodded. "I can imagine. I'm sure something like that doesn't happen often here."

Dixie shook her head. "First ever murder that I know about. And I've managed this complex for twenty-two years."

I inched forward. "That's impressive. Do you, by any chance, have security cameras?"

"We do."

"Could we see the feed from that night?"

Dixie pouted and shook her head. "I'm so sorry, Mr. Sledge, but the computer only holds about two days' worth of footage. We archive the older videos to DVD."

"And why are you sorry?"

"The police took the DVDs for the day before, that day, and the day after."

Figures. I flashed a big smile. "Well, we just happen to be looking for an apartment. And I hear that one's a great deal right now. Could we get a tour?"

She smiled back, catching on. "Nice try, Mr. Sledge. And I would have no problem giving you that tour, except the police tape is still across the door, and I have specific instructions not to let anyone in. I don't want no trouble with the police. You understand, don't you?"

I sighed. "Of course, Ms. Thompson. Can't blame you. But we had to try."

Bobo asked, "Is there anything you can remember about that day? Anything unusual? Did you see anyone out of place?"

She shook her head. "No. Sandy's apartment is on the third floor." Dixie moved from behind the desk to the window. "It's over there." She pointed across the courtyard and a little to the right. A brief flash of yellow indicated the police tape. "I don't sit here all day, so many people could have come and gone. I didn't hear anything unusual. No screams or nothing."

"Thank you, Ms. Thompson, for your time."

She turned and looked at Bobo. "My pleasure. You come back anytime. Happy to help if I can."

We left the apartment and walked back to the car.

"River City PD is next, I guess. Not that we'll get anything out of them." I opened the car door and got in.

Bobo did the same. "Try calling Mr. Jorgenson. I think he said something about greasing some wheels for us."

"Good idea." I called Jorgenson.

"Mr. Sledge, what can I do for you?"

"We're on our way to River City PD. They have video footage from the night of Sandy Akins' murder. We're hoping we'll be able to see it."

Some muffled talking came through. "I confirmed with my paralegal. We have that evidence on our list. It shouldn't be a problem. Let me know if anyone gives you any trouble."

I really liked this guy. Did I mention if I ever needed a lawyer, he'd be the one I hired?

"Thank you. We'll let you know." I disconnected and drove us to the station downtown.

Willow was on the phone and three people crowded around his desk. He saw us waiting and waved us on through, not bothering with the sign-in and visitor badges. Hopefully, he wouldn't catch any grief for that.

As we passed Kazminsky's office, the lieutenant yelled, "Sledge, come here."

I turned, walked into his office, and bowed. "At your service, oh mighty Lieutenant."

"You've moved up in the world."

Bobo stepped in behind me. "Lieutenant. How are you?"

"Mr. Johnson, I'm impressed. And that's not easy to do. And it must be you, not this dirtbag." Kazminsky pointed at me.

"Sorry, sir, I'm not following you."

"Directly from the chief. We're to cooperate completely with you on the Sandy Akins murder investigation."

I grinned. Mr. Jorgenson strikes again. Yes!

"Just don't get in our way, Sledge."

"No, sir. I wouldn't dream of it." Actually, I dream about that all the time. The River City detective squad is competent. But that's the highest compliment they'll get. Of course, the unit was much better when I was there. Just saying.

Bobo poked me and waved me to leave the office. "Thank you, Lieutenant. We won't interfere with the investigation."

We headed to Detective Morris's desk to talk with him. The two other detectives in the bullpen, both veterans, shouted out their usual catcalls. I waved, took off my fedora, and bowed.

Morris looked up from his computer. "Hey, Mr. Sledge, Mr. Johnson."

"Please. Just Sledge for me, and I'm sure Bobo will suffice for the big guy."

Bobo nodded.

"Okay, Sledge. Bobo. What can I do for you?"

I pulled a metal-framed chair to the side of Morris's desk, then sat. Bobo hovered behind me.

"Video surveillance of Ms. Akins's apartment. The day of her murder. Can we see it?"

Morris glanced at Kazminsky's office. The lieutenant stood outside his door. He nodded.

"Sure. But you'll have to watch it here. Anything else?"

"Anything new?"

Morris adjusted the rolled-up sleeves on his baby-blue dress shirt. "Not really. And honestly, I'm focused on a new case. We have the evidence we need, and the assistant prosecuting attorney is satisfied."

And after our conversation with Barker earlier, I could see why they weren't doing much more. Without another clear suspect, there was no reason to poke around. That was our job. "About that video?"

Morris led us to a small interior conference room. Its ambiance mirrored the interrogation rooms. And the chairs were no better, though the conference room had several plastic bottles of water on a credenza.

"Wait here. I'll go get the DVDs." Morris left.

Bobo grabbed a water. "You want one?"

"Sure."

He handed me a bottle. "Should we ask them about Braxton Anderson?"

"Probably. At least see if he has a record. Also, I wonder if they're working that shooting at River Bluffs or if County kept that one."

Morris returned with a laptop computer, a pad of paper, and three DVDs.

While he set up the computer, I asked, "Are you guys looking into the shooting at River Bluffs?"

Morris shook his head. "County has that one. It was outside the city limits."

"We were still inside the city limits when he shot at us."

Morris turned the computer to face us. "County considers it all the same case. We let them have it." He brought up the video program and hit play. "This is the day of the murder. Knock yourselves out. Here's the list of people we identified as they came into view." He slid the pad of paper over to us, then held up the other two DVDs. "The day before and the day after. I'll check back in an hour."

An hour to go through seventy-two hours of video? We fast-forwarded through much of it since it started at a minute past midnight. When we saw a blip in the dark, I paused the video and checked the paper. Until ten that morning, all were identified as residents. At ten-seventeen a person wearing a wide-brimmed hat and a billowy overcoat walked past the camera to the far side of the complex. The view from the camera ended before we could determine if the person went up the stairs or entered one of the ground-floor apartments. I rewound and paused the video when the person was in full view.

"What do you think? Woman? Man?"

Bobo leaned in. "Hard to tell. Dressed more like a woman. But like a woman would dress around here in March or April, not August."

I agreed. "Check the log."

"Unidentified."

We kept going but at double speed. Foot traffic increased. All residents for the next half hour. Then another unidentified person. This one with a baseball cap. Clearly a man. When he walked by, he kept his head down. Jeans. A light-colored T-shirt. Thin, but in the video we had no reference as to height.

"Do you think that's Braxton Anderson?"

Bobo shrugged. "Can't see his face or tell how tall he is."

We pressed on. Fifteen minutes later, Barker showed up and casually walked toward the other side of the courtyard. He disappeared out of the field of view. We kept the video playing. Seven minutes later, Barker came the other way. His head swiveled in all directions. He trotted out of the courtyard.

"I can see why he's their prime suspect."

Bobo nodded.

I let the video play at triple speed. Little foot traffic during the middle of a weekday. Detective Morris returned. I halted the video.

"Well? See anything interesting?"

I motioned him over to us and backed the video up to the spot of the first unidentified person.

"What about this person?" I played it in slow motion.

"We never ID'ed that person. Asked around. And as far as we could tell, that person never left, so we figured she lived there."

"She? For sure?"

Morris shrugged. "Looked like a woman's outfit, anyway. These days, of course, you never know."

"I get that. And this one?" I forwarded to the other unidentified person.

"Same story. Never ID'ed and didn't leave."

The unidentified man could have been Braxton Anderson with his hair tucked under his hat. The other one, no clue.

We thanked Detective Morris and left the conference room. In the lobby, we waved to Sergeant Willow, then took the elevator up one floor to find Geoffrey Poindexter, crime scene investigator extraordinaire, hoping he'd be able to shed some light on this case that wasn't in the reports.

Sixteen

We learned nothing new from Poindexter. Yet. We set up an appointment for the next day at Sandy Akins's apartment. Poindexter said he'd reenact the scene for us. We'd have to supply our own popcorn and sodas.

We returned to my car.

Bobo's phone dinged.

"Incoming?"

Bobo nodded. "From Jackson. Hold on." He read the text. "Bingo. Braxton Anderson's home address is **in** KC. But he's staying at his sister's apartment while she's out of the country. Jackson found some video feed."

"How did he find that?" I started the car.

"AI program that can search for facial recognition. The video shows Braxton going in and out of this apartment several times." Bobo gave me the address.

I pulled away from the curb and headed southwest of downtown. Only about four miles away, off Riverview Road.

"What's his KC address?"

Bobo read it off.

I shrugged, not knowing Kansas City that well, as I turned south on Riverview.

Ten minutes later, I pulled into the parking lot of the six-building apartment complex that was probably built sometime in the sixties. Red brick, like many buildings in Missouri. White square columns from the second floor upward. The front-facing apartments had white-railed balconies. Each building had two apartments per floor.

We got out. I opened the trunk, slipped on my shoulder holster with the .45, and slid my .40 into my ankle holster. Bobo frowned but said nothing. After putting on my sports jacket, we walked to the building Jackson had identified for Bobo. The sister's apartment was on the fourth floor. Inside the foyer, the door leading to the apartments was locked. We knew Braxton was in apartment four-oh-three, so I punched the doorbell button on the panel for four-oh-five.

An elderly lady answered.

"Hi, Mrs. Sutter." I got her name off the panel, hoping it was up to date. "It's Braxton from four-oh-three. I forgot the code to get in. Could you buzz me in?"

"Um, sure. I guess. Weren't you just up here? I thought I heard you."

"Yes, ma'am, but I had to get something from the car."

"Oh, okay."

A loud buzz. Bobo opened the door, and we entered. I stabbed the elevator button. We listened to the rattle, hum, and bang of the car as it descended. The elevator doors opened. No one inside. We entered, and I punched four. More rattling, humming, and banging, but we made it to the fourth floor. We stood to the side as the doors opened. The elevator was on one side of the hallway. I peeked out. No one was in the hall. I led the way to apartment four-oh-three.

Outside the door, we paused and listened. Nothing. Some television noises seemed to come from the apartment across and down one. Mrs. Sutter's. I hoped she wouldn't stick her head out to verify it was Braxton.

"Ready?" I whispered to Bobo.

Before I knocked, I looked up. And I was glad I did. A camera stared down at us.

From inside the apartment came a metallic clack, followed by a metallic clunk.

"Move!"

We flattened ourselves on either side of the door.

Four gunshots. Wood on the door splintered. Four holes appeared in the wall on the other side of the hall. I hoped no one was inside that apartment. A heavy thud came from inside, followed by prolonged screeching.

Bobo caught my gaze. He nodded. I pulled my .45 out and nodded back. He first tried to turn the doorknob. Locked. He slammed into the door. The lock on the doorknob, the deadbolt, and the chain were no match for Bobo. The door swung inward and banged against the wall. Bobo moved in and to the right. I followed. We saw the backside of a man climbing out of a window onto the fire escape.

I raised the .45. Bobo pulled my arm down. We ran to the window. The man was halfway down the fire escape, more jumping than stepping. His long hair bounced as he fled. I again raised my .45. And again, Bobo pulled my arm down.

I glared at Bobo. "What are you doing?"

He glared back. "What are you doing? You can't shoot a man running away."

"He shot at us."

"He won't do Barker any good if he's dead."

"I'll shoot him in the rear."

"You're not a cop, Jake. I don't think Kazminsky will overlook this one."

He had a point. The fleeing man, whom I was sure was Braxton Anderson, escaped into the alley and out of sight, though the top of his head appeared and disappeared over the fence as he ran. I sighed. That's twice Anderson had shot at us, and I hadn't returned the favor. Not fair. Bobo got to shoot at him.

I moved away from the window. "Let's look around. Maybe we can find something of use."

The apartment looked like a woman's apartment. Horse pictures on the wall. Flower vases and family photos on the mantel over the fake fireplace. The master bedroom, however, looked and smelled like a junior high boy's room. Dirty clothes scattered all over the floor. Pizza boxes, empty soda cans, and candy wrappers on every surface. Several photo frames were knocked over. If we didn't kill Braxton Anderson, his sister might when she returned from wherever she was and saw the mess.

On the nightstand was a porn magazine and a pen. The doily that had covered the table was on the floor. I picked up the pen.

"Yo, Bobo, look at this."

He came into the bedroom.

I showed him the promotional pen for Giovanni's Italian Eatery in Kansas City.

"You think he worked for Gibellini?"

Giovanni Gibellini was the mob boss in Kansas City. Over the years, foreign drug gangs had stripped the mob of any real power. Don't tell Gibellini that. He thought he was a godfather.

I pulled out my cell phone, found Bertram's number, and selected it.

After two rings, the mob hitman answered. "Hey, Sledge. How are things your way?"

"Wonderful, Bertram." I hit the speaker icon. "Got Bobo here with me. We're looking for a dude named Braxton Anderson. We think we just scared him out of his sister's apartment. You know the guy?"

"Why do you think I'd know him?"

"Because he has a pen from your boss's restaurant."

Bertram chuckled. "Yeah, I know that piece of work. He's a psycho."

Ironic, I thought. A man who makes his living killing people for money calling another person a psycho. "Tell us about him."

"You know, Sledge, I don't owe you any favors. Especially since you told the cops I killed Roth."

"You did."

"That's not the point. Why did you give them my name?"

"I only know your first name. Have they busted you?"

"Not yet."

"Are you concerned the River City cops will bust you?"

He laughed. "Not likely."

"Then what's the problem? Tell us about Anderson."

"Then you'll owe me one. You okay with that, Sledge?"

I wasn't okay with that, but then I also figured he'd have a hard time collecting on it. He'd probably stay away from River City for some time. Getting stopped for a traffic violation or something stupid would land him in jail. River City PD hadn't made much progress on proving he'd killed Johannes Roth, the neo-Nazi who had wanted to build a casino in River City. And they wouldn't without my cooperation. I'd keep that card handy in case I needed it with Bertram.

"I'm fine. What can you tell us?"

Bobo scowled. He had issues with the mob ever since they'd done a job on his family. I touched mute on the phone.

"I know you don't like the guy, but he might be able to help."

Bobo frowned and shook his head. "At what cost?"

Bertram said, "He used to do odd dirty jobs for Gibellini. But he went too far. Killed someone he wasn't supposed to.

Gibellini had two of his guys work him over. Then the crazy fool tried to go after Gibellini."

I unmuted the phone. "And?"

"I took him aside and told him he had two options. Leave town or eat a bullet."

"And he left town. And came here. Thanks."

"Oh, and the whacko's a druggie as well. Does meth."

Bobo decided to contribute. "Did you know he was in a residential facility?"

"I heard something about that. But I don't think he checked himself in to get help. I also heard someone paid him big money to go there and keep tabs on someone."

Interesting. Could that someone being spied on have been Barker Dupree?

Bobo asked, "Does he have any associates here he might talk to?"

"Yeah, there's a couple." Bertram gave us their names. He didn't know where they lived. One was a drug dealer, probably the supplier for Anderson. The other was a gambler who owed Anderson a lot of money.

I thanked Bertram and was about to hang up, but he said, "Don't forget, Sledge. You owe me."

I punched the red button.

"Can you get Jackson on those two names?"

Bobo nodded, then took out his cell phone. But he didn't text Jackson, like I thought he would. Instead, he called River City PD about the shooting. That shot the rest of the evening.

The next day we'd resume our search for Braxton Anderson and attend a crime scene reenactment.

Seventeen

Geoffrey Poindexter pulled one side of the crime scene tape from the door frame and inserted a key into the lockbox hanging from the doorknob. A little container slid out, from which he retrieved another key and unlocked the deadbolt. He opened the door, bowed, and waved us in. Bobo and I entered Sandy Akins's apartment.

A foul odor broadsided us.

I was last, so I closed the door. "Why so warm in here?"

"The super turned off the air conditioner since no one is living here." Poindexter pointed. "The kitchen is where the action was."

We waded through the clammy air toward the kitchen. Before reaching it, I stopped and examined the living room. A brushed-fabric sectional sofa took up most of the space, facing a wall-mounted television. A large, glass table sat in the middle of the sectional. The table held two coffee-table books, three purple coasters with floral designs, and a pile of nature magazines.

The odor grew stronger when I entered the kitchen. A crusty brown bloodstain covered half of the ceramic tile floor.

"Did you get permission for us to be here?" Bobo asked.

"Of course. I always do everything by the book."

Bobo and I looked at each other, brows raised.

"Sarcasm, guys. Sarcasm. But I told Detective Morris what we're doing."

I turned around. Even from the kitchen, I could see bloody imprints on the doorknob. We had only one choice: figure out who really killed Sandy Akins. No way Barker would walk without the actual murderer being caught.

"And why didn't Detective Morris come with us?" Bobo moved to the other side of the kitchen counter.

"The case is with the prosecutor's office. Everyone thinks your boy did it. All evidence points to him."

I nodded. "Tell us how it went down."

"This is mostly conjecture. No way to really determine the order of things. But... this is how I played it out in my mind." He turned his back to me. "Ms. Akins knew the killer."

"How do you know that?"

"No signs of a struggle anywhere. Nothing out of place. Just blood spatter and the blood on the floor. Oh, and your boy's fingerprints in blood on the doorknob."

Bobo walked to the other end of the counter. He pointed at a knife holder. "Six slots, all full. None missing. The killer brought his own knife?"

"That's the assumption. We never found the murder weapon. Anyway, Sledge, you're the killer. I'm Ms. Akins. My back is to you. The killer stabbed Akins three times in the back." He turned. "She turned around. The killer stabbed her three times in the stomach." He grabbed his stomach, then reached his right hand to the counter but didn't touch it. "She grabbed the counter, probably for balance. The killer gave the final blow. An upward thrust to the throat. Missed the carotid but severed the trachea. No way Ms. Akins could scream. The killer left."

Smeared blood dotted the white Formica counter close to where Poindexter made the fake grab. Streaks of blood ran down the cabinets under the counter. Most of the blood was on the floor behind Poindexter.

"Then what?" I moved around the bloodstain to the body outline and looked back at Poindexter.

Bobo's phone dinged. Incoming text message, which he ignored.

Poindexter squatted. "She fell on her butt. Heavy fall. Good-sized bruise. Then she rolled onto her stomach and dragged herself to where you're standing." He duck-walked to the outline. "Then she died. The coroner listed exsanguination as the cause of death, but I think she suffocated. Due to the knife wound, she couldn't breathe."

I remembered the crime scene photo: she was on the floor with her right arm extended over her head, but her left arm at her side. No wall separated the kitchen from the living room.

"Did she have a cell phone on the coffee table? Or her purse on the sofa?"

Poindexter shook his head. "Her phone was in her jeans pocket. Purse was in the bedroom."

"Was anything taken from the purse?" Bobo came from around the counter and joined me, looking into the living room. His phone dinged again. Another text message, which he also ignored.

"Nope. She had thirty-seven dollars and change in her purse. And a couple of credit cards."

The facts kept circling back. It didn't look good for Barker. However, the killer being known to Ms. Akins could also mean Braxton Anderson. She knew him. Question was, would she let him into her apartment?

Bobo continued staring into the living room. I rotated to match. Window to the left. Corner straight ahead. Television on the wall to the right. Sofa between where she'd lain and the rest of the living room. Was she trying to get to something?

I turned back and faced Poindexter. "What can you tell us about the killer?"

Poindexter sighed out a small laugh. "The blows to the back angled slightly down. Therefore, the killer was probably a little taller than the victim. I'd guess around five-foot-eight to five-foot-ten."

Barker Dupree stood five-foot-nine.

"And the blows to the back didn't penetrate that far. Not much strength. The knife was sharp, as the entry wounds were clean."

Dang. More evidence pointing to Barker. That man had gone weak after years in the facility. Skinny arms.

"Anything else?"

"Not technically, no. But I have one other conjecture."

Bobo turned around. "What's that?"

"Like you guys, I don't see Barker as being the killer."

I walked away from the bloodstain. The smell emanating from it gave me a headache. "Why's that?"

Poindexter walked toward the door. "Motive. Why would he kill Sandy Akins when he professed undying love for her? And there wasn't anything reported about an argument. No loud voices. And at least two of the neighbors are stay-at-home. The walls are paper-thin. They'd have heard something."

"You should have been a detective."

Poindexter blushed. "Nah. You know me. Not good with people. Much better with technology."

"You've always been fine around us."

Poindexter looked first at Bobo, then at me. "You are the most self-centered, arrogant, no-filter person I know. But you've always treated me well and shown me respect." He looked at Bobo. "And you, well, you're just plain the nicest person I know. Probably the nicest person in River City."

I'm sure Bobo blushed, but his dark face concealed it.

As for me, a compliment hid somewhere in Poindexter's comment. I took the win.

"Thank you?"

Poindexter shrugged and opened the door. We followed him into the hallway. Sure enough, two other doors in the hallway closed. Nosy neighbors. The police report stated they had talked to all of the occupants on the floor, and none of them had reported hearing anything from Sandy Akins's apartment.

Poindexter locked the door, put the key back into the lock-box, and re-stuck the crime scene tape.

I asked, "Why is this still an active crime scene?"

"Like I said, I don't believe they have the right person. In case someone else is apprehended, I may want to go over things again."

We both shook the forensic investigator's hand and left the apartment.

Before I started the car, I asked Bobo who had texted him. He took out his phone and read the messages.

"Jackson found addresses for both the people your hitman buddy gave us."

I started the car. "He ain't my buddy. Just a contact that has proved useful."

"Whatever."

We headed for the first address. More fun in River City awaited us.

Eighteen

Bobo and I didn't make it to Braxton's first buddy right away. As I drove east through downtown, "She's Not There" played on my cell phone.

I sighed.

My phone was in a holder attached to my vent so I could see the GPS. I let the song go on.

Bobo swiveled the holder and answered.

"Hello, Ms. Dupree. What can we do for you?"

"Mr. Johnson. What a pleasant surprise. I'm hoping you can come over for lunch and brief me on the case."

I shook my head. Bobo held up his hands, palms up, asking why.

"Hello, Ms. Dupree."

"Mr. Sledge. Are you able to come for lunch?"

"We're heading the opposite direction. How about we meet at Luticelli's? We're just south of there now."

A long silence. I turned north, figuring she'd agree.

"Fine. See you in about fifteen minutes." She hung up.

Bobo said nothing. I assumed he agreed with my logic that it would have been out of our way. It would be about eleven-thirty when we got to Luticelli's. I hoped Edwin T. Masewich would be gone by then.

We'd had many run-ins with Masewich. He was a suspected killer in several unsolved murders in River City, including two recently that we'd been involved in. He had an espresso at Luticelli's daily, but he usually left close to eleven-thirty.

I pulled into the parking lot and waited. If Jeopardy was at home, it would take her about five minutes longer than it did us. A few rough characters came out of the restaurant. Masewich wasn't one of them. I had no clue what he drove so wasn't sure if any of the seven or so cars in the parking lot belonged to him.

Turned out I didn't need to worry about identifying his car.

He walked out of the restaurant with a man I didn't recognize. Bobo bristled. I'm sure he was itching to get out and pound Masewich to the ground. In general, Bobo is a pacifist, but mob guys are the exception. And back when the mob had more influence and Masewich was their enforcer, he'd had a couple run-ins with the Johnson family.

"Take it easy, big guy. Not the time or place."

Bobo grunted. He gripped the door handle. If Masewich recognized us, fireworks would fly. But he never looked at us. He and the medium-height, medium-build, black-haired mystery man climbed into a GMC SUV. They left the parking lot and headed south.

A minute later, Jeopardy arrived in her four-door Audi. We got out and walked to the restaurant but waited outside for her.

"Mr. Sledge, Mr. Johnson. Nice to see you. I can't say I've ever eaten here before."

"And you probably won't ever again." I opened the left side of the double-glass door for her.

She entered, followed by Bobo, then me. I nodded to the man behind the bar. He'd seen me many times. Not sure if he was a friend of Masewich's. His expression, like every other day, was neutral, but wary. He waved us in, indicating we could grab a table.

Once seated, Jeopardy started right in. "Where are you with the case? Any... how do you call them... leads?"

"That's what you call them."

Before I could say more, a thin, middle-aged waitress threw three menus on the table. "Drinks?"

We ordered. I had to stick with Dr Pepper since Bobo was there, and it was still before noon. Bobo ordered his usual Diet Coke. Jeopardy ordered water with lime. When the waitress scoffed, she changed to lemon. The waitress nodded and left.

Jeopardy took her phone out and started typing. I didn't bother to ask. Looking back, I should have.

"You were saying?" She looked up at me with raised brows.

I glanced at Bobo, not sure how much we should say.

Bobo took the lead.

"We've identified one other person of interest, Ms. Dupree."

"Person of interest?"

"Someone who may be involved."

"Ah."

The waitress delivered our drinks. "Food?"

Her vocabulary astounded me. We'd hadn't looked at the menu, but for Bobo and me, no big deal. We knew it by heart. Jeopardy picked hers up and scanned it. I ordered manicotti and Bobo ordered chicken penne. The waitress stared at Jeopardy, tapping her pen on her order pad.

When the tapping didn't accelerate Jeopardy's perusal, the waitress cleared her throat.

Jeopardy put the menu down. "Yes, I'm sorry. I'll have the Italian salad and an order of the balsamic bruschetta."

The waitress left.

Jeopardy turned her sparkling eyes on Bobo. "Was this someone Barker knew?"

"Yes, ma'am. He knows this man. They were in River Bluffs together."

She nodded. "I see. And he's no longer there?"

"No, ma'am. He walked away not long after Barker did."

"And do you know where he is?"

"We did," I interjected. "But he got away. We have a couple of other contacts to look up. You interrupted us on our way to one. Hopefully, we'll find him."

"Hopefully." Jeopardy stared straight ahead, toward the entrance to the restaurant. She winced and rubbed one eye. When she pulled her hand away, she continued blinking the eye. "Oh, my. Mr. Johnson, would you be a dear and get me a tissue. I seem to have something in my eye."

Bobo nodded then pushed away from the table. He glanced toward the entrance, scrunched his brows, then left to go to the bathroom, which was on the other side of the restaurant.

Jeopardy flashed a wide, bright smile. She leaned forward. I had my elbows on the table, hands clasped together. The outside door opened. I started to look at who was coming in. But Jeopardy grabbed my hands and pulled them apart, then toward her. I started to pull them away, but she lifted them to her mouth and kissed each one.

"What are you doing?"

Much louder than necessary, Jeopardy answered, "Oh, Jake. I'm so glad we are together. I thought about you every day when I was away."

I jerked my hands out of hers then glanced toward the entrance. A swarm of eels crawled through my belly. A woman was walking out the door. From the back, she looked just like Allison Rogers.

"Excuse me." I pushed away from the table and sprinted toward the door, reaching it just as the woman, who I realized was Allison Rogers, stepped outside.

"Allison?"

She stopped and slowly turned. "Jake. Hi."

She put her hands on her hips.

"What are you doing here?" I let the door close and moved a little to the side as another couple was coming toward us.

"I'd ask you the same, but it's obvious what you're doing."

"What?" I put my hands up. "I don't know what you mean. We're having lunch with our client to update her."

"We? All I saw was you and Ms. Dupree."

"Bobo's in the can getting a tissue."

"Sure. Seems you're with Ms. Dupree."

The younger couple passed us, both staring. I glared at them, and they entered the restaurant.

"With her? She's our client. Nothing more."

"Not what I heard her say."

"Jeopardy Dupree is crazy. I'm not interested in her beyond being our client."

"She seems very interested in you."

Sweat ran down both sides of my face. I slipped my jacket off and draped it over my left arm. "How did you know we were here, anyway?"

"She texted me."

"What?"

"Well, she texted you, I'm guessing, but somehow it went to me."

I considered what she said. "When did you give Jeopardy your phone number?"

"I haven't."

"And you don't find that suspicious?"

Allison opened her mouth, didn't speak, then closed it again. She put her thumb on her extremely cute chin and scrunched her brows. Before she could respond, the restaurant door opened.

"Hi, Ms. Rogers. How nice to see you." Bobo walked out and stood beside me. My savior.

"Oh, hi, Bobo. So, you are here."

Bobo looked down at himself. "Yup. All of me." He smiled.

Allison's shoulders relaxed. She grinned.

I let out a deep sigh. "Now do you believe me?"

"What's there to believe?" Bobo asked.

"I'll tell you later." To Allison, I asked, "Are we good?"

She touched my arm. "I'm sorry, Jake. Yes, we're good. I just think, though, you're playing with fire."

"I agree. But we're trying to help her brother out. Who I think is a decent guy caught in a bad situation."

She squeezed my arm then released it. "Be careful with that woman. She's up to something. She has a thing for you."

"Don't all women?"

Allison gave me a "we're not going there" look. "She kissed your hands, Jake."

I raised my hands. "I didn't know she was going to do that."

"I believe you, but you need to be careful with her."

"I know. Dinner tonight?"

She sighed but nodded.

"Great. I'll pick you up at six. That work?"

She looked back into the parking lot. "You have your car back. So, absolutely, pick me up."

My red 1975 Oldsmobile Delta 88 gleamed in the parking lot two rows away. A chick magnet if ever there was one. At least it worked on Allison.

"And make sure the top is down." Allison winked at me.

"Wouldn't have it any other way. See you tonight."

She looked past me, then leaned in and kissed me on the cheek. "That woman is dangerous, Jake." She turned around and walked into the parking lot.

Bobo and I re-entered the restaurant.

"Jeopardy, what in the—"

Bobo squeezed my arm. Allison's squeeze had sent a jolt through my heart. Bobo's squeeze hurt and would leave a bruise.

"What?" Seems I'd been asking that a lot lately.

Bobo shook his head and sat.

"Mr. Johnson, you are a lifesaver." Jeopardy batted her eyes at him.

I wanted to slap her silly. Instead, I also sat and glowered at her. She smiled at me, all two-hundred pearly white teeth showing.

A thought occurred to me. After the visits to Braxton's buddies, we needed to go back to River Bluffs. I wanted to grill Barker about family life in the Dupree home before they'd become adults.

The food arrived. During lunch, Bobo and Jeopardy talked about nothing of substance. I remained silent, seething, trying to figure out what the crazy woman across from me had going on in her whacko brain.

Nineteen

Bobo and I parted ways with Jeopardy at the restaurant. We promised we'd let her know if anything broke on the case. Our first stop was the address of Anthony Harris, a drug dealer, who lived a couple of miles from Luticelli's. Both Bobo and I knew him from when we were cops.

Harris lived in an older apartment complex. Seven stories of blond brick. Three buildings built in a U-shape with a courtyard in the middle, where a neglected, though filled swimming pool shimmered in the August sun. Two kids splashed in the water and screamed at the top of their lungs. A large woman in a one-piece bathing suit lay on a grungy white pool chair reading a book. We walked past the swimming pool to the building on the far side. The woman glanced at us and returned to her novel. The kids never noticed us.

I punched the up button for the elevator. It didn't light up. Four flights of stairs later, sweat ran down my back and glistened on Bobo's head. My heart pounded. I worked out several times a week, but my routine was mostly strength training, not cardio. Maybe it was time to change that. Bobo breathed normally.

We walked to the second door on the right. Hoping to avoid a repeat of what happened at Braxton's apartment, I pounded on the door.

"Landlord. Checking on AC."

No one answered. No sounds from inside. I pounded again.

"I'm a comin'. Hold on."

Anthony Harris opened the door. He blinked rapidly then rubbed his eyes. "Officer Johnson? I ain't seen you in a couple years, brother." The tall, thin black man looked at me. "And you look familiar. Do I know you?"

"I arrested you about six times, Harris. Jake Sledge. I used to be Detective Jake Sledge. Now, we're PIs."

"And what you want with me?"

Bobo said, "We're looking for a man named Braxton Anderson. You know him?"

Harris narrowed his eyes. He rubbed a hand over his shaved head. "Yeah. But ain't seen him in a few weeks. The dude still owes me money."

I looked at Bobo. Even though I had arrested Harris multiple times, Bobo had walked the beat around the area and knew most of the residents much better than I did. To me, Harris appeared to be telling the truth.

"Okay. Sorry to disturb you. Are you keeping clean?"

"Of course, brother. Of course."

That I could tell was a lie. We walked away. Harris closed the door behind us. I stopped after a few feet, waited, and listened. Harris's muffled voice carried through the walls. I crept back to his door and placed my ear against it.

"Yeah, they came here, like you said they would." Silence for a bit. "Naw, man. I told them nothing. Said I ain't seen him in a couple weeks."

Nothing more. Faint footsteps retreated further into the apartment.

The "him" Harris referred to had to be Anderson. But if he wasn't talking to Anderson, who was on the other end of the line?

We left and went to visit Chuck Freemont, the gambler contact Bertram had given us.

While I drove to Chuck Freemont's subdivision, Bobo studied the map of the streets going into and out of that subdivision.

"Grid pattern. The neighborhood straddles Old Post Road. Freemont lives on the north side of Old Post, two blocks in."

"Got it."

We drove down tree-lined Old Post Road. Towering maples and oaks. We turned at the Hollow Oak sign and entered a neighborhood made up of one- and two-story vinyl-sided houses in grays, whites, and the occasional earth tones. All the houses featured manicured lawns, front porches, and attached garages. Typical middle-class subdivision for mid-level managers in River City, and probably some who commuted to Kansas City. Quite the contrast to the apartment complex we'd just visited.

"Left here." Bobo pointed.

I turned.

"His house is on the road two blocks up. It's the third house on the left."

"Should I take the next left and circle around?"

A dark-colored SUV answered the question. It turned onto our street from the next block. There are hundreds if not thousands of dark SUVs in River City, but this one looked like the one that had tried to run me over and the one that had picked up Braxton Anderson from River Bluffs.

I accelerated and got to the corner of Freemont's street. The SUV was parked on the wrong side of the street in front of Freemont's house. Braxton was running toward the SUV, a gym bag in his left hand and a gun in his right. He pointed the gun at us and fired on the run.

I kept going straight.

"He's getting in the SUV. Turn on the next block."

I did as Bobo instructed but had to slow for kids playing in the street. They saw me and scattered to either side. I sped up and zipped past them. At the next stop sign, I turned left. When we reached Freemont's street, the dark SUV was two blocks away. It turned right.

"Follow or talk with Freemont?"

"We'll never catch them," Bobo answered.

I wanted to try, but a car chase in a neighborhood like Hollow Oak carried way too many risks. Especially if we got close and Anderson decided to shoot at us again.

I turned left and drove to Freemont's house. "Did you see the driver?"

"Not through the back of the SUV."

I pulled into Freemont's driveway. A man opened the inside door and peeked out, then slammed the door shut.

We exited the car. "Bobo, take the front. I'll go around back."

Bobo nodded and trotted to the front door. I took off running toward the back. A white fence surrounded the backyard, but the gate had no lock on it. I went through the gate and saw a stocky, blond-haired man running through the yard toward a back gate that opened into his neighbor's yard.

"Chuck Freemont?" I yelled.

He didn't stop.

I jogged after him. "We just want to talk to you."

He still didn't stop. When he reached the gate, he tried to open it, but it was locked. The fence stood about five feet high. Freemont wore dress pants, a short-sleeved pale blue dress shirt, and wingtips. Not ideal fence-climbing attire. He hefted himself up, got his arms straight, but struggled to swing a leg high enough to clear the fence.

I reached him just as he got his first leg over. Before he could fall over the other side, I grabbed his collar and pulled him back.

He flopped onto the lawn. I straddled him and eased aside my jacket lapel, showing him the .45 in my shoulder holster. Not that I'd shoot him, unless he pulled a weapon. I was going for the effect, and it worked.

"Chuck, what are you doing?" a woman yelled.

Bobo walked into the backyard with a short, pudgy woman in her mid-forties. She had light brown hair parted in the middle that hung below her puffy cheeks.

Bobo and the lady walked up to us.

"What did you do to him?" Bobo asked.

"I pulled him off the fence. Probably saved his life."

Bobo scrunched his brows. "How so?"

"He would have fallen on his face on the other side. Broke his neck."

The woman said, "Yup, probably. I'm Louise." She stuck out her hand.

I shook it lightly. "Hello, Louise. Are you his wife?"

She nodded, then bent over and grabbed the so far silent Chuck Freemont's hand. I moved away so Chuck could stand.

"Why'd you run, Chuck?" Louise asked.

Chuck looked at me, then at Bobo. "I don't know these guys. And after that thug Braxton, I wasn't sure what they wanted."

Louise put her arm around Bobo's. "This is Bobo Johnson. Played for the Bengals. Don't you recognize him?"

Chuck's eyes widened and he smiled. Figures. Everyone smiles at Bobo. "Oh, yeah. Hey, Mr. Johnson, nice to meet you." They shook hands.

Louise pointed at me with her free hand. "And this is Jake Sledge. He and Bobo played together at Northwestern. You set some rushing record, didn't you?"

I nodded. "All because of the big guy here blocking for me."

Louise pulled away from Bobo, then tapped me on the arm. "I saw you run over plenty of cornerbacks."

"They tend to be much smaller than me."

"The hammer, right?" Chuck asked.

I nodded.

"What do you two want with me?"

Two teenage boys came out of the back door across the small cedar deck and loped toward us.

When they reached us, the taller one pointed at Bobo. "See, I told you, dude. A professional football player. That's Bobo Johnson."

Both teenagers stared at the big guy, who smiled at them.

"These are our sons," Louise said. "Tyler and Cory. Tyler's fifteen and Cory's thirteen."

"We're private investigators. And we're looking for Braxton Anderson. We have some questions for him. I assume that was him running out of your house and into that SUV."

Chuck nodded.

"Boys, you've seen the football players," Louise said. "Now, please go back inside."

Before they could leave, Bobo said, "If you have a football, I'd be happy to sign it. I'm sure Jake would as well."

"Who?" asked Tyler.

Ouch. Louise saved me from answering. "Jake the Hammer Sledge. Played one year with the Browns. Set records in college."

"Oh, cool. Yeah, we'll go get a football." The two teenagers trotted back to the house.

Granted, I couldn't be too hurt. They weren't even born when I left the NFL. And Bobo being in the hall of fame was often shown on camera at a Bengals game, especially when they played the Chiefs at Arrowhead.

"Back to Braxton. Mr. Freemont, who picked him up?"

Chuck shrugged. "He got a phone call and ran into the spare bedroom where we were letting him stay, got his stuff, then waited at the door."

"Did you see who was driving?" Bobo asked.

Both Freemonts shook their heads. Louise added, "Tinted windows. And when the door opened, Braxton was in the way."

"Did Braxton give any indication as to who was helping him?" I asked.

Again, both shook their heads.

I had a flash of inspiration. "This is the third time, we know of, that this person has picked him up. Why was he staying with you and not that person?"

Louise elbowed Chuck. "It's his fault he was staying with us. The dope likes to gamble too much and owes that guy's boss money."

"Wait a minute." I narrowed my eyes at Chuck. "That guy's boss? Who is that?"

"I ... I don't know his name. The guy who runs the Lexington Casino. You know, the one on the river north of Lexington?"

"Giovanni Gibellini runs that one." I narrowed my eyes again. "I have a reliable source who says Braxton Anderson and Gibellini are not on good terms. Why would Braxton still be collecting for him?"

"I ... I don't know. I thought I'd paid it. But Braxton told me I still owed a bunch of the vig."

The vig being the interest on a loan, and from someone like Gibellini the rate would be steep. Still, something didn't resonate.

"I'll check it out. But I don't think you owe Gibellini anything."

"Well, not now."

I raised my brows.

"Since we let him stay here, he said we're even."

Wonderful. The question remained, why couldn't Braxton stay with the mysterious driver? We had to assume the driver knew who we were, since they'd already tried to run us down. But there was no way they could have known we'd taken Barker's case; that had happened right before the first attempt. Did Braxton's actions even have anything to do with Barker Dupree, or was that a misdirection? My conclusion: the driver was someone we knew. Someone who couldn't risk being seen with Braxton.

Twenty

Allison Rogers stared at her surroundings. "Wow, I haven't been here since my parents brought me to celebrate my college graduation."

We were at Chez Martin's, the one and only French restaurant in River City, located downtown northwest of the fourth precinct. The evening light filtered through the windows fronting the restaurant. Brass candelabras hung from a ceiling depicting greenery. Gold-painted beams decorated with ornate carvings sectioned the ceiling—or *plafond*, as Allison would later call it. And no, I didn't need to look up *candelabras*. That one I knew.

I didn't want to ask her how long it had been since she graduated college because I knew it wasn't that long ago, and I didn't need a reminder of our age gap. So far, the gap had not bothered Allison, and it certainly didn't bother me. I had no issue acting younger than my age.

A waiter in a black suit with a white shirt and black bow tie stood by the table, which was covered with a white tablecloth. No pen or notepad, hands behind his back. "What can I get you to drink? Today we're featuring a wonderful rosé from near Marseille."

"Where's that?" I asked. "Isn't that somewhere near Bonne Terre?"

The waiter narrowed his eyes and smirked. Allison giggled. She touched my hand. "No, silly. France."

"Ah, that Marseille. Um, sure, we'll—"

"I'm sorry, but I don't drink wine," Allison said. "Do you have iced tea? Maybe a flavored one?"

The waiter gave his full attention to Allison. "We have a wonderful blackberry sage tea. It's supposedly for wisdom." He turned to me. "Maybe the gentleman would also like some?"

I ignored the jab and nodded. Two blackberry sage iced teas it was. And who was I to argue that I could use more wisdom, especially with our current case? The waiter left.

"Am I forcing you to be someone you're not, Jake?"

"Not at all. I don't care much for wine." And I could drink beer any other time when I wasn't with her.

She smiled. The deep blue dress she wore complemented her deep blue eyes. I wanted to get lost in those eyes.

"How was your day?" she asked.

"That's hard to say. With this case, we seem to take one step forward and a few steps backward. Lots of things are happening, but nothing seems related." I spent the next ten minutes explaining what we'd learned so far trying to prove Barker Dupree innocent. I didn't notice the waiter putting our iced teas on the table until Allison lifted her glass and took a drink.

"That is good. I think I've had this before."

I searched briefly for a straw, and when there wasn't one, I picked up the glass and tried mine. Yup, tasty. I didn't feel any wiser, though. Maybe I had to finish the glass.

"What's your next move?" Allison asked.

I started to tell her.

"Jake Sledge. What are you doing here?" Jeopardy Dupree stood by our table, hands on her hips, glaring at me, dressed to the nines in a tight-fitting dark yellow dress that ended below her knees.

"Um, I'm having dinner with Allison."

"You stood me up."

"Excuse me?"

She turned to Allison. "We had a dinner date, tonight. To discuss the case. I've been waiting at that new place inside the Napoleon Hotel. No show. Can you imagine?"

Allison squinted at her, then frowned at me. She started to stand.

"Where are you going?" I put my hands out but could not quite reach her.

"Maybe I should leave."

"No." I pointed at Jeopardy. "She's off her rocker. She needs to leave. I didn't agree to meet her tonight."

"Really, Jake. At lunch. Since Mr. Johnson was there and we couldn't be alone, you suggested dinner."

I stood and towered over Jeopardy. Intimidating a woman with my size felt childish, but the anger boiling inside me needed some kind of release. I sucked in a deep breath and waved for Allison to sit. She did.

"Ms. Dupree, I'm sorry, but you are mistaken. I did not suggest meeting with you tonight. Now please, go home. Or wherever else you want to go, but here." I felt so proud of myself for using a calm voice and not picking her up and throwing her across the room. Did she really think we had an arrangement, or was she playing a game I had not caught onto yet?

Something changed in her eyes. They went from hurt indignation to spite. An ironic grin spread across her face. "Fine. I must have misheard you." Much of her accent retreated. "We'll talk tomorrow." She turned to Allison. "Sorry to have disturbed your date, Ms. Rogers." One last glare at me, and she stalked out of the restaurant.

I collapsed into my chair. Now Allison glared at me.

"What?" I put my hands up and shrugged.

"I'd like to know if there's something between you and Ms. Dupree."

I bowed my head and sighed. "No. Nothing between us."

When I looked up, Allison had relaxed the glare, but I could see the fear of betrayal in her eyes.

"As far as I'm concerned, she's our client. Nothing else. I don't know what game she's playing or why."

"Have you been flirting with her?"

"What? Flirting? Not a chance."

"I... I'm sorry, Jake. I think it best if we back off until this case is over. I'm very confused right now."

I reached across the table and took her hand and was relieved when she didn't pull away. "Look, I promise there is nothing between us. That woman is whacko. We're trying to prove her brother is innocent of murder. Then, she's out of my life. Please." I watched the thoughts spinning through Allison's mind. She didn't know me that well, yet. And Jeopardy was a gorgeous woman. I couldn't blame her for her skepticism. But I desperately wanted us to work.

"Let's finish dinner. I'll think about it. How about we go hiking along the river on Saturday? It's supposed to be a cooler day."

I wanted to jump up and cheer, to throw my hands in the air and yell, "Yes!" Instead, I smiled and nodded. "Sounds great. I need an entire day off, anyway."

We finished dinner and talked about benign, neutral topics. The subject of Jeopardy Dupree hung between us like a sheet over a corpse we were supposed to identify. We were both afraid to lift it, fearing we'd recognize the body underneath, so we let it lie.

My statement of needing a day off could not have been more true by the end of that week.

Twenty-One

That night after dropping Allison off at her house, I drove home nursing the sting of her refusal to let me in for a movie or something. Restless, but not able to focus on anything, I tried to sleep. All night I tossed and turned. Nightmares assaulted me, involving a mixture of faceless, nameless adversaries; young men with shaved heads and swastikas; Jeopardy Dupree coming on to me; and Allison leaving me. Finally, around six, I gave up and lumbered into the living room and collapsed into my easy chair. I turned on the television and watched the sports channel. At some point, I must have fallen into a dreamless sl eep.

My cell phone awakened me, blasting "Who Let the Dogs Out." I bolted upright and snatched my phone off the end table.

"Yeah, Bobo, what's up? Why are you calling so early?"

"Early? Dude, it's eight-thirty. I thought we were going to River Bluffs today."

I glanced at my smart watch. Blank. I shook my wrist a couple of times. Still blank. The battery was dead. No working clock in sight, so I looked at my cell phone. The big guy wasn't lying. 8:35. We'd agreed yesterday to meet at the office at eight and go talk with Barker to try and tie up some of our loose ends.

"Give me twenty."

"I already did fifty this morning, Sergeant."

"Ha, ha. Minutes, not pushups." A light workout for Bobo if he only did fifty pushups. Always made me feel guilty. I did fifty pushups. About once a week.

"Got it." Bobo hung up.

I showered, skipped shaving, and threw on my tan chinos, a baby-blue, collarless, short-sleeved shirt, and midnight blue sports coat. I didn't bother putting on the shoulder holster, as River Bluffs frowned on guns entering their facility. Instead, I grabbed it along with my dark blue fedora and ran out of the house on an empty stomach. Before heading to the office, I threw my shoulder holster with the .45 into the trunk of my Delt a 88.

From the office parking lot, I texted Bobo that I was there. He came out. I let him drive. And believe me, Bobo is the only person who drives my baby other than me. I asked him to swing by Bob's Drive-in, where I purchased a breakfast sandwich. Bobo said he'd already had granola and fruit but ordered orange juice. How that guy maintained the muscle mass he did on bird food baffled me. I scarfed down the food while we drove to River Bluffs. At least no one shot at us this time.

We walked into the facility.

"Wow, you're back." I forgot her name, but I was amazed that only five days ago Braxton Anderson had shot the receptionist, and here she was. Her right arm was in a sling. Dark bags hung under her eyes. No makeup. She flashed a small smile. "I was going stir crazy. Dr. Charnow agreed to let me try a few hours a day."

Bobo said, "We're so glad you're doing better. I'd been praying for your recovery."

"Oh, thank you so much." Her smile widened. Everyone smiles at Bobo. "Are you here to see Dr. Charnow?"

"No, actually, Barker Dupree."

She frowned. "Um, hold please." She picked up the phone receiver and punched a button. "Dr. Charnow, those PIs are here to see Barker Dupree ... Uh-huh ... Yes, ma'am." She hung up. "Dr. Charnow will be right out."

Something seemed off. No reason we should have to go through Charnow to see Barker. The facility director rounded the corner. Dressed for business, she wore dark gray slacks, a white shirt, and a light gray jacket.

"Mr. Sledge, Mr. Johnson. How are you this morning?"

"I didn't sleep that well last night, but otherwise okay."

"Doing well, Dr. Charnow," Bobo said. "How are you?"

She joined us in front of the reception desk. "A little perplexed. You came to see Barker?"

"Yes." I took off my fedora. "Why would that be perplexing?"

"Well, I figured you knew."

"Knew what?"

She glanced at the receptionist, then back at us. "He was bailed out late yesterday afternoon."

Bobo and I looked at each other.

"Excuse me? Did you say Barker was bailed out?"

Bobo added, "There wasn't any bail set at the arraignment."

An older couple entered the facility. Dr. Charnow motioned us to follow her. Once in the office, she closed the door.

"Please sit."

We did.

She parked herself in her desk chair, put her elbows on the desk, and interlocked her fingers. "Around four yesterday, two county deputies came in and showed me some paperwork. They said someone posted bail for Barker Dupree."

"But there wasn't any bail," I said.

"I challenged that. And they said his lawyer, Mr. Jorgenson, right?"

I nodded.

"His lawyer had arranged bail with the prosecuting attorney."

"They said that?" I asked.

"Yes."

"The prosecuting attorney can't arrange bail."

She dropped her hands onto her desk. "I assume they got a judge to do that."

I started to protest that there was no way it could have been done that quickly, but then I considered Jorgenson's pull.

Maybe he had arranged bail. I pulled out my cell phone and scrolled to Jorgenson's number in my contacts.

"Jorgenson and Jenkins, how may I direct your call?"

"Theodore Jorgenson, please."

"Please hold one moment while I check if Mr. Jorgenson is available."

Some canned music, then a few seconds later, "This is Jorgenson."

"Hello, sir. Jake Sledge."

"Mr. Sledge, how are you this fine morning?"

I punched the speaker button. "You're on speaker. I'm with Dr. Charnow at River Bluffs. Bobo's here as well."

"Good morning, all."

"That depends, sir. Did you arrange bail for Barker?"

"No. Ms. Goodhue was insistent on no bail. Either he stays at River Bluffs or in jail. Why?"

I took a deep breath. "Two county deputies collected him from River Bluffs yesterday afternoon saying he made bail."

A long pause. "Impossible." Another pause. "I was out all afternoon. I suppose it's possible Ms. Dupree arranged something with my partner. Let me check with Cal and see if he talked to her. He's in court right now, so it may be this afternoon."

We hung up. I decided waiting wasn't an option and found Jeopardy's number in my contacts.

She answered after two rings. "Good morning, Mr. Sledge. I suppose you're calling to yell at me about last night." Thick

Southern accent. "I do want to apologize for the misunderstanding."

"While I'd enjoy yelling at you, there's something more pressing."

"Oh, and what would that be?"

"Did you arrange bail for Barker yesterday?"

"No. Why?"

I glanced at Bobo, wondering how much I should tell her.

He shrugged. "Go for it."

"County deputies picked him up last night supposedly with paperwork saying he'd been bailed out."

"What?" The question came out more as a shriek. "They kidnapped *poor* Barker? Why would they do that? Mr. Sledge, you *have to* go get him. They might be torturing him."

If actual county deputies picked him up, it was unlikely they were torturing him. Either someone forged paperwork and convinced the county to pick him up, or they were not real deputies.

"Ms. Dupree, we'll look into it. And we'll let you know what we find out."

"*Please* do. I'll have my phone with me wherever I go."

We hung up. I stood. "Can we see the video from yesterday."

She nodded. We followed her to the security office, where she worked her keyboard magic. The video played.

When it finished, I said, "They're not county deputies. Look at the hats." They wore Smokey Bear hats. "The deputies usually don't wear hats, and when they do, they're baseball caps. State troopers and some other counties wear those hats."

"The uniforms look right," Bobo said.

I nodded. "Can we see the outside feed?"

Dr. Charnow did her thing.

I leaned in and watched as a county cruiser rolled into the porte cochere. Through the tinted windows, I could not make out any faces. The driver's door opened and the man who got out immediately put his hat in front of his head, blocking his face from the camera.

"Did one of them look like Braxton Anderson?" I asked Dr. Charnow.

She shook her head. "Not that I could tell. Both men were probably late twenties, early thirties. Braxton is older than that, and he looks even older."

True that. A rough life had chewed up that man's face.

"Pause the video on the car." Both Bobo and I leaned in.

"Look there." Bobo pointed. "You can see a faint outline under the paint. I'm guessing the county logo is a magnet. And that car is at least five years old. They upgraded two years ago."

"Did you get a copy of the paperwork?" I asked.

"They only flashed it. Showed me the last page that said one million dollars and had three signatures on it."

We returned to her office then spent the next ten minutes trying to console Dr. Charnow by assuring her it wasn't her fault. The two deputies would have fooled anyone. We left, not sure where to start looking for Barker Dupree. We were playing a dangerous version of the board game Sorry!, and our adversary, whoever he or she was, had just played a "Sorry!" card on us and sent us back to start.

I grew bored with the game on my phone and looked at Bobo. He was hunched over his laptop, pecking away.

"What's up, big guy?"

"Checking the map between River Bluffs and civilization. Seeing if there are any cameras that would pick up the cruiser that took Barker."

"And?"

"Not much. Far as I can figure, ten to fifteen different routes with only a smattering of gas stations, mini-marts, and businesses. Doubtful any of them have cameras pointing out on the roads."

I leaned back in my executive chair and put my feet on the desk. Computers were Bobo's thing, not mine. I preferred reality to virtuality.

"Give Jackson a buzz anyway. Maybe he can find something."

Bobo nodded and pulled out his cell, texting our resident computer hacker. Excuse me, white hat hacker.

Another hour of twiddling our thumbs went by. Brainstorming is what I'd tell anyone who asked, like our client.

Speaking of which, I decided to give her a call and see if she'd heard anything. Maybe a ransom demand?

The phone rang five times. Finally, Jeopardy answered.

"Yes, Mr. Sledge? Any news on Barker?" Not as much Southern accent this time.

"Not yet. We're checking some leads." Hey, texting Jackson was a lead.

"Okay. Let me know if you hear anything." Another voice sounded in the background, followed by an indistinguishable low noise.

"Is someone there with you, Ms. Dupree?"

"Yes, I'm at, I'm at a restaurant having lunch."

"Sounds like a good idea. We'll do the same. Hopefully, we'll have some news by this afternoon." I listened. No other noises in the background. Didn't sound like a restaurant.

"Anything else, Mr. Sledge?"

"Nope." We hung up. I frowned and stared at the cell phone thinking. Painful exercise, usually.

Bobo looked up from the computer. "Something wrong?"

"Our enigmatic client said she was at a restaurant having lunch, but it didn't sound like a restaurant."

"Why would she lie to us?"

I shrugged. "And speaking of lunch. Lenny's?"

Bobo closed the laptop, placed it on the desk, and stood. I assumed that meant yes, so I put on my shoulder holster, jacket, and fedora.

We walked to Lenny's and ordered subs. Typical Missouri August. Bright sun partly obscured by haze from heavy humidity. For me, style superseded comfort. Plus, the jacket hid both my .45 and my pit stains. For Bobo, heat was heat. Sweat coated his shiny, dark brown head and dribbled down his temples. The dark T-shirt hid his pit stains. That or he wore better antiperspirant than I did. But not one word of complaint from the big, sweaty guy as he limped back from Lenny's carrying his vegetable sub and diet soda.

Before entering our building, Bobo asked, "You talk to Alicia recently?"

"Not since going there for dinner."

"Give her a call."

"Okay." I decided that evening would be phonathon night. Mom, Alicia, and Allison, who hadn't returned several texts I'd sent.

I'd made it halfway through my meatball sub without spilling. Quite proud of myself. My cell phone chimed out "Working in the Coal Mine." River City PD. I put my sandwich down and answered.

"Sledgehammer Detective Agency, Jake Sledge speaking. Do you have a problem that needs pounding out?"

"You're the only problem I have, Sledge."

"And a good afternoon to you, too, Lieutenant." I punched the speaker button on the phone so Bobo could hear the profound words sure to spew from Lieutenant Kazminsky's philosophic mouth.

"This is a courtesy call, Sledge. A heads-up."

"For?"

"Your client. We've put a BOLO out on him, and we're treating him as an escaped prisoner."

I looked at Bobo and shook my head. "You've got to be kidding. On Barker Dupree? Escaped? He was kidnapped."

"You got any proof of that, Sledge?"

"Two fake county deputies presented a fake bail order and took him."

"How do you know he didn't arrange that? Or someone working with him?"

"Are we talking about the same Barker Dupree here?"

Kazminsky's voice was muffled. "Just a minute. On the phone." Then back to us, he said, "Courtesy call, Sledge. For now, Barker Dupree is an escaped prisoner. You hear anything, and I mean anything, you let us know. Got it?"

I continued shaking my head. "Yeah, got it. Have a great afternoon, Lieutenant."

He hung up. How rude.

"Can you believe those idiots?"

Bobo answered, "Protocol, Jake. You know the drill."

"Yeah, whatever. I just hope they don't shoot our client. Wait a minute. Dang it, why didn't I think of that?" I dialed River City PD.

Willow answered.

"Hey, Sarge. I need to talk to Kazminsky again."

"Hi, Sledge. Again?"

"He just called."

"About the BOLO on Barker Dupree?"

"Yup."

"Please hold." And I did for about thirty seconds.

"What do you want, Sledge?"

"Braxton Anderson. Do you have a BOLO issued on him? That man is dangerous."

He chuckled. "Agreed. But he's in our holding cell. High out of his mind. Still."

"When did you bring him in?"

"Last night. An officer found him sitting against a building wall." Silence, then the sound of shuffling papers. "Apartments at West Walnut and Kelling."

"Anthony Harris's building."

"The drug dealer?"

"The very same."

"What's he got to do with Anderson?"

"Other than selling him whatever dope he's on, he might be working with him."

"You got anything we can use to grab him?"

"Nope. Can we talk to Anderson?"

"You can try." He hung up again without saying goodbye.

Bobo chuckled.

"Next stop, River City PD."

"Our favorite place." We both laughed at that.

Twenty-Two

The trip to River City PD was a total waste of time. Braxton Anderson occupied one of the cells, but he was too high to be of any use. We told Kazminsky we'd try again tomorrow. Anderson babbled about Barker Dupree killing his girlfriend. We weren't even sure he knew we were there.

I pulled into my driveway and eased into the carport. Next door, Mom sat on her porch swing, as usual. The temperature had plummeted to a wonderful eighty degrees at six-thirty. Still not comfortable. But there Mom sat and had probably been sitting since five, when the temperature hovered near ninety. I couldn't convince her that I didn't work a normal nine-to-five job. I shut the car off and sighed. It had been a while since I'd gone over for dinner, and I had nothing planned other than a couple of phone calls. What the heck.

"Hey, Mom. Got anything to eat in that shack of yours?" I joined her on the porch.

Her house looked exactly like mine. They'd both been owned by the same man who had decided Florida was a better place for him, so he'd given me a deal on the pair. That was the only reason Mom agreed to move off the farm after Dad died.

"Hi, Jake. How was your day? I think I can scrounge something up."

Understatement of the year. More than likely, her refrigerator was stuffed with a week's worth of leftovers.

I followed her into the house. Immaculately neat, a trait Alicia had inherited, not me. Two dark brown recliners with a dark green sofa between them faced a large television hanging on the wall. A Christmas present from Alicia and me a couple of years back. Alicia had pitched in a little, anyway. Bobo had helped me mount it on the wall. My mom loved Bobo, so she jumped at any excuse to have him over.

We went into the kitchen. She opened the gleaming silver refrigerator. A birthday gift from Alicia and me four years ago. As I suspected, the fridge was packed full of containers.

She studied the assortment for a minute, then selected two of them. "How about meatloaf? Made it last night."

"That sounds great."

"And I got some garlic mashed. That okay?"

"Perfect."

Mom placed the containers on the counter and loaded two plates. She slipped one into the microwave. My mouth watered. Her meatloaf would win competitions. Best I've ever had. A one-inch layer of ketchup covered the rich, spiced meat. And the garlic mashed potatoes were incredible, made with cream cheese, sour cream, and fresh garlic.

When the microwave dinged, she swapped plates. We sat at the small wooden table when the food was ready. She asked me if I wanted to say the blessing, but I deferred to her, which she did.

"You never answered me. How was your day?"

I'd already stuffed a mouthful of the delicious meatloaf in my mouth, so I pointed at my cheek and gave a tight-lipped smile. After swallowing and drinking some milk — that's right, my mom gave her little boy milk every meal — I answered her.

"Tough case. We're not making a lot of progress, and now the man we've been hired to prove innocent has disappeared, possibly escaped."

"That's rough. But you'll find him." She dug into her meatloaf.

The next hour and a half passed with conversation about the case, about Alicia and Myron, and about the hot and humid weather. After dinner, she brought out lemon pie and coffee. I passed on the coffee. Lately, I had a hard enough time falling asleep. Caffeine after seven would keep me awake. I savored the pie. The perfect tanginess and smoothness. I suspected the whipped cream was homemade.

After dessert, I helped her clean up, then told her I needed to get home. She asked if I wanted to play two-handed pinochle, but I told her I had several calls to make.

"Working this late?" We stood at the door.

"Personal calls, Ma. Alicia and Allison."

"When am I going to meet Allison?"

"Soon, Ma. I promise." I leaned down and pecked her on the cheek. "Goodnight." I left.

On my porch, I cleaned out the mailbox. Bills, junk, more bills, more junk. All the bills were on autopay, compliments of Bobo, but I hadn't stopped the paper statements from coming. Not very green of me, but computers aren't my thing. I guess I could have asked Bobo to do that as well.

Inside, I threw the mail on the kitchen table and pulled out my cell phone. Easier call first.

"Hey, big brother." Alicia answered on the second ring.

"Hey. How's things?"

"Going well. You?"

I walked into the living room and collapsed into my easy chair. "Tough case. And we're back to square one."

"Bummer. I heard you went to church last Sunday."

"Oh? From whom?"

"Bobo."

"Bobo has a big mouth. Did he tell you anything else about me lately?"

"Um, yeah, actually. He said you agreed to see a counselor. Did you yet?"

"Not yet. Been busy."

"Going to church this Sunday?"

I grabbed the remote, turned on the television, and muted it. "Doubtful. Need to move this case forward."

"When are you going to the counselor?"

"When I get a chance. Bobo gave me some names."

"Good."

Time to ask the difficult question. Enough about me. Jeez. "How are things with Myron?"

"Great."

Bummer.

"He went to church with me Sunday. Complained all the way there. Sat with his arms crossed and a scowl on his face. But guess what?"

I wasn't sure I wanted to know. "What?"

"When we got home, Julia hugged him and said, 'I'm so proud of you for going to church, Daddy.'"

"Wow. That's great." I don't think my voice conveyed much enthusiasm, but Alicia ignored that.

"Yup. And he said he'll go again this weekend."

"Progress, I guess."

"Big progress. He may come to the Lord before you." She laughed.

Ouch. That hurt. Maybe I should go to church on Sunday. My decision could wait until after I talked to Allison. And if we made the needed progress on the case.

"Well, I need to make another phone call. Nice talking to you, Sis."

"You too, Bro."

I hesitated. I knew what I should say, but the words lodged in my throat. After a large, silent sigh, I said, "I'm glad things are improving with Myron." Though I really wished he'd just go away.

"Thanks. That means a lot. Tell Bobo 'Hi' for me tomorrow. Love you. Bye."

"Love you." After we hung up, I stared at the phone for a few minutes and contemplated how to approach Allison. We had a hiking date set for Saturday. Not exactly my main leisure activity, but I'd go along just to be with her. Long ways off, though. Could I last two more days without seeing her? I could, but did I want to? Another sigh, this one long and loud. I selected her number.

"Hey, Jake. What's up?" Her voice was neutral. She didn't sound that excited to hear from me.

"Hi, Allison. I was missing you, so I thought I'd call. Like back in high school. You know, calling that girl. Talking all night. Not that we need to talk all night." I shut up. What a babbling fool.

She laughed. "That's sweet. How are things with your client?"

"I'd like to beat her to a pulp. And she may not be our client much longer."

"Why's that?"

"Fake deputies removed Barker from the facility where he was locked up. And now he's disappeared. The cops are treating him as an escaped prisoner. We're still going to try and prove him innocent, because I don't believe he did it. Even if he did arrange the escape, which I doubt. But we've hit several dead ends."

"I'm sorry to hear that." The lilt in her voice told me otherwise. She'd be happy, I was sure, if the case ended tomorrow.

However, as hard as the case had become, it was looking much easier compared to the conversations I had with these two women in my life. I'd much rather hit a few dead ends than try to figure out what the ladies wanted to hear.

"Jake, are you still there?"

"Yeah, sorry. Thinking through some complexities." Nothing to do with the case, but I didn't tell her that. "How about Friday night? Dinner again? I'll make sure Ms. Dupree knows nothing about it."

Silence.

Then a thought struck me. Jeopardy didn't know anything about my date last night. How did she find us? I said as much to Allison, then added, "And she showed up at church, too."

"Either she's stalking you or she's stalking me. My money would be on you."

"Hmm. Maybe. You need to be careful, Allie. Be aware of your surroundings. I need to do the same."

"Uh huh. Any tips?"

"When driving, look in the rearview mirror frequently. Are you seeing the same vehicle?" Another thought occurred to me. But could our little crazy woman be that technically savvy? Was she monitoring our cell phones? She had my cell number. I'd given it to her. Getting Allison's number wouldn't have been that hard. Fifty bucks and the internet and she could have found Allison's cell number. And with the cell numbers, there are ways to monitor a number with the right software, at least enough to track the location of the phone.

"Earth to Jake. You still there?"

"Huh? Oh yeah, sorry. I was wondering if our crazy client was tracking our cell phones."

"How could she do that?"

"Search the internet for that question. There are legitimate companies and software that can do that, with the person's permission."

"But we didn't give her permission. At least I know I didn't."

"And where there's legitimate software and companies, there are also not so legitimate ones."

"Scary."

"Indeed. Sorry for the rabbit trail. About Friday night? We could meet somewhere without our cell phones and test the theory."

"Good one."

"What? I'm being serious."

She hesitated. "Let's stick with Saturday. And as a bonus, how about going to church with me Sunday?"

Oh well, I'd have to entertain myself Thursday and Friday. Either work or maybe Bobo was free. "Sure. Bobo's church again?"

"How about my church?"

"Okay. Never been there. Something new. Meet you or pick you up?"

"Let's talk about it Saturday."

"Deal. See you then."

"Bye, Jake. Thanks for calling."

We hung up. Was Jeopardy tracking us? Or me? And if so, why? Even if she had a thing for me, it seemed a bit extreme. As a cop, I'd get gut feelings that often turned out correct and steered me to the bad guy. And that night, my gut churned with the feeling that Jeopardy's stalking had more to do with her brother's case than Jeopardy having the hots for me. But I could not put the two together. And if I could, then maybe that would be the break we needed in this case.

Twenty-Three

I dreamed I was shoveling coal. Surrounding me, several other faceless individuals also shoveled. Though they had no mouths, they still chanted the lyrics from "Working in a Coal Mine." Their shovels morphed into assault rifles. Faces coalesced into white men with shaved heads. They raised their rifles and pointed them at me.

My eyes snapped open. The vision lingered. Chills crawled down my back. My T-shirt clung to me, soaked from sweat. Pounding heart, rapid breathing. I pushed up and sat on the edge of the bed and ground my palms into my eye sockets to clear my head.

"Working in a Coal Mine" belted out on my cell phone.

Great. River City Police was calling me early in the morning. Never good news.

I grabbed the phone. Nine-thirty-four? What? Not that early.

"This is Sledge." The tune continued. I pulled the phone away from my ear and stabbed the green answer button. "This is Sledge."

"Hey, Sledge. Willow here."

"Sarge. What can I do for you?"

"Nothing for me, dude. But a newsflash for you."

I stood. "Lay it on me."

"Your boy Barker turned himself in this morning."

"He's there?"

"In holding. And that's not all."

I walked toward the bathroom. "Do I really want to know?"

"Probably not, but I'm telling you anyway. He confessed to the murder of Sandy Akins."

My body deflated like a hot air balloon when the fire's turned off. "Thanks for calling, Sarge. We'll be down to see him today."

"No problem, Sledge. See ya." He hung up.

I stared at the phone for a minute. He confessed? Why on earth would he do that? Unless he'd been playing us all along and had killed that nurses' aide. But I couldn't believe it, despite the evidence. Maybe I was being bullheaded. I didn't want to believe it. How would Jeopardy react? I thought about calling her but decided against it. Instead, I texted Bobo, asking where he was and why he hadn't woken me up.

He replied he was working out at the gym and thought we could use a break.

No disagreement from me.

Bobo texted again. He'd meet me at the office in an hour.

Perfect. I showered, shaved, and dressed in black chinos and black collarless shirt. Black matched my mood. I padded to the kitchen, ate some Fruit Loops, put on my shoulder and ankle holsters, and donned my gray sports jacket. On the way out, I grabbed the black fedora.

Bobo's Range Rover sat in the parking lot with a handful of other cars belonging to tenants. I walked to the building, up the stairs, and to the office. According to my phone, the total time from Bobo's text to when I entered the office was fifty-seven minutes. Not bad.

"Hey, big guy. You hear the news?" I flipped my fedora toward the coat rack. Missed. I didn't bother to pick it up. James Bond never missed. One day, I'd hit it.

"About Barker?"

"That's the news." I sat in my executive chair feeling more like I should work in the mailroom rather than own half the business.

"Yup. Willow called me."

"Yeah, me too."

Bobo studied me. "Something else bothering you?"

"Huh?"

"You look down and out, dude. Like someone stole your bowl of Fruit Loops."

"I had my Fruit Loops I'll have you know."

"Then what's eating you?"

I stood and paced the office. "You mean besides our client confessing to a murder I was sure he didn't commit?"

"Yeah, besides that."

I stopped and faced Bobo. "Weird nightmare. A bunch of skinheads were going to shoot me."

Bobo nodded. I'd almost describe it as "sagely." Oh, wise man that he was. I braced for the question I knew was coming.

"You go to that counselor, yet?"

"No." I retrieved my fedora from the floor and put it on. "Let's go."

Bobo stood. "To River City PD, I assume."

"You got it."

A deputy led Barker into the room where Bobo and I waited. Without my guns, of course. And I left the fedora and coat outside on a coat rack.

I was the man in black at that moment.

Barker sat across from us in a wooden chair, like the ones we sat in. I was amazed Bobo's held him. The deputy attached the chain that led from the handcuffs to the handcuff bar bolted onto the table, which was anchored to the floor. I thought about objecting to the handcuffs but then reconsidered, not wanting to give Barker any breaks until we heard his story.

"You look awful," I said.

Deep, dark bags hung under his eyes. Greasy, stringy hair hung down. He flipped his head. His hair flew up, then back into his face. He hung his head.

"About how I feel." Husky voice. He cleared his throat.

"They treating you okay, Mr. Dupree?" Bobo asked.

Barker shrugged. "I guess. No one's beaten me to a pulp yet."

"County lockup is pretty tame," I said. "Been there a few times myself."

"Yeah, but you're a lot bigger than me."

"The state pen, though. You don't want to go there. Not pleasant."

Barker lowered his head and sighed.

"Look at me, dude."

Barker lifted his head and locked onto my gaze. And stayed there. Good for him.

"Did you kill Sandy Akins?"

Barker looked up, to each side, and as much behind him as he could. A camera watched us from the corner just below the ceiling. I'm sure they had sound as well, which would be on, since we were not counsel.

"I have to ... I did it. That's my answer."

Bobo must have sensed my impatience. "Who were the men that picked you up from River Bluffs? Were they really county deputies?"

Barker gave a slight shake of his head but said, "Yes, they were," rather loudly.

Got it. But I couldn't figure out who he was afraid of. Who could view video from the county lockup? Maybe they couldn't, but he was overly paranoid.

I narrowed my eyes. "So, I'm guessing these county deputies were able to convince you to confess to the murder."

"Yes." He scanned the room again.

I wasn't sure who he thought might be hiding in the shadows. "And if you didn't, something bad would have happened to you?"

He nodded and whispered, "And another." His lips barely moved. I guess he thought the county employed a lip reader who watched the video. Maybe. Who knows?

"What do you want us to tell *your sister*?"

He nodded. Got it. If he didn't confess, he and Jeopardy would be in danger. Whoever was behind this whole thing would kill him. They'd become desperate. Which struck me as odd, since we hadn't come close to figuring out who it was behind the scenes.

"Tell her I did it." Barker bowed his head again. A single tear dropped onto the wooden table and left a dark stain.

"Have you called your lawyer yet?"

He shook his head.

"Want us to talk to him?"

Barker nodded. Another tear fell and widened the stain.

We needed more. "Why did you kill her?"

Slowly, he raised his head. Red rimmed his glistening eyes. "I ... I must have flipped. You know, psychotic break. Pressure from being out. It had been a long time." He looked down again. "I loved her. But something in me is very broken."

Bobo nudged me, indicating it was time to let Barker go and bring in the second contestant for truth or consequences.

I waved to the deputy outside the door and shouted, "Take him back."

The deputy came in, undid Barker from the handcuff handle, and escorted him out of the room. We waited. Everything had been pre-arranged. Barker first, then Braxton.

Five minutes later, the same deputy brought Braxton Anderson into the room. Tall, thin, head now shaved. Bloodshot, sunken eyes. The same exhausted look that Barker had. The deputy chained Braxton to the table, then left the room.

"Do I know you two?" Defiant glare. Sarcastic tone.

I wanted to slap him, but I figured the deputy might object. Maybe not, but I decided not to risk it.

"Welcome back to the world, Mr. Anderson."

"What's that mean?"

"You don't remember us visiting you in your cell yesterday?"

"No."

"Higher than a kite. Good stuff, huh?"

"I don't know, man. It wasn't—" He cut off his own statement. "What do you want with me?"

I went out on a limb. "Why did you kill Sandy Akins?"

He tried to stand, but the chain and his cuffs held him down. "You're crazy, man. I didn't kill her. That psycho Barker Dupree murdered her."

"Who are you working with to frame Mr. Dupree?" Bobo asked.

Braxton smiled. "Ain't no frame, man. He's going to pay for what he did. She's guaranteed that."

"She, huh?" I asked.

"I didn't say nothing. I ain't telling you nothing."

I didn't bother to correct his double-negative because he'd slipped. We had a gender to attach to the mystery person behind the plot to frame Barker. And as far as I could tell, Braxton firmly believed that Barker had killed her.

"You liked Ms. Akins, didn't you?" Bobo leaned closer to Anderson and rested his bowling-ball-sized fists on the table.

Anderson's eyes widened. He leaned back. "We were friends, yeah. So what?"

"Like a sister, huh?" I asked.

"Yeah, something like that. She was sweet. Treated me nice."

I leaned toward him and lowered my voice so that he had to lean forward to hear me. "When Barker and Ms. Akins became a thing, that made you mad, didn't it?"

He sat back and glowered at me. "He didn't deserve her. And then he goes and kills her."

"How do you know Barker killed her?" Bobo raised up.

"Because she ... I just know."

Bobo relaxed back into his chair.

I didn't think we'd learn anything more than the gender of his boss. I wasn't even sure what to ask to try and make him slip up again. Then a thought occurred to me. Someone else might be interested in his whereabouts and his predicament. I leaned back. "I have this friend in KC. You might know him. Giovanni Gibellini."

Braxton's eyes widened.

"When we're done here, I'm going to give him a call. Let him know where you are."

"Hey, man. That's not necessary."

"Then tell us who you're working for?"

He narrowed his eyes and chewed on his inner lip. "Guard! I'm done here."

As were we. Apparently, Braxton Anderson was more afraid of his new boss than his former one. I thought about calling Gibellini anyway, but then decided I'd text Bertram, hit man extraordinaire, and let him tell Gibellini. If someone wasted Anderson in jail, one less cockroach crawling around River City.

Back in the car, Bobo rolled down his window. "Where to next?"

"I'm thinking Anthony Harris's apartment, where they found Braxton. Make sense?"

Bobo nodded. "But maybe lunch first?"

That was the best idea I'd heard all day. "Chuckie's?" It was across the road from the apartments.

"Not my favorite, but sure, it'll do. Ain't my birthday."

Bobo wasn't into the cowboy scene. Once when he was a beat cop, we dragged him there on his birthday. They made him sit on a saddle mounted to a sawhorse on wheels while the staff and most of the restaurant sang "Happy Birthday" to him. I don't think he'd been back since.

After burgers at Chuckie's, I drove the Delta 88 across the street into the apartment complex's parking lot. We walked through the courtyard. No pool-goers. When we exited the elevator on the fourth floor a pungent, rotten smell hit me.

"What is that?"

"Smells like something died."

As we approached Harris's apartment, the smell worsened. "Did someone kill a rat and leave it in their wastebasket?" A real possibility in that place.

I knocked. "Mr. Harris. You there? It's Sledge and Bobo Johnson."

Nothing.

I banged on the door. "Harris, we need to talk to you."

The curtains parted in the apartment next door and an elderly man looked out. He shook his head and closed the curtain. Must have figured we were customers.

One more time I hammered the door and listened. Nothing but the intense smell of something rotting. Or someone?

I kicked in the door.

"Jake, what are you ... oh man, that smell."

It was a person rotting in Harris's apartment. An African American male was sprawled on his stomach on the living room floor. I assumed a man because of the short-cropped hair. Probably Harris. Bobo took out his cell phone and dialed River City PD.

We took refuge on the other side of the apartment complex to get away from the smell and watched the parking lot. Fifteen minutes later two patrol cars and an unmarked vehicle entered. Two officers and Detective Arnie Hassenberger got out of their cars and walked through the courtyard.

"Up here." I waved my arms to catch their attention. "Fourth floor. Follow the smell."

We met them at the apartment.

"Sledge, Bobo." Hassenberger slipped on gloves. "Causing trouble again, are you?"

"Not us, this time," I replied.

He chuckled, smeared some Vick's VapoRub on his upper lip and went into the apartment. We moved away and waited. A few minutes later, he emerged.

"Bad stuff. It's Anthony Harris. I recognize him, and he had a wallet in his back pocket."

"What happened to him?" I asked.

"Looks like he OD'd." Hassenberger held up a paper envelope and opened it. Inside was an empty syringe. "But we'll wait for the death investigator and his report."

"Need us for anything?"

"Just give your statement to one of the patrol officers."

And we did, then left, lunch still in our stomachs. Barely. If Harris did OD, I doubted it was an accident or even his own doing. Seemed like someone was cleaning up after themselves. I wondered if Braxton Anderson had shot himself up or had help.

In the car, I stated as much to Bobo.

"Mr. Anderson didn't remember much," Bobo said. "Could have had a helping hand."

"Now what? We've run out of people to talk to. Dropping like flies."

"As long as Barker sticks to his story, there's little we can do."

I nodded and started the car. "Got any plans tonight?"

"Visiting one of my cousins over in Grand Pass."

"Tomorrow?"

"Got a date with Ms. Goodhue tomorrow night. Nothing during the day. What's our plan?"

I drove out of the parking lot toward our office so Bobo could pick up his Range Rover and go visit his cousin. "Do you call her Ms. Goodhue to her face?"

"No."

I could feel his scowl but refused to look at him. Besides, I had to try and answer his question. What *was* our next move?

Twenty-Four

The next day I entered the office with no idea of what we'd be doing. Bobo, as usual, had arrived before me. He typed away on his laptop. I threw my dark blue fedora toward the coat rack and missed the hook. One of these days.

"What's up, big guy? How's the cousin?"

Bobo stopped typing. "In trouble, as usual. The visit was more a favor to his mother."

"Scared straight kind of thing?"

"Naw. Just a talking-to. Trying to get him to Jesus. Sort of like someone else I know."

"Who's that?" I hung my midnight blue sports coat on a hook, picked up the fedora, and placed it over the coat. Then it hit me. "You mean me?"

"Quick on the uptake as always."

I saluted Bobo and sat in my executive chair behind the desk.

Bobo pointed at me. "What's that?"

I glanced down and saw the brown spot on my otherwise pristine white collarless shirt. "The reason I wear a jacket. Coffee, I assume." I checked my tan chinos. No spots. Good.

"You have a drinking problem?"

"That I do." I rearranged things on my desk, trying to come up with our next move.

"She's Not There" rang out on my cell phone, saving me from straining my brain. I punched the green answer, then the speaker icon.

"Ms. Dupree. Good morning. How are you?"

"Fine, Mr. Sledge. And you?" Not much of a Southern accent.

"I was just about to call you and give you an update."

"I'd very much appreciate that, Mr. Sledge."

I waited to see if she'd add anything else.

"Well, Mr. Sledge, what's the update?"

"Barker turned himself in to the police."

"Uh-huh."

I glanced at Bobo, who shrugged.

"He confessed to the murder of Sandy Akins."

"Do you think he did it?"

I punched the mute button and raised my eyebrows at Bobo. "Odd response, don't you think?"

He nodded. "Doesn't seem that surprised."

"Agreed." I unmuted. "How would you like to proceed, Ms. Dupree?"

Silence for about fifteen seconds. "Good heavens, Mr. Sledge. I'm sorry, did you say Barker confessed?" The Southern accent returned in full force.

"I did."

"Oh my. And do you believe him?"

One more glance at Bobo. He mouthed, "Go for it."

"No, ma'am, I don't. We think he's being coerced into confessing."

"Wha—why?"

"To save his and your lives."

"Why would anyone want to hurt little old me?"

I thought of numerous reasons but kept them to myself. "Someone killed Ms. Akins and framed Barker. Maybe we were getting close to whoever is behind this, so they've upped the pressure." I explained how fake deputies showed up at River Bluffs and took Barker. Then I told her that the next day he'd wandered into River City PD and confessed.

"What can we do?"

"It's your money. But we can keep digging."

Silence again. This time it stretched out for about thirty seconds.

"Ms. Dupree, you still there?"

"Yes, sorry, Mr. Sledge. I think unless something new develops, I won't require your services anymore."

"Okay." That day was the seventh day of the ten-day retainer. I started to ask about that, but she interjected before I could.

"And don't worry about the rest of the retainer. Keep it. Thank you for your help. Sorry it didn't work out like we hoped."

"Sure. Let us know if Barker changes his tune."

I waited for her to say goodbye, but instead, another fifteen seconds of silence.

"Mr. Sledge?"

"Yes?"

"Now that you're off the case, how about dinner tonight? I know we can't really celebrate, but I feel obligated to thank you, anyway."

Bobo smirked. I rolled my eyes and shook my head.

"Um, I appreciate the offer, but I'm busy."

"Doing what, may I ask?"

"Do you think you're our only client?"

"What about Saturday, then. Surely, you take a day off?"

"I have plans already."

"With Ms. Rogers?"

"Sorry, Ms. Dupree, not your business. Please let us know if Barker needs help. Goodbye." I hung up.

"That was rude."

I glanced at Bobo. "Thank you for your critique of my people skills."

"What people skills?"

"Good one."

Bobo smiled. "You think we should call Mr. Jorgenson? I assume he knows, but maybe not."

"Good idea, but I have a better one."

"It's that time of the year?"

The big guy was on a roll.

"Let's go visit our favorite lawyer."

Bobo shrugged. "Nothing better to do. But I think we should call ahead."

"We'll do that in the car."

"And if he's not there?"

"We'll hit a coffee shop."

Another shrug from the man of many words. Bobo closed his laptop, and we headed to visit our favorite lawyer.

We entered the plush offices of Jorgenson and Jenkins. I wondered if they'd sell me one of the multiple leather sofas. I needed a new one. The same curt woman sat at the reception desk.

"Good morning, gentlemen. Mr. Jorgenson is expecting you."

I passed on my shtick. "Thank you, Brittany." I remembered her name. And Bobo thinks I have no people skills.

Brittany nodded and flashed a quick smile at me, then a wide smile at Bobo. Everyone smiles at Bobo.

"Oh, and Mr. Johnson, my dad freaked when I told him I met you."

Bobo probably blushed, though it was hard to tell. "Tell him I'd be happy to autograph a football or something."

"Oh, thank you so much. That reminds me." She reached underneath the desk and brought out — what else? —a football. "Will you sign this? My dad's name is Mack." She extended the football and a Sharpie to Bobo. "This is a birthday present for him. His birthday is next week."

The big guy handed me the coffee carrier holding the three coffees we'd picked up on the way. He took the football and pen from Brittany and wrote, "To Mack, From Maurice 'Bobo' Johnson. Here's to memories."

Such a sap. Brittany didn't ask me to sign the football. I guess one year didn't cut it for the McCauleys. And if they were Bengals fans, they probably didn't want a former Brown to sign anyway.

Bobo handed the football and pen back to Brittany, whose smile bloomed even bigger. I headed to Jorgenson's office. Bobo followed. We found the lawyer's door open and him on the phone. He waved us in. We sat and waited. After a minute, he hung up the desk phone.

"Good morning. Interesting predicament we find ourselves in, isn't it?"

"You heard about Barker, then?" I asked.

He nodded. "Barker mentioned you talked with him. Did he give any indication as to why he changed his story?"

"He's being threatened. Him and Jeopardy."

"By whom?"

"All we know is it's a woman," Bobo said. "Mr. Dupree wouldn't tell us, but Braxton Anderson slipped. He said *she's* guaranteed that Barker will pay for the murder."

"Interesting. And did you talk with your client? I've not been able to reach her this morning."

My turn. "Yup. And she fired us."

Jorgenson reached into a side drawer and pulled out two forms, handing one to each of us. "Sign these and consider yourselves temporary investigators for Jorgenson and Jenkins. I would like you to continue poking around. We'll pay the standard rate."

"Sounds good." We both signed and handed them back to Jorgenson. "The good news is, you have three days of us for free, still on Ms. Dupree's retainer."

"That's very honest of you. Thank you."

That's me, honest to a fault.

"I was on the phone with the APA when you walked in."

"Ms. Goodhue?" I asked.

He nodded.

I almost enlightened Jorgenson about Bobo's upcoming date with her, but Bobo must have anticipated that because he kicked the chair. I decided not to divulge the information, figuring if I did, the next thing Bobo kicked would be my butt.

"And?" I asked.

"She was trolling for our strategy, and she reminded me the plea hearing is in two weeks. Of course, she also mentioned that there's no way Barker is getting out of jail before the trial. She's petitioned the judge to rescind the million-dollar bail he set. We go to court Tuesday for another bail hearing."

"Bail?" I raised my brows. "There was no bail at the original hearing."

"You're correct. But when Barker turned himself in and they locked him in jail, the judge said he originally was going to set bail at one million. And that's what he did this morning."

"If we could prove by then the deputies who took him were fake, would it help?"

"Doubtful. Ms. Goodhue would say he arranged it."

Just what Kazminsky had said. "If you need it, video surveillance at River Bluffs shows the car is fake."

"I'll keep that in mind. Anything else?" He leaned back.

"What is your strategy?"

"Insanity plea."

"Figured."

Jorgenson shook his head. "I'm not overly optimistic, but it's the best option. At least then he'll spend the rest of his life in a psychiatric facility instead of prison." He stood. "I hate to rush you out, but I have a court appearance for another case."

We stood and shook hands. Before we left, he asked us what our next move would be.

"No clue. The best idea we have right now is to see if the KC mob will put pressure on Braxton Anderson to spill his guts."

Jorgenson walked out with us. We reached the double doors leading out of the offices. "Do you think that angle will work?"

"Maybe. Or maybe they'll just whack him in jail. Either way, it's a win for River City."

We left and headed back to the office.

I tossed a tennis ball into the air repeatedly, occasionally bouncing it off the wall above Bobo's head as he pecked on his laptop. I tried to see how close I could get the rebound to his head.

"You know if that hits me in the back of the head, you're going to eat it."

I laughed. Not that he couldn't, but he wouldn't. "Find anything interesting?"

"Something Mr. Jorgenson told us is bugging me."

"What?"

"About Ms. Goodhue asking for bail to be rescinded."

"Can you blame her?"

"No. But it will take several days. You heard Jorgenson. Tuesday, they go to court to discuss bail."

"Yeah, so?"

"Why hasn't Ms. Dupree posted bail? A hundred grand to a bail bondsman will secure it. I'm sure she could come up with the cash."

The man was a giant ball of wisdom. "What are you looking for? I can just call her."

Bobo shook his head. "Family history." He looked up. "What do you know about her background? And Mr. Dupree's?"

"Not much before her alter ego killed Daddy Dupree."

"Exactly. There's an article about Barker Dupree being sent to an institution. Not much there. His father refused to be interviewed. But they quote his sister, who says Barker has always been a sensitive person and the death of his mother hit him hard."

"Okay. Not real helpful." I tossed the tennis ball against the wall again. Bobo looked up during the rebound, and it hit him on the top of the head. He grinned at me. A Cheshire cat kind of grin.

"You wouldn't."

He stared at me for several seconds, started to stand. I prepared to run. No escape route existed. But he sat down and laughed.

"The next line from Ms. Dupree jumps out." Bobo read from the article. "She said, 'I should have protected him better, like I protected our sister.'"

Whoa. "When was the article printed?"

"A little over five years ago."

I thought about what Jeopardy said. Or was it Jeopardy? Two ideas floated through the bayou of my brain. Option one, did they have another physical sister, and had something happened to her?

"Any other articles on the Dupree family?"

"Just one announcing the father's retirement."

"Does it say who took over?"

"Some guy named Ellis Clarkson was named CEO. It said the father would stay on the board and be joined by his daughter, Jeopardy Dupree."

"Interesting."

Option two, at the time of the interview, had Connie Dupree been in charge of their mind? If so, how did Connie protect Jeopardy? She didn't kill Daddy Dupree for another couple of years. Had she killed her mother?

"Anything prior on how their mother died?"

Bobo pecked on the keyboard. "Here's something. Eight months prior to the article about Barker Dupree being committed. Their mother fell down the steps of their mansion. The death investigator ruled the fall an accident."

We needed more information on the messed-up dynamics of the Dupree family.

"I think we need to visit Barker again." I glanced at my watch. "We have time."

Bobo closed his laptop. I retrieved my jacket and fedora from the coat rack. When I opened our office door, "Working at the Coal Mine" played on my phone. I decided I'd better answer River City PD before we left. Back into the office we went.

"This is Sledge."

"Hey, Sledge, it's Arnie here. Got a minute?"

"Always, for my old pal." *Old* was not an exaggeration. If I calculated correctly, he had less than two years before retirement.

"We received an interesting finding from the crime scene investigation on the Anthony Harris death."

I punched the speaker button on the phone. "Bobo's here as well."

"Hey, Bobo, how's it hanging?"

"Arnie, doing well. You?"

"Can't complain. Or if I did, no one would listen anyway."

"About Harris," I cut in.

"Yeah, died of an overdose. But get this, no prints on the syringe. And no tourniquet. Oh, and he jabbed the needle straight in, not into a vein."

"Was it heroin?"

"It was."

Definitely odd. Not the usual way a junkie shot up. Though, if his intent was suicide, would he bother to be precise? I stated the same to Hassenberger.

"Same thoughts here, but we're opening the case as a homicide. After a few interviews, no one gave the impression Harris even used his own merchandise. The occasional joint, they said, but never the hard stuff. A dealer, not a user."

"What about Braxton Anderson? Did you talk to him?"

"That guy's a wastoid. Not much going on between his ears. All we got out of that scumbag was that Harris was alive the last time he saw him. Which he said was a couple days ago."

"Wasn't he picked up outside Harris's apartment complex?"

"Yeah, but Anderson claims he doesn't remember going there."

Someone setting him up for Harris's murder? I asked Hassenberger, but he said nothing pointed to Anderson.

"Thanks for calling. Let us know if you make progress on identifying the killer."

"Will do. One more tidbit you might be interested in."

"Lay it on us."

"Barker Dupree was transferred to the county jail in Lexington."

Not good news. That meant paperwork to visit him. We could do a virtual visit, but we still had to fill out a form and schedule it.

"Thanks, Arnie. Always a pleasure." We disconnected.

I sighed. "You mind filling out the paperwork to talk with Barker?"

"Not a problem. Is Monday okay?"

I nodded. While Bobo pecked on his laptop, I continued tossing the tennis ball, bouncing it off a different wall than the one behind him. I'm not bossy. Not even Bobo's boss. We're partners. Not lazy either. I just don't do computers. And Bobo was the fastest one-finger typist I've ever seen. His index fingers blurred over the keys. I told him I'd buy him a giant-sized keyboard. Only a couple hundred bucks. No big deal. He couldn't touch-type on a laptop because of his oversized fingers. But he refused. Said he preferred the laptop.

"We're scheduled for Monday morning. Ten."

"Thanks."

"Gangsta's Paradise" played on my cell phone.

"Who's that?" Bobo asked.

"Our favorite gangster, of course."

"I didn't know we had a favorite gangster."

"Maybe only *my* favorite gangster." Even though he tried to kill me once. I pushed answer, then speaker. "Bertram, what's up?"

"Just chillin', my man. Talked to the boss man last night about your boy Anderson."

"And?"

"Nothing happening there, dude. The big G has washed his hands of that freak."

"The big G? He's a small, wiry dude."

"Hey, sometimes you've got to stroke his ego. He likes being called that."

"Good to know. No help, though? He won't lean on Anderson?"

"Nope. But hey, I got a deal for you. Two G's and I'll remove the problem."

Bobo's eyes widened. I grinned. Nice thought, but too much money and too far outside the lines for comfort.

"Thanks for the offer, but we'll pass. For now."

"Gotcha, dude. Later." He disconnected the call.

Bobo grimaced. "For now?"

"Throwing the man a bone, that's all." I grinned. "We'll see if he comes back with a discounted price."

"Not happening, Jake."

I laughed. "Got you. I owed you one from earlier."

"Better be joking."

"I think that's a wrap for the weekend. What do you think?"

Bobo nodded. "Not one of our more productive weeks."

"No kidding. I hope something breaks next week. I'm off to the shooting range. Have a nice date." I got up, retrieved my jacket and fedora.

Bobo packed his laptop. This time we made it out the door, down to the parking lot, and into our respective cars without any interruptions. It should have been another boring Friday night. Shooting range, home to watch sports, fall asleep in my easy chair. I was wrong.

Before going to The Shooting Range, I stopped at home to change and pick up a couple of other guns. I put on khaki cargo shorts and a plain black T-shirt, then stuffed all my weaponry into a duffel bag. My head felt weirdly naked without the fedora. Better get used to it, as I wasn't planning on wearing one hiking the next day either.

I walked into The Shooting Range. The owner, a no-frills guy named Hank Nelson, waved to me. I first started going there after leaving River City PD because I no longer had access to the free range in the basement of the fourth precinct. The name struck me as odd. I asked Hank about it.

His reply: "What is this place?"

"A shooting range," I said.

"And how many other shooting ranges are there in River City?"

"Other than the two for law enforcement, none."

"Yup. So, it's not *a* shooting range, it's *The* shooting range."

"Got it. The Shooting Range."

Hank had nodded and walked away.

I put my bag on the counter, gave the attendant my license, and was assigned bay number three in the A range. At the target stand, I grabbed two targets, one with concentric circles, the other a body outline. Before entering the range, I put on ear protection and safety glasses.

I opened the first door and allowed it to close behind me. Muffled sounds of shots being fired. I opened the second door. Louder, but comfortable. The guy in bay one fired a handgun. Probably 9mm. I walked past him and the guy in bay two who was loading a rifle. I placed my duffel on the shelf, unzipped it, and pulled out a .45. A loud retort from the rifle startled me. My vision wavered for an instant. I sucked in a deep breath, held it, then let it out. Another loud retort. Then rapid retorts. Five, six, seven. I flinched at each one. My heart hammered, but I pushed on, loading the .45 magazine with my autoloader. The rifle shots ended. Handgun rounds fired. Mostly muffled. I mounted the body outline target on the clips and sent it out to twenty-five feet, then inserted the magazine into the .45.

Another deep breath. I racked the slide, aimed, and fired four quick shots. All four hit center mass with the grouping no bigger than a dime. I adjusted my aim.

A loud retort exploded from the bay next to me.

I flinched and fired, missing the target.

Rapid retorts. My vision blurred. My mind grew fuzzy. In front of me, several young men with shaved heads aimed assault rifles at me. I fired. One went down. I fired again and again and again. Someone tapped me on the shoulder. I whirled and pulled the trigger.

Nothing.

My vision wavered.

In front of me stood Hank, his hands in front of his face. I still had my gun pointed at him. Fortunately, I had emptied it.

"What are you doing, Sledge?" Hank lowered his hands and grabbed the .45 from me.

I slumped against the shelf of the bay. Hank grabbed me and dragged me out of the range. An employee passed us going in. Hank pulled off my ear protection.

"What were you thinking? You were shooting all over the place, at everyone else's targets. Then you turn on me?"

"I ... I thought." I shook my head. I couldn't tell him I saw armed skinheads in front of me. I'd sound like a lunatic. Maybe I *was* a lunatic. "I thought I saw something else. I'm sorry. I've been having these spells."

"Then why are you at a shooting range?"

The employee returned and handed me my bag. "The firearms are unloaded and cased."

"Thank you, Jeremy," Hank said. He took the bag and escorted me out of the building and to my car.

I took my bag from him and tossed it on the passenger seat, then got in.

"You need help, Sledge. PTSD isn't something to mess around with. Go get help." Hank walked back into his building.

Why did he think it was PTSD? Then I remembered. He was a veteran. Had been to Iraq and Afghanistan. I pulled out my cell phone and dialed Bobo, hoping he wasn't with Liliana Goodhue yet.

Bobo answered on the third ring. "This better be important. Just sitting down to dinner."

"Sorry, man. It's about that counselor. I ... I—something bad." I couldn't get the rest of the words out. Admitting I needed help stuck in my throat.

"What happened, Jake?"

I sucked in a breath, let it out slowly, then rehashed the incident. Bobo told me to stay put, hung up, and called back five minutes later. He told me I had an appointment in eleven days. He gave me the address and the time, and a gentle threat that I'd better go. So much for a boring Friday night. I hoped Saturday with Allison would give me the rest I needed. Again, I was wrong.

Twenty-Five

Allison directed me to turn on SE 10 Road. We'd driven forty-five minutes south to Knob Noster State Park. I turned and followed the road for a couple of miles. As soon as we passed the visitor's center, the two lanes narrowed to one. Thick woods flanked both sides of the road. I pulled into a parking lot where there were two trailheads.

We got out, and I followed Allison to the trailhead that led along Buteo Lake. A Royals baseball cap replaced my fedora. No jacket. High eighties, so no need. No shoulder holster. Not even my ankle holster. After the incident at the gun range, a little voice told me, "No guns at all with Allison." I listened to that little voice. Not something I often do. I felt naked and defenseless.

Allison wore khaki shorts that fell just above her knees and a dark green collarless shirt. Both of us sported hiking boots. It had taken me half an hour to dig mine out. They looked brand new. Black cargo shorts and a gray T-shirt completed my outdoor ensemble. With the warm day and humidity, I hoped my antiperspirant would hold up, or I'd have massive pit stains. Unfamiliar territory for me, thinking about that kind of thing. My jacket usually hid the stains or I didn't care.

I watched Allison bob up and down as she walked. During the drive, I had recounted my shooting range incident, fearing the entire time she'd decide further involvement with me should cease. Instead, she praised me for scheduling an appointment with a counselor, and she added that if I needed to talk, she'd listen.

"Ooh, look." She stopped. "A cardinal. So pretty."

"And my second favorite baseball team."

She laughed and continued walking. "Believe it or not, I'm a Padres fan."

"What? How can anyone living in River City be a Padres fan?"

"I grew up in Southern California. Been one my whole life."

A California girl. Definitely fit the mold of the ones the Beach Boys sang about. Worthy of songs and poems.

"You've lived in River City your whole life, right?"

I walked alongside her and reached for her hand. She let me take it and interlocked her fingers in mine. Progress. "Yup. Went to college at Northwestern, so hung out in Chicago for a few years. Then lived in Cleveland for one year while in the pros. Moved back after getting hurt."

"That's such a bummer. You were so good."

"You watched me?"

"I'm a huge football fan. My dad and I watched games together. By then, we lived in River City, so we had to watch whoever the Chiefs played. I was pretty young when you were a rookie."

"Thanks. Rub it in."

She laughed and skipped along the trail. I fast-walked to keep up.

"I remember that one game against the Bengals when you laid the receiver out who came across the middle. Ouch! That poor guy."

I harrumphed. "That poor guy made the Hall of Fame last year."

"I bet you would have, if you'd been able to play longer."

Of course I would have.

She stopped and looked out onto the lake. "So peaceful."

Teenagers splashed in the water and yelled at each other. Her definition of peaceful differed from mine. A soft breeze caressed my cheek. I wanted to do the same to Allison's cheek but restrained myself. We still held hands. That would have to do.

She moved on. In the woods to our right, a stick broke.

Allison glanced that way. "What was that?"

"Probably just a bear."

"What? Are there bears here?"

"Maybe." I had no clue, but it sounded good.

We continued along the trail. "Who Let the Dogs Out" played from my pocket.

"Dang it."

"What? Who is that calling?"

"It's Bobo, but that's not what's annoying me. I had planned to leave my phone at home."

She stopped. "Are you going to answer it?"

"Nope."

We continued. "Why do you have that song for Bobo? He played for the Bengals."

"Exactly."

She grinned. "Does he know that?"

"Probably not."

"What if I tell him?" She poked me and trotted down the trail.

I chased after her. She let me catch her. I wrapped my arms around her waist and spun her, then set her back on the trail. She was facing the lake. I was facing the woods.

Something moved. Something tall and thin. A person? I stared.

"What is it?"

"I thought I saw someone in there."

"He didn't have a shaved head, did he?"

I looked at Allison. Concern clouded her flawless face.

"No shaved head that I could tell. Maybe one of the teenagers. Let's go."

We walked for a while in silence, still holding hands. Her head swiveled continually. I spent most of the time looking at her.

Another stick broke. I looked to my right and noticed movement near a tree.

"I heard that, too," Allison said. "Is the bear following us?"

"Not a bear. But maybe a person." I leaned in and whispered in her ear. "Keep walking along the path. I'll catch up."

I dropped her hand and sprinted into the woods. The person took off at a forty-five-degree angle. A quick glance back showed Allison walking slowly along the path. Ahead, branches snapped like a bear crashing through undergrowth. Short dark hair, a camouflage baseball cap, a long-sleeved shirt, and dark green pants flickered in and out of view as our gap narrowed. Just when I thought I'd gained ground, the figure slipped into a thick grove of trees and bushes. The only noise, the breeze blowing through the woods. I crept toward the copse, straining to hear sounds of movement. Reaching the first bushes, a chorus of rustling leaves exploded around me. I burst through the line of bushes into the close-growing trees.

A scream.

Allison.

I plowed through bushes and skirted around trees until coming to the path. Allison lay on the ground to my right. I ran to her and knelt. Her eyes were closed, her head tilted away.

"Allison?" I placed two fingers on her neck. Strong pulse. Steady breathing. I tilted her head back toward me. On the left side of her face, a nasty bump grew on the cheekbone. Blood dripped from several gashes.

Her eyes fluttered open. "Jake?" Her eyes closed again.

I lifted her in my arms and jogged on the path back the way we'd come. It took five minutes to reach the parking lot. She opened and closed her eyes several times but seemed unable to keep them open. I eased her into the back seat and wrapped a seat belt around her to keep her from flying out of the car, should we crash.

No hospitals or urgent care centers between Knob Noster State Park and River City that I knew of, so I pushed the Delta 88 hard, breaking traffic laws. But we didn't pass any law enforcement, at least none that came after us.

"Jake?"

I risked a glance back. She looked at me. We were going over eighty, so I swiveled back to watch the road.

"Another ten minutes and we'll be at River City Hospital."

"What ... what happened?"

"I don't know. Looks like someone hit you with something."

"I ... I don't remember."

"Hang on. We're almost there."

Nine minutes later, I slammed on the brakes under the River City Hospital Emergency Room awning. I jumped out of the car, opened the back door, and gently pulled Allison out. Eyes completely open now, she leaned against me as we shuffled into the ER.

A handful of people waited on plastic chairs. I helped Allison sit in an empty chair then dashed to the desk.

A dark-skinned woman turned to me. Through the glass partition she asked, "What is the issue?"

"My friend." I pointed to Allison. "Someone bashed her in the head with something. She may have been unconscious for a while."

The woman slid a clipboard through the opening in the partition. "Please fill this out and we'll see her as soon as we can. Not too busy today, so it shouldn't be too long."

I took the clipboard and sat next to Allison. When I came to the part about insurance, I glanced at Allison and realized she'd left her purse in the front seat of my car.

"Are you okay? I need to run back to the car."

She nodded.

I ran out to the car, which I decided I should also move so ambulances could pull in, if needed. I climbed in and drove to an empty parking place, then grabbed her purse and started back toward the ER.

Halfway, I stopped and stared at a dark SUV with tinted windows backed into a space at the edge of the lot. With the heat of the day, I couldn't tell if the car was idling, but the driver sat inside. They wore a dark baseball cap, a dark shirt, and large sunglasses that only a woman would wear. Familiarity crept through my brain. An image of the person running in the woods. One of a dark SUV trying to run me over. And one of Braxton Anderson jumping into a dark SUV with tinted windows. Same person? I ran toward the SUV. Tires screeched as the vehicle drove out of the parking lot and turned north. No chance to catch her. At least I got the make and model. GMC Denali. Probably no more than a year or two old. License plate? Obscured. Of course. I turned and headed back to the ER.

Allison leaned to one side. I sat next to her and allowed her to rest her head on my shoulder.

Twenty minutes after filling out the form and giving it back to the lady behind the desk, a nurse came out and took Allison's blood pressure. The nurse examined the wound.

"Do you know how this happened?"

Both of us shook our heads. I added, "I think someone hit her with something."

The nurse helped Allison into a wheelchair and started toward the back. I followed.

"Are you her husband?"

Not yet, I wanted to say but shook my head.

"Then please wait here. Someone will be out shortly to let you know how things are going."

I wanted to protest, but the tall, bulky nurse did not appear to be someone to argue with. She wheeled Allison through self-opening double doors. I paced the waiting room. Other people came and went. After thirty minutes, my hips and back screamed at me to sit, so I did. I pistoned my right leg. Thoughts raced through my mind. Who was that person in the woods? Did she hit Allison? If so, why? Had she followed us there? I hadn't noticed anyone behind us for long periods during the forty-five-minute drive.

I got up and paced some more. My phone again played "Who Let the Dogs Out." My phone! Was that person tracking my phone? I had meant to leave it at home. And then here, in the parking lot. No way someone could have kept up with me without my noticing. But she had found us. The only conclusion that made sense, it had been the same woman who clobbered Allison.

I answered. "Yeah, Bobo? I'm at the ER with Allison."

"What happened?"

I gave him a quick summary of the events.

"Was it a woman?"

"I think so, but I can't be one hundred percent sure. The sunglasses didn't look like ones a man would wear, and the person in the woods was thin, but I couldn't tell."

The same big nurse came out. She caught my gaze and motioned me to follow her.

"Gotta go. Nurse is waving me in." I hung up.

"Ms. Rogers is fully awake," the nurse said. "She'd like to talk to you."

"How is she?"

"She'll be fine. The swelling has receded. The wound's been cleaned. It will be sore for a few days, but off-the-shelf painkillers should help." She pulled away a curtain, and I entered the area.

Allison sat on a stretcher, legs hanging over the side. A bandage covered the wound on her cheekbone. She flicked a wan smile and reached out both arms.

I held her hands and stood at the side of the stretcher.

"I'll be okay," she said.

"I'm so sorry. Do you remember anything?"

"Some. It's coming back to me. I was just walking along waiting for you when this woman appeared on the path. I didn't even hear her approach."

"It *was* a woman."

She nodded. "Tall, maybe an inch taller than me. Dark, short hair. Wearing large, dark glasses. Dressed like a hunter. You know, camo and stuff."

She described the same person I had been trying to follow. And probably the same person in the SUV in the parking lot. And it was a woman. *The* woman? The one that Braxton Anderson alluded to? Who was she?

"Did she say anything? What did she hit you with?"

"A big stick. She said, 'Stay away from Jake Sledge,' then—wham. Swung the stick at my head. I ... I had no time to react." She pulled me toward her.

I hugged her. "I'm so sorry."

"Who was she? Someone I should know about?"

I stepped back so I could see her face. "I don't know. It may be the same woman behind all the junk going on with Barker Dupree."

The nurse handed Allison some paperwork. "You're okay to go home. Call the doctor should you experience any dizziness. Do you have someone who can stay with you tonight?"

"Yes," I said. "I'll watch over her."

Allison frowned but said nothing. I helped her off the stretcher and held her arm as we walked out. She stopped at the desk and signed some papers, then we left. Before I started the car, she laid her hand on my arm.

"Wait." She dug her cell phone out of her purse.

Her phone. She had it in the car. Maybe it wasn't mine, but hers. That brought to mind Jeopardy Dupree. The inadvertent—so she says—text message to Allison. Her showing up where we were several times. But the woman Allison described sounded nothing like Jeopardy. Or her alter ego. When I encountered Connie before, she looked like Jeopardy. Which made sense, being the same person. She'd made no attempt to disguise herself or look different than Jeopardy.

Allison texted someone. Waited. A ding announced a reply. She nodded. "Jake, please drop me off, but my friend Rhonda will stay with me tonight."

"Um, okay. I'd stay in the guest room."

She patted my arm and gave a slight, reassuring smile. "It's not that. I trust you. But I think it would be best if we stay apart until your case is over."

"But ..." I stopped my protest and stared at the bandage on her beautiful face. She was right. The best way to keep her safe was to do what the woman who bludgeoned her said to do: stay away from each other. I had to find out who this crazy chick was.

I drove her home. On the way, we said very little. When I pulled up to her house and stopped, she leaned in and kissed me on the cheek.

"Please understand, it's not you. But I'm afraid I'm a distraction."

"No, you're not."

"You need to focus on finding this person and helping Mr. Dupree. You can't do that if someone is coming after me."

Again, I wanted to protest, but her wisdom held sway. I sighed and nodded, then opened my door and ran around to her side. Before I opened her door, I scanned the street both ways. No dark gray SUV. I helped her out and walked her to the door. As she unlocked the front door, a small two-door sedan pulled into her driveway.

"That's Rhonda. Thanks for the hike, even though, you know."

"When this case is over, we'll finish that hike."

Rhonda got out of her car and walked toward us. Short, stocky, long auburn hair. Probably the same age as Allison. Mid-twenties. When she reached us, she stuck out her hand.

"You must be Jake Sledge. I've heard a lot about you."

I shook her hand. "Don't believe everything you've heard."

"Oh, it's nothing but good stuff from Allie."

I looked at Allison. "Like I said, don't believe everything you've heard."

Allison smiled. "Keep me updated. I want to finish the hike."

I squeezed her hand and walked to my car. Rhonda helped Allison inside. When they closed the front door, I called Bobo and gave him an update.

"Why were you calling me earlier?"

"To invite you to church tomorrow."

I thought about it. What else did I have to do? I couldn't see Allison. If she felt up to it, she'd probably go to her church. No shooting range. The Royals stunk, so no use sitting through that torture. Alicia, Julia, and Myron would go to their church. I could join them, but that might be awkward.

"You still there?"

"Sorry, was thinking. And you know how difficult that can be."

Bobo laughed.

"Sure, I'll join you. See you at nine."

"What are you doing the rest of today?"

Great question. Jeopardy Dupree popped into my mind. What if it was her? Or someone she knew?

"I'm going to Jeopardy's. I need to ask her about today and some other things."

Silence on Bobo's end. "I'll meet you there. Not a good idea for you to go alone."

Everyone else seemed to have more wisdom than I had. But that's why I kept Bobo around. To prevent me from being an idiot. A full-time job for the big guy.

"Okay. See you in ten."

Time to confront our former client and find out what she knew about all the shenanigans going on. No need to hold back now since she'd fired us.

Twenty-Six

I paced in front of Jeopardy Dupree's home waiting for Bobo. The more I paced, the higher my blood pressure rose. Heat spread over my cheeks. I muttered to myself. Jeopardy had a camera doorbell to the side. I hoped I was either out of view or she wasn't watching it. Thoughts jumped around my brain like popping corn. Was Concentration Dupree still in Jeopardy's life? Was Jeopardy stalking me and paying someone else to follow us? Maybe Jeopardy had nothing to do with any of this. Were my feelings against her and our past run-in biasing my theories?

Bobo pulled up in his Range Rover. He got out and walked, I'd even say sauntered, toward the porch. Was that a smug expression he had? Maybe my paranoia was getting the best of me.

"Don't ring that doorbell until you take three deep breaths."

I stopped pacing. "Seriously?"

He nodded. Neutral expression. I figured if I reached for the doorbell, he'd grab my arm. And even though he was almost twice my size, he was quicker than me.

I sucked in a deep breath, held it, and let it out. Two more times I repeated the ritual. My blood pressure dropped. The heat left my cheeks. I felt calm. Not that I'd admit it to Bobo.

Bobo pressed the doorbell.

The door opened immediately. Jeopardy smiled. She wore white pleated shorts and a beige silk collarless top. A string of small pearls wrapped around her neck. She extended her right hand, but she held her left hand behind her back. Knife or phone? She either intended to stab me, but probably wouldn't with Bobo there, or she had been watching me pace on her security app.

"Mr. Sledge, Mr. Johnson. Such a pleasant surprise on this beautiful Saturday."

Bobo nudged me out of the way and shook her hand.

"The pleasure is all ours, Ms. Dupree."

She bounced and whirled, her cell phone in her hand. "Please come in."

We followed her to her sitting room.

I hated Bobo for calming me down as I'd looked forward to screaming at her and accusing her of all sorts of nefarious deeds. But that desire fled. Instead, I calmly asked, "What have you been up to this beautiful Saturday?"

She sat on the loveseat. Bobo eased into one armchair. I sat in another.

"Oh, this and that. Running some errands, that kind of thing."

"Where exactly did you go, let's say around ten this morning?"

"Why?"

I started to get up. Bobo glared at me. I relaxed back into the chair and sucked in another deep breath.

"Were you anywhere near Knob Noster State Park?"

She scrunched her brows and frowned. Strong eye contact. "I'm sorry, I don't think I know that park. Where is it?"

"Forty-five minutes south."

"Oh, no, then I certainly was not there. I went to Carrollton. They have this marvelous antique shop. I just love to browse."

A half hour north. Wrong direction. But what if she didn't know where Concentration Dupree went when that personality took over? Assuming that personality still existed and took over. But the woman in the woods, according to Allison's description, and what I saw of her looked nothing like Jeopardy or Concentration. She was several inches taller, with darker, shorter hair. Could have been a disguise. A darn good one.

"What time did you go to Carrollton?"

"I left around eight-thirty. They open at nine and I like to be there early."

I noted to myself to visit the antique shop and verify Jeopardy had been there.

"May I ask why these questions?"

"We were hiking at Knob Noster State Park and someone attacked Allison. Hit her in the head with a large stick and told her to stay away from me."

"Oh, my." Jeopardy covered her mouth with her empty hand, then let it drop to her lap. "That's horrible. Is she okay?"

Jeopardy appeared sincere in her concern. "A bump, but she'll be okay."

"That's good. I'll have to call her and ask if there's anything I can do to help."

"Not sure that would be a good idea."

"Oh." She raised her brows. "Why not?"

"She has a friend staying with her. Doesn't need any other help."

Jeopardy flashed a half smile then looked at Bobo. "And you, Mr. Johnson, any questions for me?" She stood before Bobo could answer. "And I'm sorry, where are my manners. May I get you some iced tea or lemonade?"

We both shook our heads.

Bobo stood. "No, Ms. Dupree, no questions from me. We're sorry to have bothered you. Right, Jake?"

A rhetorical question with an expected answer. I nodded and studied Jeopardy. "One more thing, though."

"Yes?"

I stood. "Can we see your garage? I'm curious about what car or cars you have."

"Why ever for?"

I paused to process that question, then figured out she had asked why in a complex manner. She gazed at me with wide eyes and half a smile, her eyelids batting, elbows bent, hands clasped together. The perfect picture of innocence. And maybe Jeopardy Dupree was innocent, always had been. What had happened to her to produce Concentration? Was she still in the claws of that destructive alter ego? We had to question Barker Monday to find out what Jeopardy's earlier life had been like.

"Well?" Jeopardy batted her eyelids some more.

"Just curious. Did Daddy Dupree leave you any classic vehicles? You've seen my car, right? I love the classics."

"Well, why didn't you say so? Yes, you'll *love* what's in the garage. Come."

Jeopardy led us to the back of the house, through a rustic kitchen but with all modern appliances. A giant granite-topped island dominated the center of the room. Above it hung an impressive collection of copper-bottomed pans. Wood-grained cabinets along one wall. Half logs backsplashed a granite countertop. Embedded into the wall above was a microwave long enough to cook a rack of ribs. Not that anyone would want to do that.

She opened the back door to the right of the kitchen. We followed into the backyard. Another impressive feature. I could barely make out the rear of the estate. Tall hedges ringed the multi-acre yard. To the left, a wide etched-concrete driveway led to a four-car garage. Jeopardy walked to the garage, flipped up the plastic lid of the entry keypad, and punched in four numbers.

Garage door number one opened. Her four-door cream-colored Audi occupied that stall, its convertible roof down. I stood at the back of the Audi and listened. No engine ticks. Not driven that recently. To the left of the Audi, an empty stall. Next to that sat a dark green Cutlass 442. Oh, baby! I guessed early seventies. A beauty. When the fiasco ended, I would have to ask Jeopardy about buying that. I doubt she drove it. And it would be a nice complement to my Delta 88. I imagined the bad guys I could catch in that classic.

I walked around the Cutlass. Impressed with the car, but disappointed that the last stall was also empty. No SUV. Four back windows let light into the garage. I moseyed over to them and glanced out. No vehicles behind the garage.

"That's a beaut." Bobo joined me at the window.

I turned and again glanced longingly at the Cutlass. "A 442. It would slaughter my Delta in a drag race."

Bobo chuckled. "Your Delta probably weighs twice as much."

"So. You weigh twice as much as me and you'd beat me in a race."

Bobo shoved me, fortunately, holding back. "I'm superhuman, little man."

"First time you've called me 'little man' in some time."

"It is. But you *are* a little man."

"Dude, to you every man is a little man."

"Not Shaq."

"Fine, you wouldn't call him 'little man.'"

Jeopardy joined us. "Very nice, isn't it?"

"It is. Do you drive it?"

"Oh, no. Daddy Dupree never let me or Barker drive that. Only ..." She turned away and walked back toward her Audi, then outside the garage.

I wondered if she was going to say only Connie could drive it. Something else to ask Barker. We joined her.

"Anything else you'd like to see?" A suggestive lilt to her voice.

No way I was biting on that. I shook my head. "Maybe when this thing is over, we can discuss that Cutlass in the garage."

"Please, let me know when."

"One question, though. Have you rented a dark SUV anytime recently?"

She opened her mouth to answer, said nothing, looked around, then turned away. Her shoulders trembled. She turned back. "No. My car works perfectly fine. Why?"

"No reason. Thank you again for showing us the Cutlass."

She flashed a huge smile, batted her eyes, tilted her head, and waited.

"You ready, big guy?"

He nodded and extended his hand to Jeopardy. "Ms. Dupree, a pleasure seeing you as always. You have a beautiful yard."

"Why thank you, Mr. Johnson. Always wonderful to see you as well."

"Thank you again, Ms. Dupree," I said.

"Oh, Jeopardy, please."

"Jeopardy. We'll be seeing you." At the back door, I held it open for Jeopardy and Bobo. Once inside, I beelined for the front door.

As we walked outside, Jeopardy said, "Have a good day. Thank you for stopping by."

I wondered if she'd figured out why we'd really stopped by. Were her two personalities completely separated? Did Jeopardy know when Connie was present and what Connie did? Was Connie making appearances, or was this mysterious woman someone else from my past?

On the way to the car, Bobo shouldered me, nearly knocking me over. "That woman is madly in love with you."

"That woman is wacko, dude. I don't want anything to do with her. Besides, she's a client."

"Was a client. No line to cross now."

I looked at him. Deadpan face. "You're not serious?"

He laughed. "Got you."

Before I climbed into the Delta 88, Bobo said, "Don't forget. You're coming to church tomorrow."

I had forgotten.

Twenty-Seven

I entered the church foyer behind Bobo. A few people said hello to me. No clue who they were. While Bobo glad-handed and talked with people he knew, I wandered toward the main worship center. Most of the white people dressed casually. The African Americans dressed more formally, like Bobo, who wore a dark green suit with a tan T-shirt underneath the jacket. I wished he'd called and told me what he'd be wearing. We were too closely matched for my comfort. I wore a green windowpane sports jacket, light purple shirt, light tan pants, and of course my light green fedora. Fortunately, our jackets were different shades of green.

At the entrance to the worship center, the pastor corralled me. "Mr. Sledge, so nice to see you again."

We shook hands. Even he had dressed casually—a dark collarless shirt and faded blue jeans.

"May I ask you a personal question?"

I shrugged. "Sure, why not?"

"What is your relationship with Jesus?"

"I haven't met the guy." I expected a mini sermon after that answer.

He nodded. "Thank you for sharing. I hope you'll get something out of today's message." We shook hands again, and he walked into the foyer.

I wandered down the aisle wondering what the pastor meant. I reached Bobo's customary seat and plunked down next to it. No sign of Jeopardy. And if she was the one stalking me, I didn't expect her, as I'd left my cell phone at home. Doubly naked that day. No guns. No phone. But I had the fedora, which I placed on the seat next to me. People in front of the stage gathered in circles of five and bent their heads. I couldn't hear anything, but I assumed they were praying. Was anyone listening to those prayers? If so, did they get answered? Always? Sometimes? I shook my head. Why was I even considering those thoughts? Maybe the setting?

Bobo joined me. He shook hands with the man on his left.

"Did you tell your pastor I was coming today?"

Bobo raised his brows. "No. Why?"

"Something he said to me."

The band gathered on the stage. A young man introduced himself as the worship director and welcomed everyone, then the band started to play. We stood. The first song went through me, not registering much. The next one, "No Longer Slaves," hit me hard. Slave? Who or what was I a slave to? Fear, the song implied. What was I afraid of? While I mulled those thoughts, the next song started. I started listening to "Death was Arrested." Did the beginning really describe me? Lost? Stuck in sin? What the heck was sin? What was I lost from? And wasn't I free as well? Free from what, though? Again, that slave question pushed other thoughts away. I was a slave to fear and sin. That's what these songs said. And believing in God could free me from that slavery? My brain hurt. That day, I realized that the worship director didn't pick songs at random.

The songs ended. We did the shake hands with our neighbor thing. I recognized most of the people around me from previous visits. Across the aisle and up a few rows, I spotted Liliana Goodhue and her father, the deputy mayor of River City. Both waved. And remarkably, both smiled. I expected that from Daddy Goodhue. But the queen of the law? She smiled at me. I glanced over my shoulder to make sure Bobo wasn't looking at her. He wasn't. His back was to her. I smiled back and gave a tentative wave, feeling a little silly.

We sat. The pastor walked onto the stage. For some reason I gave rapt attention to his words. I didn't have my phone. Nothing else to do.

"Good morning, church."

Many people responded.

"Today's message may only be for one person sitting out there. Or it may be for many. Depends on where you stand in your relationship with Jesus Christ. Maybe you haven't met

Him yet. Maybe you've spent much of your life in his presence. To be honest, today's message is for the former."

I suddenly felt singled out and elbowed Bobo.

"What?"

"Are you sure you didn't tell him I'd be here?"

"Have I ever lied to you?"

I shook my head and returned my attention to the pastor.

"What about the rest of you, those who feel they walk closely with Jesus? What do you get out of today's message?" He paused and scanned the congregation. "I'm sure you know someone who isn't as close to Jesus as you are." He opened a book. "Please open your Bibles to Ephesians chapter 2 and read along with me."

An open Bible plunked onto my lap and startled me. I glanced down and saw the passage the pastor had announced. Bobo pointed at it. I picked it up and followed along as the pastor read the first three verses. While he did, waves of shivers ran through my body. Was this me? Dead, yet living? Walking in sin? And if I didn't follow the world, what would I follow? And who was this prince of power? I wasn't following any prince I knew of. And I had to admit I carried out most of the desires of my body and mind. Though, lately with Allison, I'd found the ability to curb at least one of those desires. Allison? I missed her. Was she at her church? Was her pastor speaking only to her, like this one was to me?

The pastor proceeded to answer some of my questions. And I swear he stared at me the entire time. Sin: doing wrong. Got it.

According to whom? God, he explained. The prince of power is the devil. I pictured a tiny red dude with a pitchfork sitting on my shoulder until the pastor shattered that vision and told us who the devil really is, and that he prowled around like a lion looking for people like me to devour. He didn't really say *like me*, but that's what he implied.

"If I stopped at only these three verses and let you all go, I'd be negligent." The pastor paced the stage. "Because God didn't stop there. He didn't and won't leave us in that state described by the apostle Paul. Let's read the next seven verses."

I followed along. As the pastor read, my stomach churned. Tears formed in my eyes. Why? What the heck was going on? The words on the page blurred, but they burned into my brain as the pastor read them.

He stopped reading and let a long silence linger. "Where are you today? Are you in the first three verses, dead in your trespasses? Or are you alive and seated with God in the heavenly places?" Another long pause.

I stared at the words in the Bible, not daring to look up, afraid of seeing the pastor's eyes boring into me.

"If you are still dead in your trespasses, then thank God for his grace, for he can pull you out of the mire you're in and lift you up. He sent his only Son to die on the cross, to pay for all the bad stuff you've done. And three days later, Jesus Christ rose again, conquering death and showing us there is a path to redemption through the grace of the Father God."

I dared to look up. The pastor paced to my right. He stopped, turned, and as I feared, drilled his gaze into me.

"Surrender your life to Christ and live again. Throw off the chains the world and the prince of the power of the air have shackled you with. Let God's grace wash you clean of all that past garbage. Come to Jesus. Let us pray."

And we did. And I did. Not completely sure who I prayed to, I prayed I didn't want to be dead, didn't want to follow the devil, wanted to be the man that—and here's where it really got me—Allison wanted me to be. Allison, again. I wanted what I was hearing because I wanted Allison to accept me. What had that woman done to me? The questions from earlier steamrolled through my brain. In the background of my mind, music played. Some words filtered through the sludge clogging my mind. Amazing grace. Wretch like me. Lost. Blind. Blind to what? My chains could be shed. I could be free. I sat bent over as tears streamed from my eyes and dripped onto the Bible still cradled in my lap. Mercy. Amazing grace. What did it mean? Something about a savior ransoming me. What did that mean?

The music stopped, but the questions continued swirling through my mind. I felt a presence. No, not God. Bobo stood over me. A white cloth appeared. He'd handed me a handkerchief. I took it and wiped my eyes, then stood.

"Lunch?" Bobo asked. "Think we need to talk."

I could only nod. He took the Bible from my hands and placed it in the rack under the seat in front of him. I followed him out of the church.

We passed the pastor. Bobo didn't bother to stop and shake his hand.

"I'll be praying for you, Bobo, and for Jake," the pastor said.

I followed Bobo to his Range Rover. He drove us to Sweetie Pie's. Apparently, he thought it was funny to go to a soul food restaurant to talk to me about my soul.

I stared at the sweet potato pie the waitress set in front of me. Usually, one of my favorites, but my gut boiled and my brain felt like mush. On the way to Sweetie Pie's, I'd stared out the passenger window of Bobo's Range Rover and watched River City pass by. Bobo respected my silence. When we arrived, all the staff in the restaurant, as they always did, made a big deal over Bobo. The owners, Faith and Anthony Williams, loved Bobo. And they loved me too, but I'm sure it was because of my association with Bobo.

The big guy made small talk while we glanced over the menus. I knew he wanted to get to the issue at hand, my eternal salvation or damnation depending on how convincing he could be, but people kept coming up to Bobo and, of course, he engaged all of them. Never one to dismiss someone outright.

When the food arrived, the people respected us and let us be.

"You gonna eat?" Bobo shoveled a forkful of Southern smothered pork chop into his mouth. He watched me while he chewed.

"Not sure. Feeling a bit queasy."

Bobo swallowed. "The Holy Spirit got a hold of you good, didn't He?" He took a forkful of collard greens.

I jabbed my fork at the sweet potato pie. "I'm still convinced you told your pastor I'd be there."

Bobo put his fork down. "Even if I did, Pastor Marty prepares his sermons months in advance. I believe the Holy Spirit has you under conviction."

I took a bite. The usually fantastic dish tasted bland. My throat felt dry, so I washed the food down with Dr Pepper. No slam on the chef. All me.

"God's trying to get your attention. You get what He did for us?"

I shook my head. "All I keep thinking is I'm a slave, and the slave owner seems to be the devil."

"You got that right, brother. And that's where God comes in. He can free you from that slavery."

"How?"

"Eat." Bobo took another large bite of pork chop.

I took another forkful of pie. This time, the flavors came through, and I didn't need to wash it down.

"I ain't gonna start way at the beginning. But I got to ask, do you believe there's a God?"

I shrugged. "I guess. Someone or something had to create all this." I waved my hand to encompass the entire world. At least that's how I meant the gesture.

"Okay, so let's go in with that assumption. There is a God who created the world. Do you believe in heaven?"

I frowned and took another bite to stall.

But Bobo kept going. "What do you think happens after you die?"

"Other than my body will turn to worm food, I'm not sure."

"There's a heaven. And God is there. Can we work with that assumption as well?"

"Sure."

"But here's the problem. He don't want no one who's done wrong."

"Must be a lonely place, then."

Bobo took another bite and nodded. He swallowed. "It would be but for Jesus."

"The dude that got nailed to a cross?"

"That's the one. He was God's Son. Born of a virgin. Lived about thirty-three years of a perfect life. Was convicted in a sham trial. And then crucified." Bobo paused and took a drink of his lemonade.

"Yeah, so? What does that do for me?"

Bobo smiled. "Everything, brother. Because here's the good news. Three days later, He rose from the grave, conquering death."

"Great. So, God doesn't die. Still not sure where I come in."

Bobo cut off a piece of pork chop and ate it. While chewing he nodded. I was lost, still unable to figure out how what Bobo told me would help me break free from the metaphoric chains I supposedly wore.

"In the ancient world, the Jews had to sacrifice animals to appease God when they messed up."

"I'm surprised there are any animals left."

"That's where Jesus comes in. He was the perfect sacrifice. No more animal sacrifices were necessary. He died for all of us. All we have to do is confess him as Lord and believe that God raised him from the dead."

"Then what?"

"You'll be saved."

"From what?"

"Hell, brother. A place where God ain't. And the place if you don't confess Jesus, you'll spend eternity."

Heavy stuff. I took another bite. Tasted good. Bobo continued eating as well. We let the silence linger for several minutes while we both took care of the food on our plates.

Bobo finished first. Instantly, like she'd been waiting for the moment, our waitress, a slim, young African American, materialized at the table.

"Mr. Johnson, how was it?"

"Fantastic, as always, Jasmine."

"May I get you anything else?"

"I'm good. Jake?"

With my mouth stuffed with sweet potato pie, I mumbled, "I'm good. Thanks."

Jasmine took Bobo's plate and left.

"You ready to give your life to the Lord Jesus yet?"

I swallowed. The food, not the lump forming in my throat. Emotions I tried hard to keep down threatened to overwhelm me. I took my napkin off my lap, dabbed my mouth, then laid it on the plate. What else could I do to delay answering that question?

"Got to use the restroom." I nearly sprinted to the men's room. After relieving myself, I washed my hands and stared at the guy in the mirror. Hat hair, but other than that, no chains around me. Didn't look different than I usually did. Then why did I feel rotten, dirty, unworthy? Unworthy for whom? And it hit me again. For Allison. A question slammed through my mind. When will I be worthy enough for her? Other words floated through my consciousness. God. Jesus. Salvation. Didn't even know I knew such a big word. I left the restroom and returned to the table.

Bobo remained quiet and watched me. I squirmed under the intensity of his stare. Knowing what he wanted me to say, and knowing what Allison would love for me to say, I couldn't. Not yet. There wasn't much about this Christian stuff I knew, but one thing that seemed certain, I had to be ready to submit to God, not just say yes to make a couple of people happy, or it wouldn't be real. And I hate fake people. No way I'd become on
e.

"Not yet, big guy. I need time to think about it."

"Fair enough. You know where to find me."

I let out an enormous sigh. Not that the burden fell away from me. If anything, the weight increased. I knew I'd have to answer soon about what I believed. Allison wouldn't stick around forever.

"I want to talk about the case, but hold on a minute. Give me your phone, would you?" Bobo handed me his cell phone and I texted Allison, telling her it was me and asking her how she was.

A few seconds turned into twenty, then forty. A minute went by. I started to hand the phone back feeling hollow, when it dinged.

Allison's return text read, "I'm doing much better. Really miss you. Please solve the case." A bunch of emojis. Other than the smiley face and the heart, I had no idea what they meant. The hollowness retreated. But still I didn't feel fully satisfied. Something was missing. I liked the message and gave the phone back to Bobo.

Ignoring the niggling feeling I had, I launched into reviewing the case or cases. "I had this theory that the woman in the SUV and the woman in the woods were Concentration Dupree resurrected."

Bobo nodded. "And now?"

"I don't know. I expected to find the SUV at Jeopardy's house. Even to see her surprised for it to be there."

"Could be hidden somewhere else."

"True. But even if my theory holds, why?"

Bobo finished his lemonade. And again, nearly instantly, Jasmine appeared and refilled his glass.

"More Dr Pepper, Mr. Sledge?"

"Sure."

Jasmine grabbed my glass and scurried to the bar to refill it. I waited until she returned to continue with my theory.

"Let's say that woman is Jeopardy's alter ego. What is the motive driving her? Why does ..." I stopped. I answered why Concentration Dupree wants to kill me in my head. Because I'd outed her. I caused Jeopardy to spend all that time in the psych hospital. That made sense. But why tell Allison to stay away from me?

"Why what?"

"Never mind. New question. How does someone coming after me have anything to do with Barker Dupree being accused of killing Sandy Akins?" Bobo started to say something, but I cut him off. "Let me finish. Back to my theory. Connie Dupree is trying to kill me for no other reason than she hates me, and I had Jeopardy locked up for a long time. Thus, she was the driver who tried to run me down. She was the woman in the woods. But what does she have to do with Braxton Anderson?"

We both took drinks and stared at each other.

Finally, Bobo asked, "We've told Ms. Dupree about the woman associated with Braxton, right?"

"Maybe. I think so. Don't remember. But let's say we did. Your point?"

"To confuse you, Connie Dupree takes on the same look. We have two women, but the one trying to kill you wants you to think they are the same."

Good point. "We have two separate situations here. I'll deal with Jeopardy and Connie. But why was Sandy Akins killed?"

"How are you going to deal with Ms. Dupree?"

"You mean besides killing her and dumping her body in the river?"

Bobo glared at me.

"Kidding. I don't know yet. Let's focus on Sandy Akins."

For the next half hour, we went over all the evidence we had on the murder of Sandy Akins. Unfortunately, we ended up where we started.

"In conclusion," I said, "either Barker killed her or we have no clue who else did."

"Yup."

Great. "Ok. Tomorrow, office or meet at the county lockup?"

Bobo grinned and shook his head.

"What?"

"The appointment is at ten in Lexington."

"And that's funny why?"

"Are you going to get up early enough to be at the office long enough to make it worthwhile?"

Another good point. "Nope. I'll meet you in Lexington. I want to make a stop after that anyway."

"Where?"

"Carrollton. Check out Jeopardy's story about antique shopping."

Bobo stood. "See you in Lexington. Will be a nice change for you."

I also stood. "Meaning?"

"Seeing the outside of the lockup."

Funny guy.

"I'm going to the gym to work out. You want to come?"

I had nothing else going on, so I agreed. Gym, home, Mom's for a visit, home, fell asleep watching *SportsCenter*. The life of a big time PI. Waiting for that big break. Maybe Monday would be that day.

Twenty-Eight

I didn't sleep well Sunday night. The things Pastor Marty told me and what Bobo said tumbled around in my brain like rocks in a polisher for hours. I finally drifted to sleep around three. I punched the snooze button on my cell phone clock three times. During the fourth playing of "Sandman" by Metallica, I opened one eye. Eight twenty-eight. I sat up and turned the song off. Nearly an hour to get ready drive twenty-five minutes north of River City to Lexington. No big deal. I padded to the bathroom and relieved myself.

Shave or no shave? Decided no. I showered. In the bedroom, I stared at my wardrobe. A visit to the county lockup and a visit to an antique store. Next in line to wear was either English gentleman or Miami Vice. The vice look would play better at county but was overkill for Carrollton. Besides, after the shooting incident I had perpetrated in Carrollton several weeks ago, I decided that showing up there looking like Sonny Crockett wasn't my best play. English gentleman it was. I put on dark brown dress pants and a light brown dress shirt, grabbed my tweed sports coat and tweed hat, and headed to the kitchen for a bagel and orange juice.

I sat down and brought the bagel up to my mouth. "We are Family" played on my cell phone. Alicia. I put the bagel down and punched the green button followed by the speaker icon so I could eat and talk.

"Jake! Guess what?"

"You got up way too early and had way too much coffee?"

"No, goofball. Myron. He accepted the Lord yesterday. Went forward in church. I'm so proud of him."

Yeah, me too. Not. But I could tell it meant a lot to Alicia. "That's great. Glad to hear it. Now what?"

"It's the most important step in his faith walk. He's going to be baptized next Sunday. I'd really like you to be there for that."

Another Sunday in church? In six days? Way too far out to plan. I muttered, "Sure. I think I can make it." Bobo. Alicia. Allison. And now Myron all believed in Jesus Christ. Me? I closed my eyes and sighed.

"Jake, you still there?"

"Yeah, Sis. Still here."

"Bobo said you went to church yesterday."

"Bobo has a big mouth. When did you call him?"

"About an hour ago."

Of course. Bobo would have been up at the crack of dawn. Probably already worked out or put in a couple of hours in the office. Doing what? I had no clue.

"Yes, I went to church."

"Bobo also said the message hit you hard."

"Where are you going with this?" I took a big bite of bagel and chewed loudly.

"Are you eating?"

"Yes. I have to be in Lexington before ten."

"Did you just get up?"

I swallowed the bite of bagel and washed it down with orange juice. "No."

"Okay. I won't keep you. I have to call Mom as well. Let's talk about your faith journey sometime, Jake, okay?"

The only journey I was about to embark on was to Lexington and Carrollton. "Sure. I'll drop by later in the week."

"Okay Big Bro. Love you. Bye."

"Love you." We disconnected and I glanced at the stove clock. Barely enough time to finish my breakfast, but I did.

I sat at the table and stared into space. Those words from Pastor Marty and Bobo now had company. The words from Alicia. A faith journey. Myron accepting the Lord. Accepting? What did that mean? Bobo had said something about confessing and believing. Same thing? All the thoughts and ideas continued swirling through my mind. A tempest of faith and belief buffeted my brain. I took a deep breath to calm my anxiety and again glanced at the stove clock. Nine-thirty.

I jumped up, ran into the bedroom, and grabbed my shoulder holster. Midway through putting it on, I stopped. New images ravaged my thoughts. Guys with guns pointing at me. Gunshots drowned out all other sounds. I ducked and dropped to my knees near my bed. I looked around. The vision cleared. The sound stopped, but not the shaking. When it subsided, I stood and slipped off the shoulder holster. Couldn't have it in county anyway, and I didn't think I'd need it at an antique store. I had to go out into the world naked, yet again.

I exited the bedroom, walked down the hall, through the kitchen, and to the side door. Before opening the door, I sucked in several deep breaths and strained to clear my head of all thought. It worked. I left the house and climbed in the Delta 88, started it, and cranked the radio up, hoping the loud music would repel all those thoughts threatening to consume me.

I walked into the Lafayette County Detention Center at five minutes after ten. Bobo, of course, waited for me in the lobby.

"Nice place." I shook Bobo's hand. "Morning, big guy."

"You've never spent any time here?"

"Funny. Nope. I haven't had the pleasure."

We checked in at the desk with a uniformed officer. He took my jacket and hat. Bobo wore his usual dark T-shirt and jeans.

We knew the routines. We emptied our pockets into a plastic bin. We both carried only wallets and keys. The officer stored the bins and had us sign in.

A uniformed guard brought Barker into the visiting area, which looked like a sterile, concrete park. Hard plastic chairs were attached to steel columns holding up concrete tabletops.

"Good morning, Mr. Dupree," I said. No handshaking. No contact at all.

"Morning." Barker sat. He had dark bags under his eyes, but he otherwise seemed physically okay. He glanced around the room, locking his gaze on the camera in the corner.

"Everything going okay in here?" Bobo asked.

"Yeah. No issues. I get my meds. People leave me alone."

Bobo nodded. "Good to hear."

"What brings you two here? I thought you were done with the case."

"Your lawyer hired us," I answered. "Guilty or not guilty, he wants us to find out whatever we can."

"I see." He stared at the table.

"This visit is about history," I said.

He looked up. "What history?"

"Your sister's history. And probably some of yours."

"What do you want to know?"

"Tell us about yours and Jeopardy's childhood, to start."

Barker shook his head. "Not much to tell. Typical rich kid childhood. Dad worked all the time. Mom had her charity work and other functions. We lived in Arkansas and were raised by a nanny. Had the run of the house."

So many jokes ran through my mind. Being born and raised in Missouri, I was well acquainted with the Missouri–Arkansas rivalry. And even though River City sat much closer to the Kansas border—and yes, we had our share of Kansas jokes—all of us still made fun of Arkansas. But I resisted the urge.

"At what point did you whack out?"

Bobo grimaced. "I think what Jake means is when did your schizophrenia start to show symptoms?"

"I figured. Mid-teens. Probably fourteen or fifteen. I think everyone thought I was shy, maybe autistic. It was easy to conceal the voices I heard."

"What about Jeopardy?" I asked. "Anything happen to her as a child or teen?"

Barker nodded. "Our father abused her."

"Sexually?"

"Yup. As soon as Jeopardy bloomed, so to speak, Dad started in on her. And that's when Concentration came along."

He must have seen the questioning look on my face because he continued.

"Concentration, or Connie as Jeopardy called her, protected Jeopardy from Dad."

"Yeah, I know. She killed him but that was much later."

"Before that. When Dad abused Jeopardy, Concentration came out. She was much stronger than Jeopardy. If you ask my sister today if our dad abused her, she'll say only one time.

The memories of all the other times belong to Connie, not Jeopardy."

Mind-blowing. "Defense mechanism?"

"Exactly."

I glanced at Bobo, who shrugged. Then I asked Barker, "Do you believe Connie is gone?"

It was Barker's turn to shrug. "Who knows? Is anything happening to Jeopardy that she needs protection?"

"Not that we know of. Is she still on the board of your father's company?"

"Naw. Mr. Jorgenson sold the company when Jeopardy went away. We live on that money."

Bobo asked, "May we know how much?"

"Several hundred million. But we didn't get all of it. Only a couple million apiece. The rest is in a trust."

"For who?" I asked.

"Whom," Bobo said.

"Whatever, Professor Johnson."

Barker grinned, then answered my grammatically incorrect question. "For when we're married. First one married gets seventy-five percent. The other twenty-five goes to the other sibling when they're married."

"That might be awhile," I said.

Barker shrugged, then resumed studying the table.

"Anything else important you can tell us about your family?" Bobo asked.

Barker raised his head, a faraway look in his eyes. A single tear trickled out of the right eye. "I'm pretty sure Jeopardy, or her as Connie, killed our mother."

"We read in the newspaper your mother's death was an accident," Bobo said.

Barker shook his head. "That's the official ruling. But I know Jeopardy pushed her down those stairs."

"Why?" I asked.

"Mom didn't protect her from Dad. She ignored it. I can't blame Jeopardy, but I loved Mom, so it's hard for me to forgive her."

"Do you know Jesus?" Bobo asked.

Barker nodded. "And I know I have to forgive. But it's hard."

"I'll pray for you, Mr. Dupree. I'll pray God will soften your heart."

I sighed. Seemed I was the only one not following Jesus.

"Thank you, Mr. Johnson."

"Anything else?" I asked.

Barker shook his head. "Nothing important I can think of."

We thanked Barker and left the facility. In the parking lot, I told Bobo I'd see him in the office tomorrow.

"Where are you going now?" he asked.

"Carrollton to check on Jeopardy's story about antique shopping."

We got into our respective vehicles and left. Bobo to the office. Me to Carrollton.

I sat in my Delta 88, top down, in the parking lot of the Carrollton Recreation Park. Not much activity that Monday slightly after noon. With the first double-bacon cheeseburger, half the fries, and half the shake gone, I started on burger number two. I'm not sure how much I tasted with all the thoughts steamrolling through my head. I tried to concentrate on the case. Did anything Barker told us tie up any of the loose ends? But every time I thought I latched onto something, another Jesus thought intruded. Even Barker Dupree, potential murderer, claimed he had a relationship with Jesus. Did that make him less of a suspect? Something he told me nibbled at the edge of my consciousness, but I couldn't seize it.

Myron accepted Jesus. I knew Allison had that belief going into our relationship, and I knew it bothered her that I didn't. Bobo, of course, had been a Jesus follower for many years. My sister? I'm sure she told me several times, but I filed it and forgot. While these thoughts tumbled in the empty crevices of my brain, a sullenness settled over me. All of those people seemed happy. Even Barker, who had schizophrenia, rotted in jail, and was accused of killing the one person he loved, had a spark of something. Had that been me, I'd be angry and depressed. Sure, a sadness enveloped Barker, probably the grief of losing Sandy

Akins. But other than Braxton Anderson, everyone loved the gu y.

I brought my hand up for a bite of burger. No burger. Gone. Time to get to the antique store. I stuffed the wrappers, carton, and cup into the bag and tossed the trash onto the passenger floor. Time to find one more piece of the puzzle. A puzzle we were trying to put together with all the pieces upside down.

I drove into the parking lot of Aunt Martha's Odds and Ends. Fortunately, Carrollton had only one antique store, as Jeopardy had not given the name and I hadn't asked. Slipping in my old age. A long, brick building that was painted off-white at least fifty years ago. Eight or so cars in the parking lot. Not bad traffic for a weekday. When I entered the store, bells above the door jingled. A long aisle ran the length of the building. On both sides, you guessed it, antiques. I wondered if any of the furniture was older than my dining table. All of the pieces looked nicer, that's for sure.

A fiftyish lady, wearing a long print dress with her hair piled on her head and reading glasses dangling on a chain around her neck, approached me.

"Can I help you find something? I saw you drive up. Nice car. Obviously, a man who recognizes vintage."

"Thank you. My name is Jake Sledge. I'm a PI."

"Wow. A real-life PI? Should have figured such with the fedora and all. Lovely hat, by the way."

I tipped my hat to her. Quite the sales lady. She almost had me convinced I needed to buy something. "Were you, by any chance, working here last Saturday?"

"Darling, I own the place. I'm here all the time when it's open. And weekends are our biggest days. Yes, dear, I was here. Why?"

"And do you happen to know a woman named Jeopardy Dupree?"

She sucked in a big breath and smiled. "Ms. Dupree. One of my best customers. A lovely young woman. So charming."

"Sure. Was she here Saturday?"

"No."

"You're sure?"

"Believe me Mr. Sledge, if Ms. Dupree had been here, I'd have known it. She usually seeks me out and we spend hours looking through the store. She loves to hear me talk about where everything came from."

I tipped my hat again to her. "Thank you, ma'am. You've been a big help."

"Oh, sure. I hope Ms. Dupree is okay."

"Last I saw her, she was peachy."

"Ah, good. Now, can I show you our vintage model car collection?"

I almost declined but then thought I could use a diversion. We spent the next hour looking at model cars. Metal ones, in their original packaging, all to scale. No Delta 88s, or I would have bought one.

"I'm so sorry we don't have your car here. I think we used to have one, but that was a couple of years ago. I'll keep my eyes open for you."

"That's kind of you." I handed her my business card. "Call me if one shows up."

"I will. Nice to meet you, Mr. Sledge."

"Likewise." I left the shop.

Before heading back to River City, I mulled over what I'd learned. One more piece to the puzzle. Jeopardy Dupree either lied to me or her alter-ego planted a memory in her brain about being at the antique store. Was that even possible?

I pulled out my cell phone and dialed the River Bluffs Residential Center. When the receptionist answered I asked for Dr. Charnow.

"Hello, Mr. Sledge. What can I do for you? Are you ready to book an appointment with one of our counselors?"

"No, thank you. That's not why I'm calling. But you'll be happy to hear Bobo has booked me an appointment. It's Friday, I think."

"Wonderful. I'm so glad."

Really? Maybe she was. Who knows? "Anyway, I have a psych question for you."

"Okay. I'm happy to help."

"If someone suffers from multiple personalities, can one personality plant memories in the other personality?"

"You're in luck, Mr. Sledge. Dissociative disorder is one of my specialties. And to answer your question, no."

"Okay. Let me give you a hypothetical." I explained, without using Jeopardy's name, someone told me they were someplace, but they really weren't there.

"The person lied to you."

"But it didn't seem like a lie. The person seemed truthful. And I'm trained in spotting lies."

"If this hypothetical person, who may have a brother named Barker, loses chunks of her memory because her other personality takes over for long periods, she's grown used to filling in those gaps. To her, it may not be a lie. And to her, she might even believe what she thinks she's remembering, because that's easier than admitting she has holes in her memory."

Smart woman.

"That makes sense. Thank you, Dr. Charnow. You've been a big help."

We hung up. One piece of the puzzle fell into place. Concentration Dupree definitely still existed. But did she have anything to do with Sandy Akins? And if so, why? What was she protecting Jeopardy from?

My brain hurt. I started the car, eased out of the driveway, and drove fifteen minutes to the outskirts of River City. At River Road, I turned right. The stoplight at Meredith Drive and River Road turned red. When the light turned green, I hesitated. Straight would take me to the office. Left, to my house. Only two o'clock. As I mentioned, my brain hurt. The car behind me honked. I turned left. Being half owner of the business meant I could take time off when needed. And given that my brain had turned to mush, I needed some time off. Frustration threatened to bubble over. Too many chain links floating around.

Later, a call from Bobo linked them together.

Twenty-Nine

I dreamed about a Cleveland Browns football game. The opposing quarterback threw a pass to a wide receiver cutting across the middle. I annihilated the receiver. The ball bounced high in the air. One of my teammates caught it and ran it back for a touchdown. After the touchdown, the Dawg Pound chanted, "Who let the dogs out?"

The chant kept going. Why wouldn't they stop? I woke up and realized my cell phone was singing "Who Let the Dogs Out?" Bobo was calling me. Such a pleasant dream. I glanced at the television. A sports talk show aired. The clock on the cable box said five forty-eight. A six-month-old sports magazine lay tented on my chest as I reclined in my easy chair.

I fished my cell phone out of my pants pocket. "Yes, big guy? What's up?"

"Turn your television on."

"It is on."

"Change to channel eight."

We had the same cable operator, so giving me the number worked. Besides, had he told me to turn to something like ABC, I would have had no clue what channel that was.

"Hold on." I flipped the recliner up. The magazine slid off me onto the floor. I grabbed the remote off the small end table and changed to channel eight. The game show *Jeopardy!*

"Yeah, so? Did you beat one of the contestants, or something?"

"What show is on?"

"*Jeopardy!* So what?"

I could almost hear Bobo's head shaking through the connection. What was I missing?

"Do you remember the picture of Sandy Akins's body?" Bobo asked.

"Sort of. But I can do one better. Hold on." I went into the kitchen, sat in one of my vintage dining chairs, put my phone on the table, and changed it to speaker mode. I flipped open the folder with the Sandy Akins case notes and paged through a couple of reports until I came to the picture Bobo had referred to.

"Got it. What about it?"

"Look at her hands."

Sandy Akins lay on her stomach, her left hand sprawled open at her side. Her right arm extended above her head, straight out. The index finger curled under her hand with the thumb tucked against it.

"Sorry, I don't get it. What am I looking at?"

"How many digits are sticking out on her left hand?"

"Five."

"Right hand?"

"Three."

"What time is it?"

I glanced at the phone. "Five fifty."

"What time was it twenty minutes ago?"

He wanted me to do math? I handled it. "Five thirty. What are you getting at?"

"Five and three. Look at the picture again."

I did. Seemed Bobo was saying that Sandy was trying to tell us something about five thirty. But she'd died in the morning. And Barker had found her body around ten forty-five. I told Bobo the same.

He sighed. "Do you think Poindexter will meet us at her apartment in fifteen minutes?"

"How would I know? Want me to call him?"

"Yes. And even if he doesn't, let's meet there anyway. Before I say any more, I want to check something. And bring the photo."

We hung up, and I called Poindexter.

"Jake Sledge. How are you, my man?"

I heard background talking. It sounded like at least three other people. "Sorry to bother you, but we might have a break in the Sandy Akins case."

"Okay. But I heard Barker Dupree confessed."

"He did. But we believe it was under duress."

"From RCPD?"

"Someone else trying to cover something up."

Someone shouted, "Geoff, your turn, dude."

"Sorry," Poindexter said. "I got the gang over and we're playing D&D."

"D&D?"

"Dungeons and Dragons, dude."

"Ah. Well, then what I have to ask probably won't work out."

"Ask. How can I help?"

"Bobo wants to meet us at Sandy Akins's apartment in about fifteen minutes."

Silence, except for low-level conversation in the background. Poindexter spoke, but his voice was muffled, so he must have been talking to his friends. Did I ever mention my acute detecting skills?

"I'll meet you there, Sledge. The gang will wait for me. One thing, though."

"Sure."

"They want chicken wings."

Small price to pay. "Okay, fine. We can stop somewhere on the way back from the apartment."

"Perfect. See you shortly."

We hung up, and I drove to Sandy Akins's apartment.

I arrived at the apartment complex only a minute or so before Poindexter. He pulled in as I reached the entrance to the courtyard.

He parked and trotted through the lot to me. "I wasn't doing too well tonight, anyway."

We shook hands. "I appreciate you coming out."

He shrugged.

We entered the courtyard together. Bobo stood across the other side by the stairs. He waved. Poindexter waved back.

Outside the apartment, Poindexter retrieved the deadbolt key from the lockbox and unlocked the door. We entered, wading through warm, heavy air. Bobo walked to the bloodstained spot between the kitchen and living room.

"Over here, Jake. Bring that photo."

On the drive over, I still hadn't determined what I was missing. I handed the photo to Bobo, who rotated it to match Sandy's body position. He motioned me to look at the picture. Poindexter also joined us. We both looked.

"Where is her right hand pointing?" Bobo asked.

I examined the photo then surveyed the living room. Window. Coffee table. Sofa. Television. I looked again at the photo. "Move it a bit to the right."

Bobo did.

"Maybe the television?" To Poindexter, I asked, "Was the television on when you all got here?"

He tapped his chin with his index finger knuckle. "Yes, it was. Some soap, I believe."

Bobo walked into the living room. "No remote."

"Bagged and tagged, dude. Evidence."

Bobo raised his brows.

"Fingerprints and all that," Poindexter said. "If I remember, only hers were found on it."

Bobo went to the television and felt around the edge. The television flickered on. The number eight appeared in the top right corner. A local newscaster talked about a bad car accident on Interstate 70.

Bobo turned and stared at me, waiting. For what, I wasn't sure. I shrugged.

"Oh, come on, Jake. Your brain fried or something?"

I nodded. "It is. Too much stuff going through it. Your fault, you know."

He raised his hands, palms up.

"All that Jesus stuff."

"Jesus is the dude, man," Poindexter said.

"Amen, brother." Bobo raised his hands above his head. When he lowered them, he shuffled from foot to foot and started motioning with his right hand, like he was urging a running back to go faster.

"Just spit it out, big dude."

"Okay. We'll see who gets this first. You or Poindexter." He turned the television off and joined us. "What did her hands say?"

"Five and three," I said.

"And if a time?"

"Five-thirty," Poindexter said. "She's telling us something happened at five thirty. But I don't get it. She died before eleven."

"What was on television at five-thirty?" Bobo asked. "On channel eight."

I can be slow, but that day had been a rough one. My brain ran at tortoise speed. But when Bobo asked that question, everything flooded my mind so fast and hard I expected stuff to leak from my ears. I held up my hand to silence the crowd and pulled out my cell phone.

Dr. Charnow answered. "Mr. Sledge, how are you?"

"Possibly great. I have a question for you."

"Just finishing dinner, but if it's a quick one, I suppose that's okay."

"Sorry for bothering you. Sandy Akins. Did she ever talk about television shows she watched?"

"Not really."

I sighed. "Did she ever mention being a trivia buff?"

"Yes! Sandy had a brain like a steel trap. Remembered everything. She constantly said she should go on *Jeopardy!*" A pause. "Television show. Yes, sorry, I was thinking sitcom, that kind of thing. But yes, she said she never missed an episode of *Jeopardy!*"

"Thank you so much, Dr. Charnow." '

"Sure. May I ask why this question?"

"I think we just proved Barker Dupree is innocent. Later." I hung up.

Then to Bobo and Poindexter, I said, "Jeopardy Dupree killed Sandy Akins."

"Or maybe Concentration Dupree," Bobo said.

I nodded. "And Ms. Akins knew Jeopardy," Poindexter added. "And gave us a clue by pointing at the television with her hands at five fingers and three fingers. Wow. And we completely missed it." He looked at me. "How did you two figure that out?"

I pointed at Bobo, who said, "Divine inspiration is all I can claim. Was watching *Jeopardy!* on television today when the image of Ms. Akins's body flashed through my brain. I latched onto the five fingers and three fingers then realized what she might have been trying to say."

"Wow," Poindexter said. "Should I call RCPD and have them pick up Ms. Dupree?"

"Do you have any physical evidence that could link her to the murder?"

"We have a couple of unidentified blond hairs. We could try to get a DNA sample from her."

"Do we have enough for a court order?" Bobo asked.

Poindexter shook his head. "Probably not."

"Then give us a few more days," I said. "Go ahead and talk to Morris and let him know our theory. I can get you a hair sample from Jeopardy."

Though I wanted to move on this immediately, I willed myself to slow down. We still had no motive. Why would Jeopardy or Connie want to kill Sandy Akins? From what Barker said, Connie protected Jeopardy. How was Sandy Akins a threat to Jeopardy?

"Let's sleep on this tonight," I said to Bobo. "And tomorrow figure out our strategy to prove Jeopardy killed Sandy Akins."

The next day, we'd also find out who was trying to kill me and why.

Thirty

I had my alarm set for six, but I jumped out of bed at five-thirty after having an odd dream about swimming in a pool of greenbacks. Franklins, I think they were. The motive for the Sandy Akins murder broadsided me. Something Barker told us the day before. But my mind had been so clouded with faith questions, I'd let it fly in one ear and out the other.

A quick shave and shower. I put on a white shirt, a light brown linen suit, and a dark green tie with white dots. For that day's performance, I needed to wear dark brown wingtips as well. Not as comfy as the usual slip-ons I wore, but necessary. And the fedora—I had to leave it off, but I'd take it with me. I never understood why Columbo didn't wear a fedora. It would have completed his ensemble.

After a quick breakfast of a bagel with cream cheese, an apple, and coffee, I left the house and walked up the street to Mom's. Only six-thirty, but she always arose early.

I knocked.

She answered the door wearing a light blue, ankle-length housecoat. "Jake, what's wrong?"

"Why do you ask that?" I squeezed past her into the house.

She looked at her wrist, then glanced at the living room wall, where a round clock with giant digits and hands ticked. "It's way earlier than you normally get up."

"Important day, Ma. Hopefully closing a case." I wandered into her kitchen. She also had a vintage dining table, only hers looked more like it came out of a Victorian castle rather than a cheap diner. "Did you keep any of my toys from when I was a kid?"

She smiled. "Of course. Follow me." She led me out the side door and into the carport. Black tubs with yellow lids lined the back wall. She scanned them and pointed to one. "This one." She moved aside.

The tub labeled "Jake's toys" had two others on top of it and two others below it. I pulled the top one off.

"Holy cow. What's in this one?" I set it aside.

"Picture albums."

The next one, though heavy, paled compared to the picture albums. I lifted the tub with my toys in it and turned toward the steps to the kitchen door. Mom opened the door, and I carried the tub inside and put it on her table.

She grimaced but didn't say anything. What would some cobwebs and a few spiders hurt, right?

I pulled off the lid and rummaged through the toys until I found a red coffee can. I extracted the can and pried off its lid.

"Perfect." I put the coffee can down, put the lid back on the tub, and lifted it off the table. Mom again opened the kitchen door, and I put the tubs back as previously arranged.

Back in the kitchen, I put the lid on the coffee can and pecked Mom on the cheek. "Thanks, Ma. See you later."

She started to say something, but I left the house with the coffee can tucked under my arm. Inside my house, I grabbed my three-button raincoat and a stogie. All set for my grand finale. With everything thrown into the Delta 88, I headed to the office rehearsing what I'd say.

I arrived at Sledge Hammer Detective Agency slightly after seven. And no Bobo. Probably the first time I ever beat him to the office. On the way, I'd made two phone calls. Thomas Jorgenson and Phil Morris. They both agreed to come to our office at eight. Plenty of time to set up. Allison said she'd pass, still not wanting to be seen around me until the case was wrapped up. I told her we were close, and hopefully, in the next day or two, it would be over.

I shoved everything on my desk to the sides. From the coffee can, I pulled out six of my Batman action figures. More vintage stuff, though I'd played with them quite a bit, so certainly not in mint condition. I stood Cat Woman and Poison Ivy in the middle. In front of them, I laid the Joker. To the right, I stood Robin in his green and silver outfit with a black cap. Off to the left, I stood my green Batman with a black cape. And next to green Batman, I stood the Black Canary. The last figure I put out was Starfire. I laid her down next to the Joker. I stepped back to admire my setup.

The door opened and Bobo walked in. "Good morning. Play time?" He glanced at the coat rack and saw my raincoat hanging there. "Columbo time? Really?"

I grinned. "Detective Morris and our favorite lawyer will be here at eight. I thought about calling Jeopardy but figured that might be pushing it. Allison declined. And if I'd thought ahead, we could have put Barker on a virtual call." I turned back toward my desk and pulled out two more figures from the can. I placed Supergirl and Superman at the front of the grouping. I wished I had a Lois Lane action figure. Would have been more appropriate, but Supergirl sufficed. "Oh, and I asked Morris about bringing Braxton Anderson. He nixed that idea."

Bobo shook his head. "I'll get another chair."

"Good idea."

Bobo left the office. I had several empty offices in my building and some with old office chairs. While Bobo got the chair, I put on the raincoat and pulled the stogie out of my inside jacket pocket. For Bobo's sake, it would remain unlit throughout the performance. And for my sake at what Bobo would do to me if I lit it in the office.

Bobo returned with the chair. He arranged the three chairs equidistant around the desk, the entire time muttering to himself and shaking his head. He'd seen this from me before. I perched on the corner of the desk and waited.

At eight precisely, Thomas Jorgenson walked in wearing a dapper dark gray suit, maroon shirt, and patterned tie. And of course, he had on a dark gray fedora. "Good morning Mr. Sledge, Mr. Johnson." He took off his fedora. "Columbo, right? Love it. You're going to give us a howcatchem."

I smiled. Did I mention how much I liked this guy?

A minute later, Detective Phil Morris walked in. And with him, Lieutenant Kazminsky.

"You've got to be kidding me," Kazminsky said. "Now you're Columbo?"

"Who?" Morris asked.

"Someone way before your time." Kazminsky pointed at me. "And before *your* time."

"Reruns on streaming, Lieutenant. My mom loves that show. Columbo is one of my heroes. Along with Kojak, Spenser, and Dan Tanna. Gotta love streaming."

Bobo shook all their hands, then pulled my executive chair out from behind the desk and put it in line with the others. Kazminsky sat in that chair. I'd have to disinfect it later.

"Take a seat, everyone, and the show will begin." I put the stogie between the index and middle finger of my right hand then put my hands out palms up.

Kazminsky shot me a disgusted look. "And what's with the action figures?"

The others sat.

"All in due time, Lieutenant." I paused and then placed my right hand on my forehead. "This was a baffling case. Or is it really two cases? We'll close one of them out today, but maybe not the other one."

"Cut the impression, Sledge," Kazminsky said. "It's embarrassing."

My Peter Falk impression may have lacked quality, I admit. I switched to my own voice. It had been a while since I'd watched a show. I'd have to find the reruns again or go to Ma's and watch them on her VCR. She'd taped nearly all of them.

I angled myself so I could see my captive audience and the action figures. "Catwoman is Jeopardy Dupree. Poison Ivy is Concentration Dupree. I have them close together because, well, they are the same person." I paused. No comments from the peanut gallery.

"Black Canary is our unknown woman. I'm convinced that the woman who tried to run me over, the woman who went to River Bluffs and talked the old dude into attacking me, and the woman that hit Allison ..." I pointed to Supergirl. "Are the same woman."

"Don't forget the woman who picked up Braxton Anderson at the Fremont's," Bobo added.

I hunched a bit and pointed my right hand at Bobo, palm up. Back to my Peter Falk impression. "Good point, Mr. Johnson. Good point."

Another disgusted look from Kazminsky. Jorgenson smiled and nodded. Morris looked like a fourth grader in an advanced calculus class.

Back to my regular voice. "Yes, and that ties Black Canary to green Batman. Otherwise known as Braxton Anderson. But is that mysterious woman Connie Dupree?"

"Who?" Morris asked.

"Sorry, Concentration Dupree. She goes by Connie."

"Ah. And that's the alter-ego of Jeopardy Dupree, Barker Dupree's sister?"

"You are correct, sir. To round out the cast of characters, Robin represents Barker. The Joker is the late Daddy Dupree. Starfire is the late Sandy Akins. And of course, Superman is me."

Kazminsky let out an evil laugh. "I guess you didn't have a Penguin figure."

I ignored Kazminsky and pressed on. "Let me take you back a few years." I pointed to The Joker and to Poison Ivy. "Connie Dupree killed Daddy Dupree. Why, you ask? Connie Dupree emerged from inside Jeopardy's sensitive psyche because Daddy sexually abused her. I'm guessing things reached a boiling point a few years ago and Connie did him in."

"And how does that relate to the Sandy Akins murder?" Morris asked.

"Great question, young man." I again put my right hand to my forehead, then dropped it. "At River Bluffs where Barker Dupree spent several years, he and Sandy Akins fell in love. A strange pairing for sure, but they did. And three weeks ago, Barker Dupree left River Bluffs. And here's the linchpin in this whole case. He was going to ask Sandy Akins to marry him." I paused for dramatic effect and surveyed the audience.

Morris spoke up first. "Why is that the linchpin?"

Kazminsky answered for me. "Puts in question any motive Barker would have to kill her. Except he's a whack job, so that won't fly."

I put both hands out, palms up. "Except there's another piece of recent evidence that sheds light on the motive." I nailed Peter Falk with that sentence.

Even Kazminsky grinned.

I continued. "You see, Barker told us about a trust fund his dad set up for Jeopardy and Barker."

"I'm aware of that," Jorgenson said. "The first one to get married will get seventy-five percent of the late Mr. Dupree's estate. And the other one gets twenty-five percent upon marriage."

"And how much is that estate worth?" Kazminsky asked.

"Roughly four-hundred and fifty million dollars."

"Whoa." Morris looked at Kazminsky. "And if Barker and Sandy Akins got married, he'd get over three-hundred million, leaving Jeopardy only a little over a hundred million."

"Only," I said. "But yes, you're right."

"You're saying Jeopardy Dupree is the killer?" Kazminsky asked.

"Technically, I'm saying Connie Dupree is the killer. Again, she's protecting Jeopardy. She sees Barker getting that money as a threat to Jeopardy."

"But all the physical evidence points to Barker," Morris said.

I walked around behind the desk and picked up the Catwoman figure. "What color hair did Michelle Pfeiffer have as Catwoman?"

"Blond," answered Bobo.

I looked at Morris. "Did Poindexter talk to you yet?" I didn't think so given the early hour.

Morris shook his head and confirmed my hunch.

"Part of the evidence collected from the scene were several unidentified blond hairs. Jeopardy Dupree has blond hair." I paused again.

The amazed and stunned crowd was awed into silence. Okay, not really, but it was half a minute or so before anyone spoke.

"That's not enough for a court order," Kazminsky said. "We can't just show up at Ms. Dupree's house and ask for a hair sample."

I hunched over and gave Kazminsky my best Columbo stare. "Ah, Lieutenant. You're right. You can't." Another long dramatic pause. "But I can. And that's exactly what we're going to do today. Bobo and I will visit the lovely Ms. Dupree, and we'll bring a hair sample back to Poindexter. And when he matches that to the ones found at the scene, she's all yours."

Stunned silence again. Maybe stunned. Maybe awed. Or maybe tired of my act. Not sure.

"And you think she'll just let you in her house?" Kazminsky, ever the skeptic.

Bobo turned to him. "Yup. She will. Ms. Dupree has a thing for Jake."

Kazminsky shook his head. "Why?"

"One of the mysteries of the universe," Bobo answered.

Thanks, partner. I cleared my throat. "That's case number one. Let's now turn to case number two. This one still has us baffled. Why is this woman—" I picked up Black Canary. "—trying to kill me? And why did she attack Allison?"

"To keep you from proving Barker innocent?" Morris asked. "Are you sure that's not Connie Dupree?"

"Not sure, no. But she has short black hair. Jeopardy is a blonde."

"She could be wearing a wig, you moron." Kazminsky of course.

"Yes, she could. But this mystery woman is also considerably taller than Jeopardy and her voice is different. No hint of a Southern accent."

"Hired by Connie Dupree?" Morris asked.

"Yeah, we thought about that as well. Same for Braxton Anderson."

Detective Morris shifted in his chair. "Do you think Connie Dupree or this mystery woman killed Anthony Harris and tried to kill Anderson?"

I nodded. "Cleaning up. Getting rid of those who could identify her. Again, points to Connie Dupree or a friend of hers." I waved my arm over my desk. "That's it. Thanks for coming. We'll get a hair sample from Jeopardy and deliver to Poindexter as soon as we can."

Kazminsky stood. "Thanks for the show, Sledge. I hate to admit it, but it makes sense. Let us know if you need anything." He waved to Morris and walked to the door. He opened it, then looked over his shoulder. "But Barker Dupree stays at county until we have another viable suspect." He left the office.

Morris stood and nodded to me. I nodded back. He followed Kazminsky out the door.

That left Jorgenson, Bobo, and me.

"Impressive show, Mr. Sledge. And I thought the Peter Falk impressions were spot on."

"Thank you, sir."

Jorgenson stood. "However, keep in mind, not only is Barker Dupree my client, but so is Jeopardy. If you get her arrested on the murder of Sandy Akins, more than likely, I'll be representing her."

I hadn't thought of that.

"And as Ms. Dupree's future lawyer, I will tell you that if you do acquire a hair sample from her, it will not be admissible in court unless she willingly gives it to you knowing why she is doing so."

Major bummer. I didn't think telling Jeopardy we wanted to see if her hair matched one found at the murder scene would compel her to volunteer a sample. I hung my head. All that work for nothing.

Jorgenson put his fedora on and shook Bobo's hand. He reached out for mine. I grasped it. "But don't be too crestfallen. I shouldn't be telling you this, but I fear Ms. Dupree is a danger to herself and probably others. If the hair sample matches, more than likely, River City PD can use it to convince a judge to order a DNA sample from Ms. Dupree."

I let out a long sigh of relief and smiled. "Thank you for your honesty, Mr. Jorgenson."

He tipped his hat to me and left our office.

I waited a few minutes, then pulled out my cell phone and dialed Jeopardy.

"Mr. Sledge, how lovely to hear from you this morning."

"Ms. Dupree. I hope you're well, today."

"Peachy. To what do I owe the pleasure of your call?"

"Bobo and I would like to come over and brief you on a break in the case against your brother. I believe we can prove his innocence."

A sharp intake of breath and a little squeal. "Oh, that's too wonderful. Please do come. Anytime."

"See you in about fifteen minutes."

Thirty-One

Again, Bobo drove his Range Rover. I don't think he trusted me to drive, afraid that someone's muffler backfire would send me into a tailspin and I'd freak out. Whatever. It saved me gas and avoided the possibility someone would ram my car. Again.

"What's the game plan?" Bobo stopped for a red light at the corner of Willson Drive and Riverside Avenue. A straight shot south on Willson Drive to the outskirts of River City, then right on County Road 13 to the Dupree estate.

"Stick close to me. When Jeopardy comes close, accidentally shove me into her." I did air quotes for "accidentally."

"And?" Bobo accelerated.

"I'll grab a few strands of hair and yank."

"When she asks why you did that?"

"I'll stumble or something. Tell her it was an accident."

We cruised through the lights at W. Walnut Street and Westline Road. Light traffic for a Tuesday pre-lunch.

"What are we going to tell her about the case?"

"We have a suspect. We're gathering final evidence. Should have things wrapped up this week."

"Are you telling her that before or after you snag her hair?"

"Does it matter?"

"It could. Depends on if Connie knows what's going on when Jeopardy is herself and Connie is suppressed."

"Good point. Let's hope opportunity comes early."

"We'll pray opportunity comes early."

"Yeah, that too."

We drove in silence for ten minutes. We caught a red light at Eden Boulevard. Bobo slowed. One car ahead of us.

"You give any more thought to our conversation?"

"What conversation?" I looked out the side window. "We've had many."

"About your faith."

"Oh, that. A passing thought here or there." I didn't want to reveal the constant reel running through my head of everyone I knew who had a relationship with Jesus. Bobo would pounce on that like a mountain lion on a wounded fawn.

"I'm praying for you, Jake." He pressed the accelerator, and we continued south. "What do you think about Myron giving his life to Christ?"

What did I think? How could a just God accept that cockroach? Probably not best to voice that thought. "I don't know.

We need to see evidence that something changed and that he didn't just do it to make Alicia happy so she wouldn't throw him out again."

"Fair point. Let's go visit this weekend."

"Just show up unannounced."

Bobo said nothing.

"You didn't?"

He grinned.

"We're invited this weekend is what you're saying?"

"Maybe."

"Don't maybe me. Come on, big guy. Spit it out."

"Alicia is throwing a small party for Myron's baptism on Sunday. After the baptism we're going to her house."

"We?"

"Yes. We. We are going to Alicia's church. And we are going to Alicia's house after church. That 'we' would be you and me, and hopefully Allison, if we've wrapped the case."

Bobo slowed and turned onto County Road 13.

"You've been busy," I said.

He grinned again. And that was that. Sunday I'd be going to Alicia's church and then her house to celebrate her slimeball husband's baptism. Bobo rarely says we're doing something. Usually, he asks and may try to convince. But when he says it, well, it's happening. The only way I could refuse would be to leave town and hide. Not worth it. I'd probably like everyone there but Myron, anyway. And on the plus side, Allison might g o.

Bobo pulled into the driveway of the Dupree estate and parked near the house. We got out and walked up the steps to the front door.

When opportunity knocks, one must be ready to answer. Jeopardy opened the door, squealed, and threw herself at me. I caught her, stumbled back, grabbed several strands of blond hair, and yanked.

"Ouch." Jeopardy pushed away from me. "Why did you pull my hair?"

Heat spread over my cheeks. "Oh, sorry, my ring must have caught in your hair." I shoved my right hand into my pocket before she could see I wasn't wearing a ring. I could feel her hair between my fingers.

She narrowed her eyes at me but then smiled and jumped up and down several times. "I'm so excited that Barker will be freed." She turned and skipped into the house. "Please, come in. Tell me all about it."

What I really wanted to do was turn around and leave. We had what we came for. Lingering now would serve no good purpose and might cause issues. I started to turn. Bobo pushed me, and I stumbled inside.

"We'd be happy to tell you about it, Ms. Dupree," he said as he followed me in.

No escape. But I'd show him. I'd make him talk. Ha.

We followed Jeopardy to her sitting room. I never understood what a sitting room was. I sat in every room in my house.

As soon as we entered, Jeopardy bounced some more. "Tell me. Tell me. Tell me. Who killed that poor girl?"

I looked at Bobo. He looked at me. I shrugged. "Go for it, big guy."

He scrunched his brows, then smiled. "Unfortunately, Ms. Dupree, since it's an open case, we're not allowed to give any details."

"Ah. It's just little ol' me. I won't tell anyone."

And little ol' Connie, who might know everything you know. Or who might emerge and decide it's a great time to take a vacation to the Caymans.

"Sorry, Ms. Dupree. All we can say is that we have crucial physical evidence that will tie the suspect to the murder scene. Hopefully, it will be enough to exonerate Barker."

Good strategy, I thought. Use big words to totally confuse her. And it worked. She gave Bobo a questioning look. He remained silent.

She shrugged. "That's so exciting. I'm happy for Barker. My poor brother has suffered so much. Can I get you both something to drink? Lemonade, maybe?"

Maybe hard lemonade. I also kept that to myself, not wanting a bruised shoulder from Bobo's massive fist. We both shook our heads.

I finally spoke. "We still need to go downtown today. Drop something off. Otherwise, we'd take you up on your kind offer." See, I can play nice as well.

"Okay. Will you see Barker, today?"

"No, sorry. We saw him yesterday. He's at the county lockup facility in Lafayette."

"Oh? And how was he?"

"Still sticking to his story. But he doesn't know what we've found out. Unless his lawyer has told him."

"Mr. Jorgenson knows?"

"Yes."

Anger with a dash of hatred flashed through Jeopardy's eyes. She said nothing but stared hard at me.

Bobo jumped in. "Are you okay, Ms. Dupree?"

Jeopardy shook her head. Her eyes softened. "What was that, Mr. Johnson?"

"Are you okay?"

"Peachy. Why?"

I looked at Bobo. He looked at me. His turn to shrug.

"Time to go, big guy." I stepped forward. "How about another hug. I'll try not to pull your hair this time."

I didn't think it possible to smile as big as Jeopardy did. Almost Joker-like. Kind of creepy. She stepped forward and threw her arms around me. I hugged her back.

"Thank you so much, Mr. Sledge."

I pried her arms from around me, then tipped my hat to her. "We'll see you later, Ms. Dupree. And at that time, I'm hoping the case will be wrapped up."

She shook Bobo's hand. "Mr. Johnson, always a pleasure."

"Likewise, ma'am."

We left her house. She stood on the stoop. I watched her through the mirror as she watched us until we went around a bend in her long driveway. Nothing happened.

I'm not sure what I expected. Her to morph into some hideous creature? I pulled my hand out of my pocket and waved the strands of long blonde hair.

"Nice." Bobo turned onto County Road 13 and drove to the River City PD. I wondered if Connie and / or Jeopardy felt the nails driving into their coffin.

Thirty-Two

After dropping off the hair sample with Poindexter, Bobo and I grabbed lunch at Bob's Drive-in on the way back to the office. I scarfed down two double burgers. Bobo ate a chicken sandwich. We split a bag of fries, though Bobo ate more, as usual. And we had milkshakes. Yes, both of us. Mine chocolate, Bobo's strawberry. No diet soda.

We spent several hours in the office twiddling our thumbs, until Bobo had enough boredom. Next stop, the gym, where we worked out, then departed to our respective houses. Another TV dinner night. This one Salisbury steak. Woohoo. I cleaned the cardboard container of everything edible and tossed it.

Off to the living room, where I collapsed into my recliner and flipped on the sports channel. Boring. I surfed until I found the Royals' game. They were playing the White Sox. About the seventh inning I drifted off with the score tied three apiece.

I dreamed that a beautiful woman knocked on my door. When I opened my door, her back was to me. I reached for her, assuming it was Allison. She turned around. A hideous, scarred, and disfigured face. The woman laughed at me and started knocking again on the door. I awoke and realized the second set of knocks actually happened as a third set followed. Then someone rang my doorbell. I contemplated getting my gun. Maybe the zombie apocalypse had started. I decided to risk it .

Another set of soft knocks. I opened the door.

"Mr. Sledge, how are you this fine evening?"

"Jeopardy?" I studied her eyes. They seemed to smile with the rest of her. She wore a beige pantsuit, right hand in the jacket pocket.

"What are you doing here?"

She pushed past me and walked into the house. A musky-sweet smell.

"How quaint. I thought you were a big-time football player. Such a small housc."

I closed the front door. "What are you doing here?"

She whirled. Her eyes burned with a hard edge. She spoke with little hint of her Southern accent. "I came to see you, of course." She walked toward me.

I sidestepped. She kept coming. I backed up until I hit the hallway wall. She didn't stop until her body touched mine.

"Maybe you should back up a little?"

"And why would I do that, Mr. Sledge?" This time she spoke with an exaggerated accent.

"Please?"

"Ah, Mr. Sledge. I know you have feelings for me." She reached her left arm up and wrapped it around my neck.

I started to pry her arm away when I felt a jab in my thigh. She smiled. With her right hand, she tossed the syringe away behind her. My eyes grew heavy. I teetered. She stepped away. I tried to take a step, but I'm not sure if I ever did. Things went black.

I halfway opened my eyes and jerked my head up, then opened my eyes all the way. I tried to move. My hands were tied behind my back. Zip ties bound each of my ankles to a kitchen chair leg. Jeopardy, or should I say, Connie, sat to my right. She grinned at me.

"Concentration Dupree, I presume?"

"You are a brilliant detective. Long time, no see Mr. Sledge." She grinned again. "However, we've spoken on the phone recently. Several times."

I rattled the chair. Moved my hands. The binds held. I could probably break the chair, but I decided to let things play out a little longer.

"Not that long ago. I saw a flash of you earlier today, at your house."

Another grin. "That you did, but I let Jeopardy come back."

"It must have been a struggle to get me into this chair."

She nodded. "It would have been, but I had help."

I looked around as much as I could.

"They're gone. I sent them to do something else for me."

"Were they wearing their fake deputy uniforms?"

She stood and leaned against the edge of the table. "My, my, you are a good detective. I believe you might have actually figured everything out. And that's why I'm here. We couldn't let things go any further."

She leaned toward me. "Jeopardy isn't too observant. But I am. You don't wear rings. You pulled my hair on purpose, didn't you?"

My turn to grin. Was the "we" Connie and Jeopardy? Or Connie and the men she was using?

"I have a question for you before you kill me."

"Kill you? Oh, Mr. Sledge, much to my disappointment, I can't kill you. As long as you meet my one condition."

"Can't or won't?"

She paced the kitchen. "If you do what Jeopardy wants, it's can't. If not, it's will."

She returned to the chair, put her elbows on the table, placed her chin on her fists, and stared at me.

"What does Jeopardy want me to do?"

"Marry her, of course."

That statement hit me like a two-by-four to the side of the head. But it also knocked all the dangling chain links together. All but one.

"That was you in the SUV who tried to run me over, wasn't it?"

She nodded, glee dancing in her eyes.

"If Jeopardy wants to marry me, why did you try to kill me?"

"That was before Jeopardy convinced me to let her work on you."

It all came together. Connie Dupree had been all of them: the woman in the SUV, the woman at River Bluffs, and the woman who attacked Allison. And why did Jeopardy want to marry me? Other than my irresistible charm and stunning good looks? The reasons went along with why Connie Dupree killed Sandy Akins. Over three hundred million reasons. If Jeopardy married first, she got the lion's share of Daddy Dupree's fortune. Mystery solved.

Unfortunately, Sandy Akins's murderer had me tied to a chair. All I had to do was agree to marry Jeopardy.

"And if I agree to marry you, or Jeopardy, you'll let me go. And after you let me go, what's to stop me from turning you over to the police?"

She flashed me a Cheshire Cat grin and pulled out her cell phone.

"Remember the two that helped me get you into that chair?"

After a few stabs at the phone, she pointed the screen at me. What looked like two county police officers sat in a car. The one in the passenger side held his arm out with his phone pointing at them.

"Yeah, so what? The same two that extracted Barker. Big deal. Are they going to beat me up?" I would have loved the opportunity to go toe-to-toe with them. They didn't stand a chance.

She shook her head. Into the phone she said, "Point the phone the other way."

The fake officer did, and my heart rate doubled. The phone screen showed Alicia's house. She pulled the phone away and stabbed at it, then pocketed it.

"Those two are not nice men. Both have long histories of violence. If you agree to marry Jeopardy and try to walk away from it, then— "

"Yeah, I get it." Time for plan B. The only problem was I didn't have a plan B.

My phone played "Who Let the Dogs Out?"

"What's that?"

"My ringtone for Bobo. Remember him? Big guy. Seems all sweet and everything. Until you threaten someone he loves. And boy does he love my sister."

The song continued. She picked up my phone and looked at it. The song stopped. She put it on the table. "What's it going to be, Mr. Sledge?"

"If I say no, do you think Jeopardy will let you kill me? I think she likes me."

"Likes? She's madly in love with you. But you misunderstand something. Jeopardy isn't in charge. She's my other personality. I'm the real person."

I didn't see that coming. Nor did I know if it was true. Could the other personality think it's the real personality? I'd have to ask Dr. Charnow about that. If I got the chance.

"We are Family" played on my phone.

"And who's that?" Connie snatched the phone off the table. "Ah, your sister."

I nodded. "Bobo probably called her to see if I was there."

She shrugged and put the phone back on the table.

"Bobo's next move will be to come here and see if I'm okay."

Connie scratched her head and frowned. "We can't have that." She picked my phone up again and pointed it at me.

It took me a second too long to understand what she was doing. She turned the phone back around and started stabbing at the screen.

"What should we say to Bobo and to your sister to let them know you're okay?"

I sighed. Stupid face ID. But an idea hit me. "To Bobo just say 'Hey Bobo, sorry I missed your call. Was asleep on my easy chair. What did you want?"

She pecked away. I hoped she'd type verbatim what I said.

"Sent. And your sister?"

"Sorry, I was sleeping. Will call you tomorrow. Give Jules a kiss for me."

More stabbing at my phone. "Sent."

"Can I have some water? Not sure what you injected in me, but I'm getting pretty dry."

She went to my kitchen cabinet. While she opened them looking for a glass, I tried to get my hands free. Since she used zip-ties on my legs, I figured the same on my hands. I strained trying to break the tie. She turned with a glass in hand. I stopped straining.

"Open up."

I thought about using my head to spill the water on her, then stand and bowl her over. She pushed the glass to my lips. I opened my mouth and drank. She pulled away and sat down.

"How long do I have to make this life-altering decision?"

She placed the glass on the table and looked at my phone. "Bobo says 'Okay.'"

I shrugged.

She pulled her own phone back out of her jacket pocket. "It's nine-twenty. At ten one of three things will happen." She put the phone back and stared at me. Then she lost focus on me and stared beyond me. Her eyes came back into focus, and she shook her head.

"What will happen?"

"Huh? Oh yeah, three possible paths. You agree to marry Jeopardy. Those two disappear and no one gets hurt. You don't agree, and I call those two and they come here to deal with you."

I chuckled.

"What's so funny?"

"You think those two dipsticks can take me?"

"You're tied up."

"They're going to carry me out on my chair?"

"I have another hypodermic."

Good to know. I played a couple scenarios through my head generally involving me charging her, knocking her down, and somehow, using my mouth to get the hypodermic and injecting her. All of the scenarios ended up with me failing. Even if I got it, how would I take the cap off, stick it in her, and plunge it using my mouth? More than one scenario ended with me injecting myself.

"And the third case?"

"I don't call them at ten and they do nasty things to your sister, her husband, and your niece."

I lunged forward in my chair, shoving the table into her. She rocked back in her chair and almost tipped over but caught herself.

"Nice try." She shoved the table back at me and pinned it against me. "What's your answer?"

"I still have forty minutes."

"Thirty-eight."

I went out on a limb, and in hindsight probably too thin of a limb with the possibility of it breaking and me falling to my death, but I was angry.

"What's to stop me from agreeing to marry you and then strangling you in your sleep one night. Then I'd hunt down those two dipsticks and break every bone in their bodies."

She nodded. "I tried to convince Jeopardy you might become violent. She's convinced you're not that way, and you'll eventually come to love her like she loves you."

I dropped my head. "I think I'm going to puke." What she said rang true. I don't think I could kill a woman in cold blood. Breaking every bone in those two fake deputies? That I'd happily do. I could have justifiably killed Connie the last time she attacked me, but I didn't. Knocked her silly, sure.

"Don't think I'll clean you up, if you do."

I didn't bother to look up, and I didn't puke, though my stomach churned and bile burned my throat. The options spun through my brain. If I said no, I'd probably die at the hands of either this psychotic woman or the two fake deputies. If I said yes, Allison would kill me. Probably not, but certainly our relationship would end. Maybe we could move to Utah.

I sighed and looked up. "If I agree to marry Jeopardy, what happens to you. Do you go away for good?"

She frowned. "Jeopardy asked me that same thing."

"And?"

"I promised I would stay away when you were around."

That was something, I supposed. Jeopardy as only Jeopardy, though a conniving little imp, I could tolerate.

"Still thinking." I sat and stared at her. Every so often I glanced at the clock on the stove.

At 9:30, Connie stood and paced the kitchen.

At 9:35, someone knocked on the front door. Bobo?

"Who's that?" She put her right hand into her pocket.

"How would I know? Answer it and find out."

She plastered herself against the wall and peeked through the opening to the living room. I have three diamond-shaped windows at the top of the door. I strained to look at the door and could barely see it out of the corner of my eye. The motion detection light had come on.

"I don't see anyone."

Therefore, not Bobo standing on the porch waiting for someone to answer. Only someone under five-six or so could stand there and not be seen. Oh, no, not Alicia. Please don't be Alicia.

Another knock.

My front window had heavy curtains. I always kept them drawn since I rarely spent daylight hours at home.

Several rapid knocks sounded.

Could be mom. I feared Alicia may have called Mom to come check on me.

The back door burst inward, and Bobo filled the entryway.

Connie turned.

"Watch out, she has a needle." I felt like an idiot yelling that. Gun, knife, bomb. Sure. But needle?

People think because Bobo is so big he's slow. People are wrong. He covered the ten or so feet between him and Connie in two giant steps. Connie pushed off the wall and brought her right hand out. She stabbed at Bobo and caught him in the stomach. He backhanded her and knocked her against the wall.

Her head hit the frame of the doorway. A loud crack. She slid to the floor.

"You feel faint?" I asked Bobo. I wanted him to get me loose before he collapsed.

"No, why?"

"She stuck you."

He bent over and extracted the hypodermic from Connie's hand. She moaned. Her head lolled to the side. Bobo came over to me and stuck me in the shoulder.

"Hey. What the heck..."

No sharp poke.

He grinned and showed me the still capped needle. I laughed.

The front door opened. Detective Morris walked in, obviously off duty as he wore jean shorts and a T-shirt. Behind him came two uniformed officers, one a man, and one a woman.

Bobo retrieved a paring knife from a drawer and cut me loose.

The clock on the stove said nine fifty. Alicia!

Thirty-Three

I jumped off the chair and ran to the bedroom, grabbed my shoulder holster, and ran back into the kitchen.

"Let's go. We have to get to Alicia's in less than nine minutes."

"Why?" Bobo asked.

The female officer cuffed Ms. Dupree and lifted her up.

"What's going on?" Jeopardy's Southern accent returned.

The officer told her she was under arrest and led her out of the house.

"Come on." I walked toward the back door, which now hung by one hinge with a chunk missing from where the deadbolt had been. Small price to pay for Bobo's rescue.

Bobo grabbed my arm. "Leave the gun here."

"Are you crazy? There are two bad men outside Alicia's house."

"Leave the gun here."

We entered a stare down. Something I never won against the big guy.

"Are you armed?" I asked.

Bobo nodded. I trotted back to the bedroom and tossed the shoulder holster with my .45 onto the bed, then trotted back through the kitchen to the back door. Bobo was talking with Morris. I heard him say something about calling in backup to go to Alicia's.

Bobo followed me. "I'll drive."

Still didn't trust me with firearms or a vehicle.

"Where's your Range Rover?" I stood in the driveway.

"Parked a block away."

I ran down the sidewalk to his SUV. He trotted after me.

"I'm sure she's fine." Bobo unlocked the car and got in.

I jumped in as well. "Drive!"

Bobo started the Range Rover and pulled away from the curb. He drove the speed limit.

"Go faster."

He sped up to five over the speed limit. Not exactly what I meant.

"I guess you understood that text message. Connie Dupree sent it."

Bobo slowed and coasted through the stop sign. One more mile to Riverview Road, then north about three miles to Alicia's.

"To be honest, I was annoyed at first."

Bobo hates it if anyone says "Hey, Bobo." His father used to say that every night when he came home from work. He'd walk in the house, throw his arms open and say, "Hey, Bobo." Young Bobo would run into his arms. But through the course of the evening, Bobo's dad became drunk, and usually beat his mom, or Bobo, until Bobo grew bigger than his dad.

In eighth grade, his father went after his mother. Bobo stopped him. His dad slugged Bobo in the mouth. Bad mistake. Bobo pounded his father nearly to death. His mother stopped Bobo from finishing the job. That ended his dad's reign of terror. He moved out after that and died of a heart attack about a year later.

"Alicia called me and told me you'd sent the code for being in trouble."

During our last case, my niece Julia had been kidnapped as a way to get me to stop pursuing the bad guys. After I rescued Julia, Alicia and I set up a distress signal. If either of us texted the other using "Jules" as her daughter's name, that meant the one who texted was in trouble.

Bobo stopped at the light, looked both ways, and turned left onto Riverview Road against the red light. "I then called River City PD and asked for Morris, who wasn't working tonight. But I got his home number. He agreed to meet me at your house. I figured it would be those two fake deputies." He stopped at a stop sign and looked over at me. "Didn't think a woman would get the best of you." He grinned.

"Funny. She stuck me with a hypodermic and knocked me out. Go a little faster, would you. Connie said if she doesn't call those two fake deputy clowns by ten that they will mess up Alicia and family."

Bobo floored it and we flew up Riverview Road. Two lights and we made them both. We came up over a slight hill before Alicia's house. Red and blue lights strobed the neighborhood. At least four patrol cars blocked the street. Another unmarked sedan sat near the curb across from Alicia's. Neighbors stood on their lawns watching the show. Bobo drove as close as he could, then parked on the curb.

I jumped out of the SUV and sprinted toward Alicia's. A woman officer put a hand up and told me to stop. At all of five-feet-seven-inches and maybe one-twenty, she wasn't going to stop me. I blew past her and ignored her yelling.

Alicia flew out of the house and ran down her steps toward me. When she reached me, she leaped into me. I caught her and hugged her close.

"Jake, you're alright. I was so worried."

I put her down and held her at arm's length. "You okay? Is Julia okay?" I didn't bother asking about Myron. Probably should have, but oh well.

"Yes, everyone's fine."

"What happened?"

Bobo joined us as did the woman officer. I glanced at her and muttered an apology. She waved it off and walked back to her post.

"After I called Bobo because of your text, I looked outside and saw a car sitting with what looked like two uniformed officers." She pointed at the sedan.

From across Old Post Road two officers, one in a River City PD uniform, the other in a county uniform escorted a man who also wore a county uniform.

Alicia continued. "I sent Myron out to ask them what they were doing. He came back and told me they said they were on a stakeout of someone in the neighborhood. I called Bobo back and told him that."

"And I warned her that they may be fake," Bobo said. "I asked her to describe the car. When she told me it was an unmarked car, I told her they probably were fake. Uniformed officers don't do stakeouts in unmarked cars."

From across the street and one house down from Alicia's another pair of officers, again one River City, one county, escorted another man in a county uniform. Both trios reached different squad cars about the same time and shoved the fake county officers into the back seats.

"After Bobo hung up, I called the county police number and asked them if they had any officers staking out our neighborhood. The person on the phone said no. And I told them there were two county police officers who told us they were on a stakeout. The lady on the phone said they'd send someone to investigate."

"Where's Julia?" I asked.

"In bed. It's after ten. She slept through the whole thing."

A tall, beefy county police officer joined our group. "Ms. Brown, thank you for calling us. Not sure what those two Bozos were doing, but we'll take them in for impersonating an officer and try to find out."

"County or River City?" I asked.

"County, since it's us they were pretending to be. And you are?"

I stuck out my hand, which the officer shook. "Jake Sledge. I'm Alicia's brother."

He nodded then looked up at Bobo. "You I recognize. Bobo Johnson, right?"

Bobo grinned and shook the officer's hand.

"Why are you here?"

"Ms. Brown is like family to me. Came to make sure she was alright."

"Cool. Ms. Brown, we'll let you know if we need anything else." The officer nodded to Alicia who smiled back. He walked away.

"Anyway," Alicia said, "About ten minutes later, all these police cars came and surrounded the sedan. Their lights were flashing, but no sirens. The two in the car took off running. One north across Old Post and the other into the houses across the street. The four police cars stopped, and men jumped out chasing them."

Alicia hugged me again. "I was so worried about you. What happened?"

Before I could answer, Bobo said, "A woman zip-tied him to a chair."

"Really?"

"She drugged me first. And those two fake deputies helped her put me in the chair."

"What woman? Not Allison."

"No, Jeopardy Dupree. Or I should say Connie Dupree. Her brother is the one accused of murdering that nursing assistant from River Bluffs."

"Oh."

Myron walked out of the house toward us. He spoke briefly to one of the River City officers, then joined us.

"Glad to see you're okay, Jake. Alicia was worried." Myron put his hand out.

I stared at it for a couple of seconds. Bobo elbowed me. It hurt. I grasped Myron's hand. "Likewise. Glad you all are okay."

Bobo said, "Brave of you to approach those two."

"We thought they were cops." Myron looked at me. "Alicia said you're coming to church Sunday for my baptism. That's cool."

I nodded. Like I had a choice.

"We're having a get together after. I hope you'll come to that as well."

"And bring Allison," Alicia said. "I want to meet her."

Now I really didn't have a choice. But at least with the case wrapped up, I'd get to see Allison again. And I'm sure she'd be happy to be invited to a church to see a baptism and then to my sister's house. With her there, I figured I could tolerate it.

Thirty-Four

I drove the Delta 88 into the parking lot behind River City Christian Church and parked. About fifty other cars partially filled the parking lot, though we were a little early. We had the top up because Allison didn't want her hair messed up. It didn't matter to me. Curly locks falling to her shoulders or a rat's-nest of blond hair, she looked beautiful. I turned in my seat and stared at her.

"What?"

"Do we have to go in? Let's just drive west until we hit the ocean."

She blushed, smiled, and patted my arm, which still gripped the steering wheel. Then, to my disappointment, she slid her hand off my arm and turned the ignition key, shutting down the purr of the Delta 88.

"It's your brother-in-law. I know you have mixed feelings for him. But you need to be there for your family."

Mixed feelings? Nothing mixed about them. I detested the worm. "For Alicia and Julia's sake, I guess you're right."

"And after the party—"

I frowned.

"After the party that we are going to, then maybe we can talk about going west."

A smile pulled across my face. Hope!

I pushed open my door, swaggered to her side, opened her door, and bowed with a grand gesture. She stepped out, grabbed the sides of her emerald-green shin-length dress, and curtsied.

The dress featured a high collar, short sleeves, and a bow at the neck draped down the front. Ultra conservative, but to me more gorgeous than any revealing outfit I'd ever seen.

During our phone conversation the night before, when I broke the news that we'd solved the case, leaving out the part about Jeopardy wanting to marry me, she mentioned she'd wear her green dress. Of course, that meant I had to wear my green windowpane sports jacket, with a light green dress shirt, tan pants, and the light green fedora. We were a couple of leprechauns.

I put my arm out, and she hooked hers around my elbow. We walked to the red brick fortress of a church, overdressed compared to the other people entering. Inside, we passed through a small foyer and entered the main worship area. I stopped. Oak benches with brown fabric pads were aligned in two columns of ten. It didn't look quite as comfortable as the chairs at Bobo's church. In the second row from the front, I noticed three familiar heads: Myron on the end, then Julia, then Alicia.

"You gonna stand here all day, or go sit?" said a deep, growly voice from behind.

I turned and grinned at Bobo, then put my hand out to the one and only Liliana Goodhue, who looked stunning as always, in a dress not too dissimilar to Allison's, only Liliana's was dark brown.

"Ms. Goodhue, so nice to see you. Though I question your judgment hanging with this unsavory character."

"Mr. Sledge." She grabbed my hand, shook it once, dropped it, and turned to Allison. "Ms. Rogers, a pleasure to see you again. I heard about the attack. How are you doing?"

Allison shook Liliana's hand. "The headaches are gone. Doing well, thank you. And you?"

"Wonderful."

Bobo hugged Allison. Then to me he said, "Go on. Say hi to your family."

"Yessir." I walked down the center aisle toward the front, Allison's arm tucked around my elbow.

About halfway there, Alicia turned around. She jumped up and ran to me, throwing her arms around my midsection. I hugged her back, wondering if the church allowed running in the worship area.

"I'm so glad you came. Thank you so much. It means the world to me."

With that greeting, how could I feel annoyed about being there?

Julia ran up the aisle. "Uncle Bobo, Uncle Jake." At least she hugged me first, then Bobo.

Myron stood and waited for us to reach the row.

Allison saved me from having to say something to Myron, as I had no idea what you say to a person about to be baptized.

"You must be Myron. I'm Allison. Praise the Lord for your confession of faith."

Myron shook Allison's hand. "Nice to meet you."

I waited for a jab about her being too beautiful or sweet, or something for me. It didn't come from Myron.

Bobo stepped forward and also shook Myron's hand. "Congratulations. I've been praying for you."

"Thank you, Bobo." The look in Myron's eyes simultaneously conveyed a little fear and a lot of relief.

Bobo put a hand on Allison's shoulder. "Hard to believe, isn't it, that this wonderful woman is dating him?" He pointed at me.

Everyone laughed. Well, almost everyone. I didn't. Thanks, partner. To his credit, Bobo broke any tension, but at my expense.

Liliana introduced herself and we all sat. Me next to Alicia. I had to push Bobo out of the way. Not an easy feat. Then Allison, Liliana, and Bobo on the end.

"Can I sit on Uncle Jake's lap?"

Alicia shook her head. "I don't think he wants you crawling all over him."

"I don't mind."

Julia jumped down from the pew. She gave Alicia a wide berth. Smart girl. And she jumped onto my lap, where she sat until the music started.

In contrast to Bobo's church, the music consisted of a man and a woman. The man played an acoustic guitar and the woman sang. Fantastic voice.

We stood, and everyone but yours truly sang along with the woman.

After the congregation sang several songs, the pastor, a man in his late fifties, with perfect salt and pepper hair, walked behind the ornate, oak pulpit. He opened a thick Bible and put it down.

"Folks, we are blessed today that a new convert, who was saved in this very church, is going to be baptized. But first, let's hear from God's Word. Please open your Bibles to Philippians chapter 2 as we continue our study of this marvelous book."

People around the church opened their Bibles or their Bible app. I did nothing until Allison elbowed me, then put her phone between us, opened to an app displaying the Bible where the pastor had said. I read ahead and immediately felt woozy and uncomfortable. It grew even worse when the pastor started preaching.

"Friends, we live in a world consumed with self. A world that says you be you, and don't let anyone tell you otherwise. But friends, that is not what our Lord teaches us. Last week, we made it to verses one and two. Today, we'll look at verses three through eight."

For the next half hour I listened to the pastor, who I'm sure got my life history from Alicia, speak directly at me. His words pierced my heart. Was I really that selfish? I served others. But did I serve others for their sake or mine? I could be humble. But maybe being humble isn't something we turn on and off. Maybe what this dude conveyed from the Bible was that humility is a state of being. All the time.

The torture finally ended. Myron got up and walked to the side of the church and through a door. The dark blue curtain behind the pastor opened revealing a water-filled tub with a plexiglass front. The preacher explained the reason behind baptism. Being raised to a new life. Would Myron really come out of the tub a new person? For Alicia's sake, I hoped so. And for Myron's sake.

Myron and a young, beefy man, who I learned was the youth pastor, climbed into the tub. Myron had changed into shorts and a T-shirt. The youth pastor wore hip waders over his clothes. Clever. He positioned himself alongside Myron, put his hand on his back, and raised his other hand. He said something to Myron we could not hear. Myron nodded, then gripped his n ose.

"We are buried in death." The youth pastor let Myron down backwards into the water until he was completely submerged.

"And raised to new life in Christ." He lifted Myron up out of the water.

Myron threw his arms into the air, then hugged the youth pastor.

My mind wanted to scream, "Faker." But my heart didn't allow me to. And much to my dismay, tears formed. I swiped the back of my hand over my eyes.

Allison grasped my arm and hugged herself to my side. I looked down at her. She smiled. A sad smile, one with hope that I'd be following Myron soon. Would I?

We drove as a mini caravan to Alicia's. Myron, Alicia, and Julia squeezed between them led in Myron's ten-year-old pickup truck. Followed by Bobo and Liliana in his Range Rover. Finally, me in the Delta 88. The top down, Allison's hair flying in the wind. Repeatedly, I checked myself to keep my eyes on the road, as my gaze drifted to her. She turned and smiled at me, then motioned for me to watch the road. Running into Bobo's Range Rover would probably not end well.

We made it to Alicia's house without incident. I jumped out and opened Allison's door once again.

She climbed out and pecked me on the cheek. "Try to enjoy yourself. Be nice."

I pasted a smile on my face and followed her into the house. Mom had stayed back and prepared for the gathering. She waved to us all as we entered the house. A bunch of guys that looked similar to Myron gathered around Myron in the living room, slapping his back, shaking his hand, jostling him. Mechanics from where he worked, I surmised, being the brilliant detective that I am.

The rest of the crowd gathered in the kitchen. I stood in the hall. Allison hugged Alicia then chatted with Liliana. Bobo hugged Mama Sledge, Alicia, and Julia. He then joined the group of guys in the living room. His presence tripled the decibels from that group. Bobo shook all their hands, grinning ear to ear, always the sucker for fans.

Someone said to Myron, "You know Bobo Johnson, and you never told us."

I moved to the living-room side of the kitchen entrance to listen to Myron's response. What would the worm say, given the history between him and Bobo?

"Yeah, well, Bobo is Jake's partner."

"That's right. You and The Hammer don't get along, do you?"

I liked that dude, whoever he was. He remembered my nickname.

"We didn't," Myron said. "I'm hoping that will change."

I sighed. What was I supposed to do with that?

Alicia leaned out the doorway, glanced at me, then at the living room. "Lunch is ready. Let's go." When Alicia speaks, people move. And they did.

I let everyone go past me. A couple acknowledged who I was and shook my hand. Bobo glanced at me but got in the food line in the kitchen. I entered the empty living room, sat on the edge of the sofa, and stared at the television. A pre-season NFL game was on, but I don't remember the teams.

Julia approached me. "Uncle Sledge, are you coming in for lunch? Mama made chicken salad." Her smile puffed her pudgy cheeks.

"In a bit. I'm waiting for the line to die down."

"Okay." She ran back into the kitchen.

Five minutes later, Allison came out with a cardboard plate loaded with a sandwich and various raw vegetables. She sat next to me and stared at me.

"What?"

"I know this is hard for you, from what you've told me about Myron." She nibbled her sandwich.

Alicia's chicken salad is to die for. My mouth watered. My stomach rumbled. I sighed.

Allison swallowed. "Jesus can change anyone's life. Even Myron's. Give him a chance."

I shook my head. She frowned.

"It's not Myron," I said. "I'm happy for him. I hope this new faith really does change his life." I left off the "for his sake."

"Then what is it? Why are you sitting here alone?"

"I'm not alone. You're here. My plan worked." I forced a grin.

"Ha-ha. Nice try. What's bothering you?"

I stared at the television and sighed again.

"Look at me."

Not really a difficult request to grant. I looked at Allison. She'd smoothed her hair. I rather liked the wind-tossed look she had when she stepped out of the car. But flowing over her shoulders worked, too. I ran my gaze over the rest of her.

"My eyes, Jake. Look me in the eyes and tell me what is going on."

I raised my gaze to her eyes but said nothing. Thoughts swirled in my mind. I lost myself in the sparkle of her eyes, allowing myself to sink into their depths.

"Speak."

I clawed back to the surface. "Fine. What Bobo said at the church was a joke. I get that. His attempt to lighten the mood. He's good at that. But I can't get the thought out of my head. Why are you dating me? According to the preaching, I'm a self-centered, self-serving sinner with no hope. Why do you hang with me?"

Moisture filmed her eyes. She put her plate down on the coffee table then put her hand on my arm. "There is always hope. You're not that way at all around me. I see who you can be. Especially if you come to Jesus. And no, I'm not trying to force you into a decision."

I nodded.

She sucked in a deep breath. "Just be with others like you are with me."

"But I don't feel the same about others as I do about you."

She blushed and squeezed my arm. "See? It's not that hard for you."

I stroked her cheek with the back of my hand.

She grabbed my hand and kissed it, then flashed a stern look. "Now get in there and be with your family. And be nice."

What choice did I have?

Thirty-Five

My alarm went off. I reached over and hit the big red stop on my cell phone clock app. I'd been wide awake since around four. In and out of weird dreams about Myron, Jesus, church, Allison, and even Jeopardy. In all of them, I did what I wanted to do, and someone got hurt or angry or saddened. All my fault.

I shuffled into the bathroom and did my thing. A quick breakfast of the usual: toasted bagel, cream cheese, orange juice. I glanced at my phone. Ninety minutes before my appointment. No use going to the office first. I tossed my gray sports jacket and black fedora onto the sofa and fell into my easy chair. Black chinos and a black collarless shirt completed my outfit. Fitting color for my first counseling session. It felt like I was attending a funeral. And maybe I was. Maybe the real me had died and needed resurrecting.

"Working in a Coal Mine" played on my cell phone. I muted the volume on the television and pressed the talk button.

"This is Sledge."

"Mr. Sledge, it's Phil Morris."

"Detective. How are you? And please don't call me mister. Makes me feel old."

Morris chuckled. "Deal, Sledge. And how are you doing? Haven't talked to you since your ordeal."

"Doing okay. Happy the case is over."

"Speaking of the case, I have good news and I have bad news."

"Lay it on me, Detective." I let the footrest down on the easy chair.

"The good news is the APA has agreed Barker Dupree isn't our man. She dropped the charges."

APA was the assistant prosecuting attorney. In this case, the one and only queen of the law, Liliana Goodhue. I wondered if Bobo had any influence over that decision.

"Great to hear. And the bad news?"

"There's more good news. A judge granted a warrant based on the matching hair sample. We collected DNA from Ms. Dupree. The results confirmed a match. But ... that's not enough for the PA to charge her."

Wow, this one went all the way up to the prosecuting attorney. "Why?"

"That's all we have. The PA said no way he was going to battle against Jorgenson on first-degree murder with a hair sample and nothing else."

Disappointing, but I saw the logic. Jorgenson could argue Jeopardy had visited his brother's future fiancée. No witnesses placed Jeopardy there on the day of the murder. The mysterious woman on the video looked nothing like Jeopardy.

"Nothing found searching her house?"

"Nope. If she killed Ms. Akins, she disposed of any evidence. But ... there is more good news. The PA did agree to charge Ms. Dupree with home invasion and aggravated assault. He also asked me to ask you if you want to charge her with attempted murder."

"No. She didn't try to kill me. She wanted to marry me."

Morris laughed.

"You find that funny, Detective?"

"Don't you?"

I had to admit I did. "Anything else?"

"Yes. The PA is also charging her with conspiracy and attempted murder of the receptionist at River Bluff. And he's handing her case over to the feds around the kidnapping of Barker from River Bluff."

Maybe, just maybe, Jeopardy would do jail time. "What about those two yahoo fake deputies?"

"We gave them to the feds. Kidnapping charges. The PA said he can charge them with impersonating an officer, if necessary. One was on parole, so he's back in the slammer, anyway. I heard from a buddy at the FBI that they're singing like canaries, hoping to make a deal."

"Nice." I felt relief. If they had come after Alicia or Julia, I'd have killed them. And that would have been a mess. Partner of Ms. Goodhue's boyfriend or not.

"That's it. Just wanted to let you know where things stood. You'll have to testify, but I figure you knew that."

I grunted acknowledgment. "Has she been arraigned yet?"

"Yeah. That's the other bad news. She's pleading not guilty by reason of insanity."

I shook my head. "Thanks, Detective." We disconnected. No surprise there. Hopefully, this time, Ms. Dupree's stay in the state psychiatric hospital would be for a long time.

And speaking of Jeopardy, something she, or Connie, said bothered me. I dialed River Bluffs and asked to talk to Dr. Charnow.

"Mr. Sledge. I heard you proved Barker innocent. That's great."

"Yes, we did. I have a question for you."

"Sure."

"Jeopardy, or Connie, told me that she, that is Connie, was the real person and Jeopardy the alter-ego. Could that be true?"

"Unlikely. However, a alternative personality can think they are the real person. That's not unheard of."

I scratched my head. "Really? Interesting. Thanks again for all your help."

"I'm glad things worked out."

I hung up and glanced at my watch, jumped off the chair, grabbed my jacket and fedora, and left for my appointment. The call from Morris and my call to Dr. Charnow had given me the distraction I needed. But on the drive to the counselor's office, my stomach twisted into a knot, and a pain invaded the base of my skull.

I parked on the curb outside the office building at the corner of N 9th Avenue and W 7th Street in downtown River City. I studied the stone sign outside. A law office. An engineering office. Two accountants. Some other companies with obscure names. I had no idea of their line of business.

One placard touted "Christian Counseling."

I walked into the foyer of the building. Offices lined both sides of a long hallway. All of them glass-fronted. I checked the directory on the wall. Second floor for the counselor. I inched up the stairs, pausing after each step. My heart hammered. I tried to swallow, but my desert-dry throat refused to cooperate.

Inside the second-floor hallway, I found a water fountain and guzzled a gallon of water. I hovered outside the shaded glass office. The words "Christian Counselor" formed an arch on the window. Dr. Leslie March's name was stenciled inside the arch. I stared at it. Leslie. Man or woman? And which did I prefer? I always liked talking to women. But did I want to reveal my deepest, darkest secrets to a woman? Did I even want to tell those to a man?

I opened the outer door and stepped through.

"Hi, may I help you?" A young man with black hair tied back into a ponytail sat behind a glass partition.

"Um, just a minute." I retreated to the hallway where I drank another gallon of water.

Thoughts ping ponged through my head. I tried to latch onto one. I questioned why I agreed to come. What would this person, man or woman, be able to do for me? Things had improved. No neo-Nazi sightings in the last several days. Real or perceived. But I'd promised Bobo. And I'd almost killed Hank Nelson at the shooting range. I moved back in front of the office door and stared at it. Two minutes and I'd be late for the appointment. If I waited three minutes, then I could justify not going in, right?

I felt a presence beside me. Someone put an arm around my shoulder. I glanced left and up.

"What's up, my brother from another mother?" Bobo squeezed my shoulder. "You want me to help you with this?"

I nodded, not able to form any words.

Bobo led me into the counselor's office.

Check out the case before Final Jeopardy:

Jake Sledge—former football star, ex-cop, and River City's most dangerous private investigator. He's got a fedora, a smart mouth, and twin .45s he's not afraid to use. When a kidnapping case explodes into a conspiracy involving corrupt politicians, the mob, and a white supremacist gang, Jake will stop at nothing to save his family.

Chilled to the Bone: A Jake Sledge Mystery

Thank you for reading *Final Jeopardy: A Jake Sledge Mystery*.

Please leave a review on **Amazon**, **Goodreads** and/or Book-Bub. Every review helps.

Join B.D. Lawrence's Email list and ***Get a Free Jake Sledge story***

https://www.bdlawrence.com/stories/#partners

Did you enjoy *Final Jeopardy*? Click on the link above or go to B.D. Lawrence's website to download the novella ***Partners in Crime: A Jake Sledge Mystery*** to read another thrilling story featuring Jake Sledge and Bobo Johnson.

And don't forget to download and read ***Double Jeopardy*** to learn the backstory of Jake Sledge and Jeopardy Dupree.

Click this link for ***Double Jeopardy*** or go to **https://www.bdlawrence.com/1991-2/#jeopardy** to download the short story.

Acknowledgements

Thank you so much to Amy, Christina, Marie, and Tamelia of the Scribes Mystery Writing Group. Your input was invaluable and made Final Jeopardy a better story.

B.D. Lawrence has always loved reading fiction. Ironically, his worst subject in high school was English. One night, sitting in a master's level computer programming class, daydreaming about vigilantes, he decided to give writing a try. Out of that came his first novel, which went nowhere. That was many years ago. During his writing journey he's dabbled in mystery, suspense, science fiction, fantasy, and drama. He is currently focusing on stories of justice, vengeance, and redemption.

Sign up for B.D. Lawrence's newsletter at www.bdlawrence.com. You'll receive monthly updates on upcoming books, access to short stories, book reviews and other articles.

www.ingramcontent.com/pod-product-compliance
Lightning Source LLC
LaVergne TN
LVHW050927080826
845145LV00001B/236

* 9 7 8 1 7 3 7 4 9 7 1 4 1 *